LONG TIME COMING

ELIZABETH BRIGHT

*For the women who were told the responsibility for men's sins
rested squarely on their bare shoulders—
May you only know joy when the sun touches your skin*

PROLOGUE

JEREMIAH

Fourteen Years Ago

It was the kind of night we planned missions around. A new moon and cloud cover that dampened the starlight but didn't threaten immediate rain. The lake was indistinguishable from the sky in the inky darkness.

"They dump bodies here," Uncle Hiram said. The boat seesawed as he strained against the duct tape binding his wrists behind his back.

I arched a brow even though I doubted he could see my expression in the dark. "A church elder is aware of mob activities? How does that fit in with the prophet's revelation to shun the sinning world?"

"Las Vegas is too close to the compound to safely ignore. To protect the flock from sin, one must first know it. My sacrifice is for their benefit. The power of the priesthood protects me from going astray."

Sanctimonious motherfucker. I should have kept him gagged. But then how would he repent of his sins?

"Your banishment did not rest lightly on my soul, Jeremiah. I hope you know that. We had always hoped you would one day repent and return to the Lord."

My rowing did not cease. Every stroke took us further from land. "I begged you and Father on my knees for forgiveness. I swore to never commit the sin again. What more does repentance require?"

"Ah, my son." Uncle Hiram's voice was full of sorrow. "The Lord told us you were of impure heart and must be banished. I wept and begged for you to be spared, but His answer was unyielding. You are a son of perdition."

Hypocritical motherfucker. I snorted. "How convenient."

The prophet's revelation that men must have multiple wives to reach the highest kingdom of Heaven had not taken into account that the birthrate hadn't changed across civilizations since the beginning of time —at least, not without human intervention. With every man being promised three wives, there weren't enough women to go around.

"Is that what this is?" Hiram asked. "A soul for a soul?"

I didn't answer. My soul wasn't worth the cost, but Hannah's was.

"How is my wife?" Hiram asked gently.

Suicidal motherfucker. I squeezed the oars to keep from strangling him then and there. "My *sister* is none of your business." *Fourteen fucking years old.*

"Our marriage was sealed for all eternity before God and the prophet. That is a bond no man can break. Not even you, Jeremiah."

"Then I will leave it in God's hands."

We were here. I pulled in the oars, laid them under the seats, and dragged Hiram to his feet.

"This is murder!" he shouted.

"This is a choice," I corrected. "The FBI has been trying to build its case for years. Turn yourself in. Confess your sins. Accept the consequences."

Our faces were close enough together that I could see his lip curl in a sneer. "And if I don't?"

I spun him in front of me, with his back to my chest, and he faced the vast nothingness before us. Water slapped against the boat.

Hiram sucked in a breath. "I can't swim. You would murder an innocent man with his hands tied behind his back?"

"No." I flicked open my blade and sliced through his bonds. "But I would tell a guilty man to take a swim."

His scream pierced the silent air as I tossed him overboard. Droplets of cold lake water sprayed my face and torso. I squinted into the darkness. He had landed a few feet from the boat.

"Help me!" He slapped the water futilely, spluttering, and went under. A moment later he bobbed to the surface again, choking. "Help me!"

I didn't move as he sank again. He strained to get his face above the water, gasping, and propelled himself closer to the boat. I grabbed the back of his shirt and hauled him to the side. He clung to the edge, coughing.

I squatted down so we were face to face. "Make your choice, Hiram."

"You offer me prison or eternity with my Heavenly Father?" A coughing fit shook his body. "I serve the will of God. I denounce you as a vessel of Satan. Repent, Jeremiah, for the Kingdom of Heaven is at hand. It is not too late."

I stood.

"Your soul will burn in hellfire for this!" Hiram shouted. It was the first time I heard true fear in his voice.

"I'm already damned, remember? I'll see you in hell."

I slammed my heel down on his fingers.

1

LENNON

IF THERE WAS ONE THING BEING MY MOTHER'S DAUGHTER had taught me all too well, it was that every girl needed her own "fuck you" money. No matter how rock solid you thought that job was, no matter how loyal you thought that man was, no matter how secure you thought that living situation was, the day would come when you were forced to choose between walking out or being walked all over.

For me, that day was today.

Again.

"Fuck you, Hector," I hissed into the phone cradled between my shoulder and ear as I unlocked my mailbox. "Benny said I could have the apartment through the end of the year. It's only May."

"I know you're angry, Lennon. Believe me, this wasn't what Benny wanted." His tone was as placating as ever.

Hector was Benny's emotional fixer. Benny hated giving anyone bad news, so he paid Hector to deliver it for him and deal with the aftermath. When Benny had to cancel my birthday weekend? Hector was the one I heard from, and the one who picked out the diamond earrings to make up for it. He reminded me of oil—he smoothed over all the unpleasantness so nothing stuck to Benny but left you a mess.

"Well, if this isn't what Benny wanted, then maybe we should work together to find a way to give him what he *does* want," I snapped.

"What Benny wants is to not find himself in jail. All his financial accounts are frozen, and he has been warned not to leave the city. Benny owns this apartment outright. It's his only real estate in New York that the feds can't seize—yet."

Frowning, I scooped out my mail. I smelled the postcard before I saw it, a familiar comingling of sweet vanilla and bright orange blossom that had for years been my signature scent. Now it turned my stomach. I wedged the stack of mail under my arm—out of sight, out of mind—and breathed through my mouth. One problem at a time.

"Maybe I could stay here with him?" I wheedled. "I won't be any trouble at all."

"It's in everyone's best interest for you to stay as far away from this mess as you can. They don't know about you, and Benny wants to keep it that way." He paused. "For your own sake, of course."

I rolled my eyes so hard they nearly fell out the back of my head. "Of course."

It wasn't that Benny *didn't* care about me, because he did. And I cared about him, too. Sure, he was thirty years older than me and refused to part with his wispy comb-over no matter how often I told him I adored his bald head and he was fooling nobody, and yes, we both knew that if he didn't provide me with a rent-free, prewar apartment with park views and the occasional cash gift I would suddenly be unavailable. But that was the fine print of an unwritten agreement.

What mattered was that he made me smile, I made him laugh, and Wednesdays and Sundays—the days I saw him—were now my favorite days of the week. Hector chose the apology diamonds, but Benny paid for my audiobook addiction. That might not be fairytale love, but it was more than a girl from Chesapeake Trailer Park could reasonably expect from life.

I chewed my lip. "He's going to be okay, right, Hector?"

"Don't worry, honey," he soothed. My lips flattened. The way he said it was more insult than endearment. Like I didn't have two brain cells to rub together to create a spark of intelligent thought. "This will all blow over. The feds don't have any real evidence of wrongdoing."

He did *not* say that Benny hadn't actually committed any wrongdoing. And I had enough friends in low places to know that the FBI couldn't freeze your accounts without getting a warrant, and warrants required reasonable suspicion of criminal behavior. Hector didn't have to say any of that, though, because Benny had said a *lot*.

Unfortunately, I was a good listener.

The same realization must have hit Hector, because he said, "You need to make yourself scarce for the next couple of months. The feds aren't the only ones who have questions. Benny has friends who would hate for certain information to fall into the wrong hands."

The back of my neck prickled. "Am I in danger?"

"This is an investigation. People are going to be poking into his business and his personal life, asking questions. Benny would appreciate it if you weren't available to answer those questions."

"Right." I slapped the mailbox shut. That wasn't exactly a straight answer to the *am I in danger* question. "But where am I supposed to go?"

Hector chuckled. "You're a resourceful girl, Lennon. You'll figure something out. The further away from this life, the better."

I blinked at my mailbox. Brass, with pretty filigree swirls around the apartment number. People didn't make shit like that anymore. I had worked so hard to build this life for myself, this life with a safe place to sleep and pretty mailboxes, and now I was being forced out of it because a goddamn *man* made a mistake? Okay, not just any man, this was Benny and he was a sweetheart, but still—

He owed me *something* for the inconvenience.

Hector had one thing right, anyway. I was resourceful. I had a good emergency fund stashed away, but that would only go so far. I didn't have a typical nine-to-six job. My livelihood was cobbled together through cam streams, catalogue and fit modeling when I could get it, and whatever Benny left on my nightstand.

I had enough money to walk, but I didn't have enough money to hide.

"You can't tell me Benny doesn't have cash on hand because I know that's not true." Benny kept money everywhere he could. I also knew he kept gold and silver bars and coins in a safe behind the mirror that faced the bed.

There was a pause. I held my breath, my hand clenching my keys so tightly that my freshly done nails dug into my palms, only releasing it when Hector heaved a deep sigh of resignation.

"Be at the café on Sixth Avenue at nine tomorrow. I'll bring an envelope and a burner phone. You turn on the phone only once a day to check for an update from me. Understood?"

"Understood."

Fuck, fuck, fuckity fuck.

Entertaining men was the last thing I felt like doing, but Hector had made it clear that my cam girl activities did not fit his definition of lying low. This would be my last stream until Benny was in the clear—which could be months from now. I needed to say goodbye and pause the monthly payments from my subscribers.

I dumped my mail and snacks on the kitchen table before heading to my bedroom to get ready. There was a certain kind of man who got off on watching a woman do wholesome things in a supremely slutty way. Generally, that man was older, worked fourteen-hour days, and lonely.

Benny, in other words.

He was my top supporter by a long shot, but not all my subs were middle-aged men. A handful of straight women subscribed because they found my topless cooking videos and flower arrangements strangely soothing *and* informative.

I donned a blue 1950s style dress, red lipstick, and

my black lace mask, and pulled my wavy brown hair into a high ponytail. Flesh-toned fishnet stockings and round-toed blue heels completed the look. *Welcome to the Donna Reed Strip Tease.* Benny would be thrilled. I blew a kiss to my reflection and took my camera to the kitchen.

After setting the camera up to record, I got to work on dinner while I waited for subs to join the livestream. Bone-in chicken thighs with crispy skin, carrots roasted in thyme and oregano, and mashed potatoes with plenty of cream and butter. I was cooking for two.

While I prepped the chicken, I broke the news that I wouldn't be livestreaming for the next couple months, but hoped to be back in the fall. Subscriptions would be paused but not cancelled—unless they wanted to, of course.

Tips poured in along with lamentations that I would be missed. My phone dinged—the first tier had been reached. "Eek," I squealed, wiggling my fingers to show they were coated in olive oil and garlic. "Let me wash my hands first. I don't want to get salmonella on my dress."

After thoroughly washing my hands and drying them, I turned my back to the camera and slowly unzipped my dress. With a little shimmy, it fell to the floor, leaving me in my lacy black bra and thong, and the stockings held up by garters.

When I ended the livestream thirty minutes later, I was down to just the thong. My panties always stayed on for cooking shows. Call me a prude, but vaginas and food didn't mix.

After changing into my comfiest sweats, I divided the dinner into two portions. One went into the fridge for Benny. The other went to Mrs. Bianchi on the eighth floor. At eighty-three years old, she'd been living all alone in her rent-controlled unit for three decades after her husband died of a heart attack. Six months ago, I'd found her wandering the hallway, lost and confused. I'd been making her dinner twice a week ever since.

What was she going to do without me? And what was I going to do without Benny?

I ripped open a package of Skittles, dumped the contents on a white porcelain plate, then popped open a can of Diet Coke and poured it into a fancy wine glass over ice, topped with a lime wedge and pretty green glass straw.

With my phone tucked into my bra, the stack of mail tucked into my armpit, and my wine glass balanced somewhat steadily on my plate, I took my dinner to the window, dragging a chair behind me. I dropped into it with a soul-weary sigh. *Finally.*

Tossing the mail aside, I kicked my wool-socked feet up on the windowsill. God, this view. This was what rich old white man money got you. Fourteen floors up, a deep bay window with three eight-foot-tall glass panes that looked out over the park. It had never truly been mine, this view. I had always been on borrowed time here.

My eyes burned hot enough that I almost wished I could summon up a tear or two to ease the sting, but unfortunately, I wasn't much of a crier. I popped a lime Skittle into my mouth instead. Skittles and Diet Coke: dinner of scrappy trailer trash, if not actual champions.

Shit, shit, shit. I had to be out in forty-eight hours. Not just out of the apartment—out of New York. Hector might as well have told me to leave the fucking planet. This city had been my home since my emancipation at sixteen, and I'd rarely stepped outside the city limits since. Mom would probably let me stay with her if I kicked in some money, but as far as I knew she was still with Rob. I fucking hated that guy.

No. I was not going back to the trailer park with my tail tucked between my legs. No fucking way.

Anyway, if someone truly started looking for me, that was the first place they'd go.

I pulled my phone out of my bra to see if Benny or Hector had contacted me. Part of me was hoping this was all a misunderstanding. No such luck.

I tossed my phone aside, popped a red Skittle into my mouth to steel my nerves, and scooped up the mail. Junk, mostly. The Memorial Day sales catalogues were in. I'd posed for Lululemon and J. Crew months ago. That was no guarantee I'd actually made the final pages —I was paid for my time regardless—but there I was. I allowed myself a quick flip through. If I looked too long, flaws were all I'd see.

There was also a brochure for some wellness retreat-spa-ranch thing in Wyoming. I'd gotten about three of these in the last nine months. They must be desperate for customers. *Come to Mercy River! Indulge in massage and skin treatments. Book an appointment with our on-site physical trainer or relax in your private cabin.* The photos were breathtaking. Mountains and green pastures, a cozy cabin, horses. I studied each one like I might actually go there someday. Stalling.

I didn't want to look.

But I picked up the postcard anyway, pinching a tiny corner between my thumb and index finger like it could bite me if I wasn't careful, and read the message.

Now we can be together.

Ha. No fucking thank you, Mr. Delusional Stalker.

I let the postcard fall from my fingers to the floor and stared out the window. Autumn was the city's best season, but there was something to be said for the lush green of Central Park in summer, too, and I couldn't feel the humidity from up here. Beyond the park was the skyline, high-rises gleaming in the soft glow of golden hour.

Goddamn, I loved this city, but I needed to disappear. Hide out until this all blew over in some sheltered Podunk town where no one knew my name. I studied the Mercy River brochure again. The "About Us" page told the story of five military friends banding together to open the ranch. The scenery truly was gorgeous. Mountains...That would make a great backdrop in photos, right? Horses...Sure, why not. A spa...Yes, I could definitely get on board with that.

And most importantly, two thousand miles away from this city and anyone who knew me.

2

JEREMIAH

THE ONLY THING MORE ANNOYING THAN WRANGLING COWS was wrangling cowboys. Especially when those cowboys were also ex-special forces who would be mightily offended if I were to use a whip or rope on their hides, and even more especially when those cowboys were the only thing standing between me and my breakfast. Our Monday meeting started at nine, but it was 8:57 now and two were missing.

"Where is Seb?" I groused.

Liam Cole grunted, which could have meant he didn't know, or it could have meant he knew but didn't want to narc. In all fairness, Liam should have been the one wrangling cowboys, not me. It was his ranch, after all. But Liam preferred cattle to people, so here we were.

Mercy River Ranch had been in the Cole family for four generations. The ranch had nearly gone under with Liam's parents, until Liam's younger brother, Daniel, had the bright idea to turn the ranch into a nonprofit retreat for veterans, military, and first responders suffering from the mental scars that came from doing the kind of work we did.

Daniel and Liam Cole, Sebastian Ashcroft, Mateo Alvarez, Holly Delaney, and me—we had all served on a SEAL team together years ago. Now we were cowboys together. I was the general manager. Liam and Mateo oversaw the cattle operation. Holly and Seb handled the nonprofit.

Liam filled his mug then raised the silver urn to me, brows arched above big dark eyes that somehow looked bigger and darker than ever. I held out my own mug, squinting at him as he topped it off. Why did he look so...pretty?

I peeled my gaze away. "Mateo? You see Seb this morning?"

"We've got two minutes," Mateo said, always the optimist. "He'll be here."

"Unless he's dead," Holly chirped as she breezed through the doorway.

She headed to her usual perch on the front desk, but with her arms full of sleeping chicken, she couldn't pop herself onto it. Mateo patted his lap and, without missing a beat she placed one boot on his thigh, using him as a stepping stone. His hand circled her ankle and his biceps flexed as he gave her a boost. His other palm ghosted her calf to steady her, but she didn't need it. Graceful as a ballerina, she twirled onto the counter and settled above him, her legs hanging next to his shoulder. Mother Clucker didn't even blink.

I shook my head. "He's not dead."

Holly shrugged like it didn't matter to her either way, even though I knew it did. "He might be dead."

"I'm not dead." Sebastian finally made his appearance. "I'm not even late."

There was a fresh bandage on his arm, which meant he had been out in the mountains this morning. Rock climbing or mountain biking, probably. That was what I told myself, anyway, because the alternative was he'd jumped off a cliff wearing nothing but a nylon wingsuit like some kind of deranged Batman. I tugged at my hair, frowning at his bandage. You'd think the only survivor of a rescue gone really fucking wrong would handle his own life with a little more care.

I bit back the safety lecture that wouldn't do any good and muttered, "Call next time."

"Sure, Dad," Seb lied with a smirk, because he thought it was hilarious that I was a mere six months older than him and still demanded check-in calls. Maybe if he stopped scaling mountains in the stupidest way possible, I'd be less nervous about it.

"Coffee?" Liam offered, and I found myself once again puzzling over what was different about him.

"Sure, I'll take a cup. Thanks," Seb said.

Liam set his own mug down to fill Seb's, leaving a smudge of pink on the rim where his mouth had been. There was a beat of silence as we all realized what it meant.

"Are you wearing makeup?" I asked, baffled.

Liam crossed his arms over his chest and stared back at me. "Blair," he said succinctly.

I should have guessed. Liam's thirteen-year-old niece had decided her future career at age seven and never once wavered from it. She had done all our faces at one time or another, but her Uncle Liam was her favorite. Maybe because she didn't know what a broody grump he really was. He liked to keep his grunts and growls just for us. With Blair, he had the patience of a saint.

Mateo studied him through his round glasses. "She's getting really good. Your cheekbones, dude. Damn."

Liam grunted in acknowledgment, but his lips tilted in the closest thing to a smile he got.

My stomach growled. I had been up since four, and the protein bar I had washed down with my thermos of coffee had burned off hours ago. The welcome desk where we held our Monday meetings was close enough to the dining hall that I could smell the biscuits and bacon waiting for us.

"It's 9:02." I flicked my clipboard. "Some of us have work to do."

"Ha." Mateo's dimples flashed in a grin. "You're a poet and you don't even know it."

Seb and Liam groaned in unison. Holly's dark eyes bulged out comically.

"Mateo," she hissed. "You were a *Tier 1 operator*. You blew the entire electrical grid of the East Coast when you were nine years old just to test a theory. Russians call you T'ma."

"What's your point?"

"You can't say shit like that. It's embarrassing."

He shrugged, bumping his shoulder against her calf. "Someone had to say it. We were all thinking it."

"No," Liam said. "We weren't."

"Well, you should have been." Mateo shook his head like we had all let him down. "Have some fucking whimsy once in a while. Especially you, Jay. You've been an old man since the day you were born."

I pinched the bridge of my nose. Worse than a whole herd of stampeding cows, every last one of them.

"We have two new guests checking in today," I said before anyone else could run their mouths about something that had nothing to do with work. "We'll put Tyler Wood in Hydra. Lennon Graves will be in Orion."

It was more of a reminder than new information. Tyler had made the reservation a month earlier, but Lennon's had come through only two days ago.

Seb nodded. "Cabins are ready for them. Saw to it yesterday."

I checked it off my list and moved on. "How about the trails, Holly? You were out there this weekend. Are they safe for us to take guests on horseback yet?"

"The lower ones are clear." Holly ran the back of her index finger down Mother Clucker's wing. "The higher ones still have snow, but it's not too deep. Should be clear in a week, unless we get another storm."

I nodded. This close to the Wind River Range, we couldn't rule out a freak snowstorm even in June. It was rare, but it happened. I tapped my pen on my clipboard. "All right—"

The door chimed as someone entered the lodge lobby, and we all turned to look.

And I forgot how to breathe.

The woman's steps faltered as she took us all in, but then she tilted her chin and strode forward. Her gaze darted from face to face, pausing to assess before moving to the next one. And then her eyes found mine.

"Hi. I'm Lennon Graves. I'm checking in."

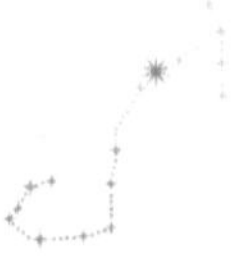

NINE YEARS ago I had walked into a café in Fallujah and found myself thrown right back out again by a blast that took down half the building. In between entering on my feet and leaving on my ass, there had been a split second where my gaze had landed on a shaking, scrawny kid barely out of his teen years and known without a shadow of a doubt that I was about to get blown up.

Lennon Graves felt like that split second—an epiphany that came a moment too late for self-preservation. I was as certain now as I was then: I was about to get blown up.

She was pretty—jaw-droppingly, chest-achingly pretty—but that wasn't it. It wasn't that she was a woman, either, when I had been expecting a man, as most of our guests tended to be. Mercy River was a working ranch, but in addition to our cattle operations, we provided a respite for veterans, active military, and first responders who needed a moment to catch their breath. Some stayed three days and others stayed three months.

This woman didn't look like she should be here three minutes. Something was off about her. Maybe it was the way she'd braced as her gaze darted around the room at each of us, like she expected to be recognized. I'd never seen her before in my life—she didn't have the sort of face you'd forget—but what did it mean that she thought I might? I didn't know.

And that meant I didn't trust her.

"It doesn't take five cowboys to check in one guest," I said pointedly. Seb, Liam, and Mateo took the hint, greeting Lennon quickly before they headed out. Holly apparently decided the term cowboy didn't apply to her, and she leaned a shoulder against the wall.

Lennon stared at her. "Is that a chicken?"

"No," Holly deadpanned.

I gave her a narrow-eyed look over my shoulder before turning back to Lennon. "I'm Jeremiah Bell. This is Holly Delaney. Welcome to Mercy River Ranch. Check-in is at two," I informed her.

Her face fell. "I could have sworn it was eight."

"The lodge opens at eight. Check-in is at two. It was in your confirmation email."

She pushed her hand into her enormous bag and rummaged around. The bag was a simple design with no logos or fancy hardware, but I knew leather and that bag right there likely cost more than a ranch hand made in a week. The sunglasses she tossed on the counter *did* have a big ass logo glinting on the side, and even I recognized the name Prada. It made me wonder if those big rocks studding her ears were real diamonds.

Mercy River was mostly funded by donations and the cattle operation. Guests rarely paid their own way, although insurance usually kicked in about fifty percent. Lennon hadn't provided insurance information on her forms, but it was common enough for insurance to reimburse the person directly that I hadn't thought much of it.

Lennon had money. Another reason not to trust her.

It is easier for a camel to go through the eye of a needle, than for a rich man to enter into the kingdom of God. I had a healthy suspicion of any mortal mouthpiece that presumed to speak for the divine, but that lesson at least had held true.

With a triumphant huff, she whipped out her phone, presumably to verify the email. Her brow didn't exactly furrow, but the squint of her eyes made it seem like it had. I tapped the sign next to the computer to get her attention. She blinked at it.

"Wi-Fi password will be provided at check in?" she read out loud, making it sound like a question instead of a certainty.

"That's right," Holly said firmly. "At two p.m."

Lennon studied her for a moment, immediately determined I was the weaker link, which was accurate because anyone standing next to Holly was the weaker link, and turned her big doe eyes on me pleadingly.

I caved before she even asked. "Your cabin is ready. No harm in getting you settled now."

"Thank you," she said over Holly's soft snort. Holly knew as well as I did that getting Lennon settled at the ranch was an hour-long process, and doing it now instead of at two meant other things were *not* getting done.

Breakfast being one of them.

I took her I.D., matched it against what we had in our system, and added in the license plate from her vehicle. Swiping the cabin keys from the locked wall cabinet, I glanced over at her. "You want the Wi-Fi password now?"

She rolled her lips together, then shoved her phone back in her bag with a firm shake of her head. "No. No, I do not."

Not the reaction I was expecting. The way Holly's eyebrows went up, I knew she was thinking the same thing. "Where did you park?" I asked.

"Just out front."

I nodded. "I'll meet you there."

She headed out the front door, and I grabbed our welcome packet: a map of the grounds and other handy information, such as meal times, activities, rules, places to go in town, and the Wi-Fi password.

Holly put a hand on my forearm, waylaying me. "Something is off with her."

I nodded. We were on the same page there.

Outside, Lennon leaned against a black mid-size SUV. Brian, one of our ranch hands, tipped his hat to her as he passed on his way to the dining hall and then did a double take. His expression turned quizzical, but at her blank stare, he shook his head and kept moving.

"Morning, Jay," he greeted, reaching for the door behind me.

"Morning, Brian," I returned, but my attention was focused on the woman standing still as stone.

Everything about her was all wrong, and if I were a

betting man, I'd put good odds that she had never seen a day of military life. First responders cared about duty and service. I'd never known a person with money to show a lick of interest in either. But maybe I was letting her pretty face cloud my judgment. Maybe she did belong here at Mercy River Ranch. Because her eyes...

Her eyes had that hunted look.

3

LENNON

THERE WAS NOT A SINGLE THING IN THIS ONE-ROOM LOG cabin *not* constructed of knotty pine. The wide-planked walls. The ceiling that came down a few inches closer than I would have liked. The floor beneath the colorful braided rug. Even the furniture was the same golden pine. I had seen pictures of the cabin on their website I had pulled up through the link on the postcard, but seeing it and being inside it were two very different things. It gave me the feeling of being in a tree hollow. Like a claustrophobic squirrel.

Jeremiah cleared his throat, and I gave him my sweetest, *I'm-a-low-maintenance-girl* smile. A lie. I wasn't low-maintenance. I wasn't easygoing. I had clawed my way out of a world very few girls ever managed to leave and then spent the next decade working my ass off to stay out. I was excruciatingly aware of every cent it cost to maintain this lifestyle that I had never quite allowed myself to become accustomed to.

"It's cute," I said brightly.

He arched a golden-brown eyebrow—the exact shade as the pine that surrounded us. It wasn't weird that I noticed. With that same color coming at me from all angles, it would have been weird if I *hadn't* noticed. But judging from the way that eyebrow nearly disappeared into his matching hairline, *cute* wasn't the look he was going for. It was a ranch, after all, and he was an honest-to-goodness cowboy. Men were so delicate about these things.

"Cozy," I amended. "It's very cozy in here."

His lips twitched beneath his mustache as if I had amused him. A man of few words, this cowboy. I didn't hate it. The mustache, that is. The jury was still out on how I felt about his way of saying a whole lot without using his words. But I didn't hate the mustache, and that *was* weird, because normally I was not a fan of facial hair at all. But it suited him. He looked like Westley from *The Princess Bride*, before the farm boy went all Dread Pirate Roberts. Golden hair and blue-gray eyes like a stormy sea, but a decade older and a mustache that didn't make me wish for a razor.

He hooked his thumbs into the front pockets of his

jeans. *Why are you staring at me?* his raised eyebrows seemed to ask.

Because I feel like it, my smirk silently answered.

The polite thing to do would be to break eye contact, say something about the weather, and turn away. But I didn't do that. I kept right on staring at him because he was staring back at me, and suddenly it felt like the most important competition of my life, and dammit, I wanted to win. Everything about my life felt out of my control right now, but this? This I could control.

He dipped his chin, studying me. I was a tall girl, but he still had a good two inches on me. Were his cheeks a little pinker now? He was going to crack first, I could feel it. Any second now, the awkwardness would make him say something—

Unless he doesn't know this is a staring contest. Maybe he simply thought he had a very rude, very odd guest on his hands and was trying to be professional about it.

Oh, god.

I never blushed—shameless, my mom called me, and she didn't mean it as a compliment—but my skin prickled like it almost remembered how. I cleared my throat. "So."

Jeremiah grinned, the smile lighting up his face like Christmas morning. Oh, goddammit. He'd known. Only winning could make a person glow like that. With an annoyed huff, I crossed my arms under my chest and turned away.

He chuckled softly. "Now, don't be like that. We already have one sore loser around here, and I don't think the ranch is big enough for the both of you."

"Is it Holly?" I'd gotten a vibe from her. She hadn't liked me on sight, and that made me inclined to believe she had other faults as well. I ignored the part about the other sore loser in this scenario being me. He wasn't wrong, but I saw no reason to admit that.

"It doesn't matter who it is. We don't need two of them."

I snorted. "Yeah. It's Holly."

He ignored me. "Do you want to settle in now, or do the tour of the ranch? If you need a minute, I can come back later."

"Now is fine. I just need to use the bathroom first."

"I'll wait for you on the porch."

I made use of the small bathroom, which was not wood-paneled, but instead tiled floor to ceiling in green and white porcelain squares. The sink vanity was too small to hold more than a bar of soap and a toothbrush, but at least there was a bathtub. I was a hot-soak-after-a-long-day girl through and through.

I paused on the way out and took another look around. It *was* cozy, actually. No TV, but there was a mini-fridge and a coffeemaker. Jeremiah had set my luggage next to the (pine) dresser that definitely wouldn't hold everything I brought.

The décor was simple but thoughtful. A gorgeous

black-and-white photograph of Yellowstone National Park hung over the small (pine) desk. The cushion on the (pine) chair was a dark green that matched the flannel curtains hanging in the window. Across the room, the quilt on the (pine) bed was the same dark green. The color added to the whole *you live in a tree now* aesthetic.

My home for the next two months. New York, it was not. For a moment, I felt completely lost. Discombobulated. Everything had happened so fast. Once Hector decided I should disappear, he went all in. He hadn't wanted to tip the feds off to my destination, so he'd flown me all the way to Seattle. One of Benny's associates had met me at the airport there with a car he claimed was registered to his ninety-year-old grandmother who wouldn't miss it, and I'd backtracked to Mercy River Ranch.

Four days. How could my entire life change so much in four days?

I took a breath and squared my shoulders. I could do this.

Starting over was my specialty.

"THERE ARE NINE GUEST CABINS, all of them spread out here on the east side of the property. They're close together, but the trees provide privacy."

Jeremiah gestured to the log cabins that peeked out between the towering evergreens as we climbed into the golf cart. From the outside, they were all identical. Quaint structures, like something out of *Little House on the Prairie*, each with a green roof and a front porch with two rocking chairs. I suspected the inside had the same pine bed, dresser, and desk, and the same green curtains.

"Seven of the cabins are full right now. There's one of your neighbors right now, as a matter of fact," Jeremiah said, nodding in the direction of a man heading down the path to one of the cabins.

I slipped on my oversized sunglasses before lifting my hand in a wave. The man jerked a shoulder in response. Slowly I lowered my hand. "What's with him?"

"That's Caleb. Got here a few days ago. Most guests keep to themselves the first week or so, I've noticed. It takes time to reset the nervous system."

That made sense. The website had made it clear that this wasn't a dude ranch for family vacations or city slickers looking for a cowboy adventure. It was first and foremost a working ranch, and a wellness retreat on the side. Kind of like the monastery my friend Kimmy went to every February for a two-week electronic detox. They couldn't even talk there—the monks had taken a vow of silence, and the guests were expected to be respectful of it. This wasn't a vacation. It was an escape. That was why I was here, too, even if my reasons were forced upon me rather than chosen.

"As I was saying," Jeremiah continued, "you'll have plenty of time to get to know the other guests. Some are more sociable than others, but you'll see them at meal times."

"Oh." The golf cart bumped over a dip in the dirt road, kicking up red-brown dust, and my stomach lurched with it. "Is there room service?"

His assessing look told me the answer before he spoke, so I wasn't surprised when he said, "No room service. Let us know if you're sick and someone will bring you food and get you medical care."

I nodded uneasily. With the exception of the cowboy who had looked at me a little too long this morning, his forehead furrowed like he was trying to figure out where he knew me from, no one had recognized me yet. That didn't surprise me. Mercy River was a blue-collar town. I very much doubted the locals spent their free time watching my naked floral arrangement livestreams or thumbing through clothing catalogues.

But the guests...they could be anyone from anywhere. A New York socialite who had seen me with Benny. A Los Angeles photographer. Some random middle-aged man from Chicago who paid my monthly subscription fee.

Still, the odds of someone recognizing me from my modeling work or social media were almost nonexistent. I knew that. But somehow I couldn't seem to convince my nervous system I was safe. Which was ridiculous because I wasn't the one in danger. Unlike Benny, I was fastidious when it came to my taxes. The cash he left in the mornings appeared with or without fucking, which made it a gift, not payment. Totally legal.

"The east side of the property is the bunkhouse for the ranch hands and owners' cabins," he went on. "Where the road meets in the middle is the lodge. That's where you'll find the dining hall, the library, and the game room."

"What about the spa?"

He gave me that assessing look again. It did not bode well. "The health center is behind the lodge. We have a physical therapist on staff, and a massage therapist, too. The gym has free weights, barbells, and some cardio machines, but it doesn't get much use. Most people find that after a long day of ranching, lifting heavy objects and putting them down again with no real purpose loses its appeal."

Okay, the website had definitely oversold the amenities here. "So I guess a facial isn't going to happen?"

"What's a facial?" he asked, and I truly could not tell if he was fucking with me.

But that didn't stop me from fucking with him right back.

"Oh, you haven't tried it yet? It's the latest skincare craze. Semen does wonders for skin tone. Tightens everything right up."

It took him a beat to work through what I meant, but when he did, a mottled red crested his cheeks. "You're joking. People wouldn't—"

"People absolutely would." I snickered. "Have you met people?"

The flush deepened. I couldn't help but stare. I had never seen a full-grown man—much less a cowboy—actually blush. I hadn't blushed in a decade. Nothing fazed me anymore. I took pride in that. But seeing this man who was older than me, rougher than me, turn bright red at a little sexual innuendo made me nostalgic for the little girl I had been before I'd installed a deadbolt on the inside of my bedroom door.

"I've *met* people," he muttered. "Usually I shake their hand. I don't do...*that*."

I burst out laughing. "I think that's the kind of thing you have to work up to. Consent is important."

His lips parted and he stared at me as if he were wondering how a person might go about asking for something like that in a spa.

"You know I'm joking, right?" Suddenly I was hyper-aware that if the roles were reversed, I would be asking to speak to his manager right about now. Probably. That mustache might slow me down a little.

"What you city folk get up to is none of my business."

"No one does that for skincare." *I don't think.* "Just sex."

The look he gave me made it clear he didn't think that was better. There wasn't a great way to end this conversation I had trapped us in. This was so unlike me. I didn't ramble on about kinks for the pleasure of watching someone squirm. I was the queen of small talk! Especially with men. Mostly that meant asking questions and parroting their own words back at them with wide-eyed wonder as if I were awed by their existence and dying to know more, all while perfectly roasting a chicken and stripping my clothes off.

Maybe I could roll myself right out of the golf cart. We couldn't be going more than five miles an hour.

"I could have gone my whole life without knowing that," he mused. "I only had another forty years or so to go. Damn shame."

Wonderful. This rough and rugged cowboy had at least a decade on me, and I had come along and stolen the last vestiges of his innocence. I eyed the ground speculatively. The dirt looked hard, but I could probably land on my feet.

His large hand cupped my triceps, preventing my escape. "Don't even think about it. If I have to live with this conversation, so do you. You want to meet the horses? Stables are coming up."

4

LENNON

THE SILENCE WOKE ME UP. I LAY THERE, DISORIENTED IN the quiet darkness, staring at what logic required to be the pine ceiling, but there was no way to know for sure because not even the faintest sliver of yellow streetlight cracked through the window.

Back in New York, the city sounds had become a soothing white noise. Blaring car horns, the steady whoosh of the subway beneath my feet, and the hum of human voices all blended together. Sunglasses on, head down, I tuned it out until it didn't exist for me. But the Wyoming silence was deafening.

With a groan, I rolled onto my side, but it was no use. I was wide awake. Fucking jetlag. I fumbled for my phone next to me on the bed, but the screen didn't light up. Dead, because I had fallen asleep listening to an audiobook. And the charger was in the car. I groaned again and then swung my legs out of the blankets and rolled to my feet, swiping my keys from the nightstand.

The braided rug was thick and warm, but the pine floor was freezing as I tiptoed to the door.

"Shit! Shit!" I whisper-hissed like I was afraid of waking the squirrels before shoving my feet into the Uggs I had left by the door.

Being June, it hadn't occurred to me that the outside world would be a few degrees colder than my cozy cabin. The car was parked only ten feet from the door—today I would move it to the gravel parking lot behind the lodge, per the ranch's policy—but I almost high-tailed my ass back inside to grab my hoodie. Or at least some pants.

But the stars.

Holy shit, the *stars*.

Trillions of them, each one a silver pinprick of light in the velvet darkness, a sky so cluttered with stars that it was impossible to distinguish one constellation from the next—although the only constellation I could reliably find was Orion's belt. Hell, I couldn't even find the rest of him. Most nights in the city, I didn't bother to look up. The light pollution hid the stars. Even my mom's trailer was too close to Norfolk to get stars like this.

Out here, there were more stars than sky. I was dizzy

from the breadth of it. The sheer *vastness* of it. My head rolled back as far as I could take it as I gaped at the heavens, my breath white wisps of steam.

I was awed.

I was humbled.

I was—

"Where the hell are your fucking clothes?"

I was annoyed.

Because now that I had nearly jumped out of my own skin, I was suddenly very aware of how cold that skin actually was, and I was not all that thrilled about it because now I had to stay cold until I had proved my point. Also, I didn't appreciate being barked at like a disobedient child, hence the point to prove, which was that I did whatever the hell I wanted because I was the boss of myself.

I kept my head tilted to the sky, not moving a muscle. My bare skin goosebumped so hard, I swear to god I could feel the hair growing back on my legs. "Didn't anyone ever teach you that sneaking up on a girl in the dark is a bad thing to do?"

Jeremiah didn't say anything, but his approaching footsteps turned purposefully loud. I bit my lip to hide my grin and lowered my gaze back down to earth so fast that I was momentarily lightheaded. I swayed dizzily. Large hands grasped my biceps, steadying me.

The inky darkness had faded to a pre-dawn violet-gray, and my eyes had adjusted enough to make out his expression in the dim light. Concern. Aggravation. Attraction.

Or maybe that was just me.

"Why are you skulking around my cabin?" I demanded.

"Heading to the pasture to bring the horses in. I come this way every morning." When he was sure I wouldn't keel over, he dropped his hands from my arms and gritted out, "Where are your clothes?"

"I'm wearing them," I said pertly.

His gaze raked over my tiny sleep shorts and tank top. He speared his fingers through his hair and tugged at it with a growl of irritation that gave me great joy. Maybe it was bratty of me, but in my real life, I didn't have the luxury of annoying men. Being here with Jeremiah was freeing. I didn't need his approval. I didn't need his money. I could say and do whatever I wanted.

"Not enough," he gritted out. Before I could think of another snappy comeback, he'd taken off his own coat and wrapped it around my shoulders.

Oh my *god*, that felt good. But admitting that would knock me off a high horse that I had already grown pretty attached to, so I said, "That's not necessary. I'm just grabbing my charger from the car." I moved to take his coat off, but his fists tightened at the collar, holding it closed. My lips parted in surprise.

"Try it," he said pleasantly. "See what happens. I'll

have you off your feet and back in your cabin before you can blink."

"Don't threaten me with a good time," I purred back, batting my eyelashes.

The flat look he gave me was worse than a scold. I stared up at him, wondering if he'd really make good on his promise. He glared back, his mouth clamped shut but his face saying a whole lot.

I decided he would, and not in a fun way.

"Fine," I huffed.

Immediately, he stepped back, giving me space, and I wished he hadn't. It was freezing out here, and proximity to his big body had been like standing close to a fire. But that high horse wasn't going to ride itself, so I pranced over to the car like I could still feel my thighs.

He said nothing as I beeped the key fob, the sound cutting through the stillness like an air horn. He said nothing as I grabbed the charger and a pack of Skittles from the console and stomped past him back to the cabin. He said nothing as he followed me up the steps to the porch.

The second I crossed the threshold, I whipped around to face him. He leaned against the doorway, watching as I shrugged out of his coat and tossed it to him. "Thank you for the favor I never asked you for."

He said nothing to that, too. Just touched the brim of his cowboy hat and nodded before disappearing into the ponderosa pines.

Leaving me to wonder how saying nothing at all said so much.

By the time I had pulled on jeans and a T-shirt, the sky was a brilliant pinky-orange, and I was ravenous. My phone claimed it was 5:37, but my stomach insisted it was nearly eight. I had always been a morning person and thrived on routine, starting every day with a Pilates class before breakfast, and right now my body could not be less interested in sleep. It wanted movement and food.

And maybe an overly protective cowboy for extra warmth.

Benny had gone from paying for my time to paying me to stay away, and I wasn't under any illusions that we would pick up where we left off when I returned to the city. Maybe he'd actually be in jail, although I doubted it —people with money didn't tend to end up there—and I really hoped not. Either way, he wouldn't care what I got up to. Would it be so bad to get over a millionaire by getting under a cowboy? A vacation fling was like Skittles and Diet Coke. It wasn't healthy, and it couldn't replace chicken and vegetables in the long term, but sometimes it was exactly what you needed. A little treat.

My stomach growled. The lodge didn't open for breakfast until eight, but maybe I could grab a piece of fruit from the kitchen or something to tide me over. I needed to park my car there, anyway. If the lodge was locked, I'd head into town—but that was a forty-minute drive, and my stomach might eat itself in the meantime.

I pulled on my ancient hoodie and headed out. It hadn't occurred to me that I'd need a coat or warm clothes in June, and my packing consisted of shorts, T-shirts, every pair of underwear I owned, and the occasional dress for nights in town. Everything else I'd packed up into a rental storage unit.

The lodge was a quick four-minute drive from my cabin. I parked in the gravel lot behind the lodge designated for overnight guests and staff. The door was unlocked, so I slipped past the sign at the welcome desk with posted hours and headed for the dining hall. The overhead lights were off, but the big windows provided plenty of morning sun to guide me, and I could hear pots banging and low chatter coming from the back, so I knew someone was around.

A quick peek through the small, square window of the swinging door told me I had found the kitchen. I could make out gleaming metal tables, a tall man with a long dark braid at the griddle, and a girl with lavender hair pulled into a bun standing with her back to the door, a large silver bowl tucked against her side, her whole body vibrating as she stirred its contents vigorously.

I pushed through as she said, "So then he said *I'm coming to the cottage.* Can you believe that? Amos, the way I screamed—" She turned as she spoke, saw me standing there, let out a startled yelp, and nearly threw the bowl at me. A glob of batter shot out of the bowl and landed with a plop at my feet.

"Um, hi." My hand arced like a rainbow in an awkward wave.

The girl looked me up and down with wide brown eyes. "Well, shit," she laughed. "You're gorgeous."

My body tensed. Did she recognize me? Or was that nothing more than a compliment? I cleared my throat. "Hi," I said again. "And, um, thanks. I was wondering if—"

"You're a guest." The man at the griddle pointed his spatula at me. "You can't be back here. Breakfast is at eight."

He was my height, wearing a black AC/DC shirt with cutoff sleeves that showed his muscled biceps and weathered brown skin, although there wasn't a single thread of silver in his long black braid.

"Right," I said, my tone conciliatory. "But I was hoping I could maybe get a banana or something? Would that be okay?" I gave him a pleading smile, the one that never failed to make men puff out their chests and be my hero.

But Amos did not appear inclined to rescue me. He folded his thick arms over his round stomach and stared me down as if he had never heard the phrase *the customer is always right* in his life. "Breakfast is at eight."

The girl rolled her eyes. "Don't listen to him. Of course you can have a banana. We have plenty."

She set the bowl down on one of the silver prep stations and spun on her toes to the back counter, which was piled with apples, bananas, oranges, and uncut melons. She plucked a banana from one of the bunches and ripped off a paper towel that she dampened at the sink.

"Here you go." She handed me the banana and then squatted in front of me to wipe up the spilled batter.

"Thank you. And sorry for startling you." I cracked the banana's top and peeled it back. "I'm Lennon," I added.

"I'm Cecily Shepherd. And that grump over there"— she indicated Amos with a jerk of her purple bun—"is Amos Tallbull."

"Nice to meet you both. Thanks again for the banana." I raised it like a salute. "I'll get out of your way now."

"Wait!" she blurted.

I paused, eyebrows raised.

"You could..." Her brown eyes darted to Amos like she knew he wasn't going to like this and back again. "You could stay. I mean, you're hungry, right? We've already fed the cowboys and ranch hands, so now we're making our own breakfast before we get started on the guests'."

"Really?" I looked at Amos, who I suspected was the boss of the kitchen.

He grunted, arms still crossed. "You stay? You help. *Then* you can eat."

"Amos!" Cecily hissed. "You can't make Lennon cook. She's a guest—" she broke off, biting her lip, then squinted at me curiously. "You *are* a guest, aren't you? No offense, but you don't look like a ranch hand."

I nodded, relieved she didn't recognize me but feeling silly for thinking she would. "I'm here through July."

"So what?" Amos said. "All the guests help out at the ranch. It's part of their healing process. Helps them discover a new purpose or something. Anyway, we're down a hand. Miguel is out for the week visiting family."

"I don't mind helping," I said quickly. "What are we making?"

"Scrambled eggs, bacon, biscuits," Amos barked. "I'm on eggs and bacon. You can help Cecily with the biscuits."

My stomach sank. Cooking and baking were two different skills, in my mind. I never used a recipe when I cooked, preferring to season food to my taste. Baking required precision. But I forced a smile. "Sure." I pulled my hair back into a braid, fastened it with the black band I always kept on my wrist, and moved to the sink. "Let me wash my hands first. Do you have a recipe?"

Cecily nodded at the sheet of paper pinned to the wall. "Right there, but I've got it memorized."

I looked it over as I dried my hands. Fractions. Those were the worst. Always moving around and making no sense. So fucking sneaky. "How about you tell me what you want me to do and I'll do it? That way I'm not running back and forth from the prep station to the recipe. Go slowly, okay?"

She shrugged. "Sure. No problem."

I smiled at her. "I love your hair, by the way. It's my favorite color."

"Really?" She rubbed her hairline with her forearm. "I was about to change it to red. I like to cycle through the rainbow. But I guess I'll keep it purple while you're here."

My smile widened and I bumped her hip with mine. "Cecily, I think this is going to be the beginning of a beautiful friendship."

5

LENNON

HAVING NOTHING TO DO HAD THE ODD EFFECT OF MAKING me want to do *something*. After making breakfast for two dozen ranch hands, the staff, and the guests, I'd headed back to my cabin for a little rest and relaxation.

Five minutes into my audiobook, I was itching for something to keep my hands busy.

I didn't know how to do nothing. Even my vacations were work. Benny's rent-free apartment was the closest I ever came to a steady paycheck, and I never once forgot that. When every cent you made was dependent on making people want to be around you, turning it off even for a moment meant eating nothing but cereal for a month. I was always *on*.

Hustling was second nature to me. I'd been doing it

since Terri Allen had knocked on our door looking for a babysitter.

"*Your mama home?*" *she'd asked, peering over my shoulder. I knew she saw Mom's bare feet dangling over the couch armrest when her shoulders rolled forward. "She sleepin'?"*

I nodded, and Terri's face fell. Then she straightened, her expression canny as she sized up my nine-year-old self. "What are you up to this evening?"

"Making sure Mom doesn't burn the house down," I said honestly. Mom didn't do drugs, but she drank, and she had a disconcerting habit of leaving things burning and then passing out. The stove, a cigarette, a candle. I'd learned to keep a full watering can under the sink for emergencies.

"She been sleepin' long?" Terri asked.

"Only about ten minutes."

Terri smoothed her hands over the white button-down and pleated black pants that the diner made her wear. "She'll be down for a while. It wouldn't be much trouble for you to watch them both, would it? I got an extra shift at the diner, and I can't say no. You're a good kid, Lennie. Mia loves you."

I hesitated, glancing over my shoulder at Mom. "She's grouchy when she wakes up hungry."

"I'll bring you dinner after my shift. Anything you want."

"Ice cream?" I asked hopefully.

She laughed. "Ice cream would melt before I got it here, sugar. How about French fries and a burger? Some pie, too." *She tweaked my messy ponytail. "Cuz you're so sweet."*

She needed me. It was a powerful feeling, one I didn't want to let go of quite yet. "And five dollars."

"Five dollars? That's a lot of money." She bit her lip like she was hiding a smile.

I took that as a challenge and folded my arms. "So don't smoke for a day."

She burst into a raspy laugh. "Damn, sugar. You got fire. You keep hold of that, you hear me? In this world, you're gonna need it."

She wasn't wrong.

I popped out my earbuds and stretched. Maybe I'd go down to the animal barns and pet a horse or something. Mercy River Ranch had a lot of animals. There were the horses, of course, and chickens, goats, two pigs, and a llama. Supposedly there were cows, although I hadn't seen a single one.

It was warm and sunny as I ambled down the dry, brown path that led to the barns. The daily temperature fluctuation definitely took some getting used to. Frigid mornings, hot afternoons, and in the distant mountains, I could see blinding white patches of snow. It took my breath away. Sure, New York had trees and grass, and Central Park. But there, nature was polite, like it had been wrangled into submission. Trees grew only where allowed.

Nature was so *present* here. So wild.

And also kind of a bitch, because it stabbed me in the toes. I winced and pulled the twig out from where it had lodged in my shoe. Sandals were probably a mistake on a ranch, but the only other shoes I'd brought with me were a pair of three-inch heels and two-hundred-dollar designer sneakers that I couldn't afford to replace right now. The sandals had cost me twenty bucks at Target, so sandals it was.

Even with its wide entryways allowing sunlight to spill inside, the stable was darker than the day, and I had to blink a few times for my eyes to adjust to the sudden dim.

"You all right, ma'am?" a concerned male voice asked.

I blinked again. A ranch hand stepped out of a shadowed stall, pitchfork in hand. The same one whose gaze had lingered a little too long outside the lodge on my first day here. Logically, I knew he hadn't recognized me. Cam girls were a dime a dozen, so even if he spent time on that part of the internet, it was highly unlikely that my naked cooking and floral arrangements were his particular kink.

But I still didn't like the way he stared. Not then, and not now.

So I gave him my brightest smile, like he didn't bother me in the slightest. "I'm fine, thank you. Just wanted to say hello to the horses." I glanced around at the empty stalls. "Apparently, I came at the wrong time."

"The horses spend most of the daylight hours working, either ranch work or trail rides for the guests. If they're not working, they're in the pastures. We don't keep them inside when the weather is nice." He moved closer. "I'm Brian Carpenter."

"Lennon Graves. Nice to meet you." I pivoted away from him on the pretense of investigating a stall. I peered over the chest-high door.

"I know who you are."

He stepped closer, and the hairs on the back of my neck stood on end. I could feel his body heat invading my space. *Ugh.* I knew his type, and I hated it. Harmless when it came right down to it, but they got off on giving women the impression that they weren't. Scaring women made them feel powerful.

I gripped the stall door like I was wringing his neck, but I glanced over my shoulder at him with a smile still firmly in place. His gaze was glued to my ass. He didn't even try to hide it. Just slowly dragged his gaze upward to meet my eyes. My skin crawled.

I wouldn't give him what he wanted. I wouldn't show fear.

But I wasn't going to poke at him either. So much of staying safe came down to one simple, infuriating rule: *Don't antagonize them.*

And right now, I was a little scared. This man, knowing who I was? Knowing why I was here? I shuddered to think how he would wield that power. How he would twist and abuse it to make me do things I didn't want to do. I could leave if I absolutely had to, but Hector had paid for my stay here. Finding new living arrangements would eat into my savings, and if things went south with Benny, I was going to need those savings to restart my life.

So I let my smile ride the line between curious and flirtatious as I said, "Oh? Have we met?"

He smirked. "Nah. Not officially." He paused just long enough to make me wonder, and then added, "We don't get a lot of women staying here, for whatever reason. Maybe the work doesn't affect them in the same way. Maybe the really hard shit, the stuff that leaves scars, a man does it for them. Equality, am I right?"

What work? What the hell was he going on about? I'd kept mostly to myself and the kitchen since my arrival and hadn't seen more than a glimpse of the other guests. But from the ranch's website, I would have thought that women were their target market. I masked my confusion behind my smile. My cheeks were starting to hurt.

"You're right," I placated. I'd gotten good at that. I hardly even tasted the vomit anymore.

He grinned like he had won something. "If you're looking for a chore to pitch in on, I wouldn't mind the company."

Apparently, part of the allure of staying at a dude ranch was learning how to be a real cowboy. I got the appeal...sort of...but I wasn't spending a second more with this douche canoe than I had to. I held out a sandaled foot. "I'll have to pass, I'm afraid. Wrong footwear for the job."

He looked down at my feet and chuckled. "Next time, then. Come find me when you're ready to be a real cowgirl. I'll show you how to save a horse." He winked and tapped the brim of his hat.

Gross.

"Sure thing," I lied brightly, like I was just a dumb city girl who had never heard the phrase *Save a horse, ride a cowboy.*

I let my smile fade as he walked past me down the main drag, still squeezing the stall door to ease my frustration. Nothing he had said was overtly sexual or threatening. If I complained, they'd tell me I was overreacting or being too sensitive. But his body language and the look in his eye…He'd *wanted* to make me uncomfortable. And he'd succeeded.

His footsteps faded. He was almost gone—

"Hey, Jay."

"Brian."

I whipped around and my gaze collided with Jeremiah's. How long had he been standing there? He faced me close enough to have heard every word, his blue-gray eyes stormier than ever as he studied me, one large hand on Brian's chest to waylay him as they stood shoulder to shoulder. Then all I saw was his profile as he turned his face to Brian, lips moving. Whatever he said was too low for me to hear, but Brian's spine snapped straight and his head jerked. Jeremiah's fingers curled over his shoulder, and he gave him a little shake. Brian nodded.

I didn't bother to pretend I wasn't invested in the little drama as they parted. Brian disappeared into the sunshine without looking back. Jeremiah paused, hands on hips, like he was thinking about following him, but then shook his head and looked at me. We kept our eyes on each other as he approached.

"Anything you want to say?" he asked.

"Nope," I said, popping the p.

His lips parted like he was going to argue, but then he shook his head again. "If you change your mind—"

"It's fine. Nothing happened that I can't handle."

One hand went to his belt, the other hooked onto the back of his neck. He frowned down at me. "You shouldn't have to."

"There are a lot of shouldn'ts in this world, Jeremiah. People shouldn't have to go hungry or homeless. People shouldn't have kids they can't love or care for. People shouldn't steal or murder." He made a scoffing sound and looked away. "Honestly, shouldn't is boring. So unless you have a solution for all those shouldn'ts, I'm going to focus on *can*. I *can* refuse to let the big cowboy with the small mind live rent-free in my brain. I *can* let the little things go. Or I *can* make him an extra-special batch of laxative cookies." I shrugged. "There are *so* many options here."

The *shock* on his face. "No. You can't."

I laughed. "I think you mean I *shouldn't* because I assure you, I absolutely can. *Shouldn't* is not *can't*. Life is a lot more fun when you don't confuse the two."

"Giving a man the shits is not my idea of fun." Arms crossed, he glowered down at me with stern disapproval.

I held up my hands. "What can I say? Twenty-nine years of sharing a planet with your species has broadened my horizons. Laxative cookies are absolutely my idea of fun. I mean, just *imagine* it."

His gaze went sideways and his chin tipped. He scrubbed a hand over his mouth, but not before I saw his lips twitch. Oh, he was imagining it, all right.

"Lennon." He speared his fingers through his hair and tugged. I'd only been here two days, but I seemed to have that effect on him a lot. "I don't want to have to ban you from the kitchen. Can I trust you to behave?"

"Oh, absolutely not," I said cheerfully.

He studied me, then shook his head. "Yeah," he muttered. "I guess I knew that."

I smirked. Of course I wasn't going to poison Brian. Why did it feel so good to push Jeremiah's buttons? Maybe the jet lag had throttled my filter. I had a talent for making people like me—men and women—but Jeremiah wasn't paying me for my time. I could say whatever I wanted. I could *be* whoever I wanted. He could fuck off if he didn't like it.

But he didn't fuck off.

And I suspected that meant maybe he did like it. That he liked *me*, against his better judgment. Because he sure as hell didn't trust me.

That didn't bother me, either.

Trust was overrated. The only person who would never let you down was yourself.

THE GUARDIAN

She's perfect.

I shouldn't be surprised. We've been friends for almost two years now, so I know her pretty well. Still, I'm not naive enough to believe everything I see on the internet is real. People pretend to be something they're not all the time. You think you're bonding with a fellow Taylor Swift fan you can swap friendship bracelets with, but instead it's a forty-seven year old geezer who wants you to send him topless photos.

Men are such a disappointment.

Deep, deep down, I was afraid she would be, too. Never meet your heroes, right? But Lennon isn't my hero. She's my friend.

But I've been fooled by people before. I've been hurt and betrayed by people who claimed to love me. Sometimes the loss still ached, deep and low in my belly. The doctor said that wound had fully healed, and whatever pain I feel now, it's all in my head. But when I look down at my body, the scar is still an angry red above my pubic hair. I know, deep in my bones, that the pain won't heal until that scar is a pale silvery line.

I rub silicon gel across the six inch line the way Lennon told me to do before settling into my bed to watch my favorite TV show. Vitamin E oil doesn't really work, apparently, and neither does cocoa butter, no matter what the influencers try to sell you. Lennon knows all kinds of stuff like that from working with makeup artists as a model. It's one of the things I like about her, that she doesn't gatekeep shit like that. She's a girl's girl. The older sister I never had.

And now she's here. She's really here. Maybe I should be surprised that this is all working out so perfectly—it's not like anything else in my life has ever gone to plan—but I'm not. I feel peaceful. Like I'm finally on the right path. Everything is falling into place. Finally.

She's so happy here. I *knew* she would be. It's exhausting working the way she does, sharing so much of herself. All these men watching her videos, saying disgusting things to her, they don't deserve her. They don't understand her—and they're dangerous. She doesn't realize that, but I do. I know exactly what men are capable of, and I'm not going to let them hurt her.

Mercy River. It was the name that called me here two

years ago, broken and desperate. This town and this ranch are my safe haven. She feels the same way. I know it.

Someday, when I tell her everything, she'll thank me for being her guardian angel. The one person who truly saw her.

I settle back into my nest of pillows and blankets as the theme song plays. The four women embrace, comforting and protecting each other against the world.

That's going to be us. Friends forever, long after the romantic relationships fade. We're going to grow old together. Like soul mates.

6

JEREMIAH

LENNON GRAVES HAD TROUBLE WRITTEN ALL OVER HER. Whether she was *in* trouble or she *was* trouble was yet to be determined, but I had a feeling I would soon find out.

She was in the goat yard with Seb. Randy and Michael, two guests who had already been with us for a of couple weeks, were also around. Randy, a white guy from Vermont, was active Army, on medical leave for the summer. Michael was a Black EMT from Atlanta. Both were wearing work boots with their jeans because it didn't matter if they were from the city or country, the nature of military and first responder work had taught them the importance of appropriate footwear for the job. Some of our guests came here in sneakers, but most wore boots of some kind.

Lennon was here in sandals. Fucking *sandals*.

Holly came to stand next to me. Neither of us spoke as we watched the scene unfold. The ranch currently had seven goats—all rescues, all escape artists, and all extremely food-motivated. Goats were curious, intelligent animals and had a tendency to get into trouble when bored. A lot like Seb, actually, which was why he claimed them as his project. Right now, Seb was reconfiguring their obstacle course, and goddammit, he was handing Lennon a hammer.

I took an unconscious step forward like I intended to snatch it back.

Holly cackled. "Oh, this should be fun."

"She's going to break a toe," I muttered. "I don't like it." Because I didn't like the idea of *anyone* getting hurt on our watch, and that meant Lennon, too. Not *especially* Lennon. Her safety only felt more urgent because of those fucking sandals, that was all.

"Well, I don't like it either. Any of it." Holly kicked at a pebble with her ranch-appropriate cowboy boot. "There's something not right about her, Jay. You know she's not military. Why is she here?"

"She could be a first responder."

Holly shot me an *are you kidding me?* look.

"Fine. I don't know why she's here." And hell, that

bothered me. If she wasn't military or a first responder, how had she even heard of Mercy River Ranch?

I watched Lennon nod at something Seb said and then carefully place a five-inch nail on a wooden beam. She glanced up at him for approval, and when he nodded, she tapped the head with the hammer in quick, light movements. Then she pulled her fingers away and used three hard strokes to send the nail the rest of the way home.

I let out a breath and rolled my shoulders down from my ears. But they tensed right back up again when Seb clapped her on the back, and she grinned at him. Something that felt like a growl rumbled through my chest, but I swallowed it down.

"Maybe Seb knows something," Holly smirked.

I grunted. I didn't like not knowing Lennon's story, but somehow I hated the thought of her confiding in Seb even more. "Our guests' reasons for being here are not our business unless they make it our business. You know that."

We took privacy seriously here. Most of our guests opened up eventually, with each other, if not with us. Sharing what had brought them to Mercy River was part of the healing process. But it had to be done on their own terms. Guests didn't owe us their stories or their pain.

"Every rule has an exception. I'm not suggesting we find her mother's maiden name and social security number. Just a basic background, that's all. A quick tappity-tap on your keyboard and we'll know if Lennon is someone we need to worry about. Maybe she killed someone. Maybe she robbed a bank and is hiding out."

I snorted. Lennon had moved on to the next nail with more confidence this time. It gave me a funny feeling in my chest, the way she smiled.

"Maybe she works for a development company looking to turn Mercy River Ranch into ugly mansions for Hollywood stars."

That gave me pause. The ranch and its acres of open land had caught the eye of more than one greedy developer. Mercy River wasn't for sale, but there were people in the world that believed everything had a price, and if that price wasn't willingly given, then it would be taken by force. Those were the ones you needed to look out for, the ones that hid their dirty work behind a pretty face.

And Lennon's face was damn pretty.

Reading my silence correctly, Holly pushed her point home. "Keep an eye on her, all right? Let Lennon worry about protecting her privacy. We protect the ranch."

There was no need to respond, so I didn't. Holly knew my past. She knew I had once mistaken a wolf for a friend, and my sister had paid the price. I would never make that mistake again.

With her task completed, Lennon looked around for

something else to do. Randy waved her over. "You want to give them a treat?"

Oh, hell. My gaze shot to Seb, who was up on the ramp with Michael, fixing the rope-and-plank bridge. He wouldn't get to her in time. I was already on the move when Seb called down to them to wait, but it was too late. Randy handed Lennon a paper cup filled with goat treats. The goats, not being stupid, advanced. She backed up to the fence and they followed.

I broke into a run. The goats weren't usually biters, but their sharp hooves would slice her unprotected toes to shreds. Maybe she would have done something sensible, like throwing the cup away from her, if they hadn't knocked it out of her hand. It fell to her sandaled feet. With a little shriek, she turned toward the fence and found me on the other side, a four-foot tall wall of metal mesh separating us.

Our eyes locked.

She reached up. I reached over. "Jump, Lennon."

She jumped. I caught her under the armpits and heaved her upwards. Her thighs slid against the plastic top rail as I hauled her over the fence to safety. She clung to my neck, her body shaking.

"Hey." I stroked the ridge of her spine to where it started to curve and then back up again. Her body was sun-warmed and strong beneath my palm. I hated that I noticed. Hated that I didn't want to stop touching her. It wasn't a problem I normally had. What a terrible time for my body to wake up. "You're okay."

She snorted. "I'm okay, but *they* won't be when I make handbags out of their hides." There was a suspicious tremor in her voice. Her shoulders shook again.

I dipped my chin to get a better look at her. Sparkling dark eyes looked back at me. Light brown irises that turned to green rings around her pupils. Her lips tilted up. Laughing.

She wasn't scared at all. Lennon was *laughing*.

Hell. I speared a hand through my hair and tugged. "It's not funny. You could have gotten hurt."

"But I wasn't." She laughed again.

"You okay?" Randy called through the fence.

I glared at his worried face. "She's fine." I glanced up at Seb, who was watching us with a smirk. "She's okay," I said, louder for his benefit, not that he seemed all that concerned. He nodded and waved. Was I the only one who took guest safety seriously?

With an annoyed growl, I grabbed Lennon's hand and tugged her along as I strode toward the lodge.

"Where are we going?" she asked, her tone curious but not distrustful.

"To get you some fucking shoes."

LENNON REGARDED Bartholemew's Ranch and Home with the wide-eyed look of Dorothy leaving her black-and-white world and opening the door to Technicolor Oz. "I have never bought shoes from a store that also sold baby chicks. This place is amazing."

She hadn't spent much time in rural areas then. I filed that tidbit of information away. The address she gave us to hold the reservation was in Virginia, but that didn't tell us much. "City girl?"

She made a noncommittal sound.

"Where did you serve?" I asked casually. I suspected she wasn't military, but I couldn't imagine her as a firefighter or an EMT either. Cop was out of the question.

She smirked at me over her shoulder before turning her attention to the rack of boots. "Cowboy, the only thing I serve is face."

I blinked. She served...face? What the hell did that mean? "Like...Salome?"

"Who is Salome? Is she a model?" She picked up a boot, studied it, then returned it to the rack.

What did models have to do with anything? "In the Bible. Salome dances for the king, and he likes it so much that he tells her he will grant her one favor. She goes to her mother and asks what she should request. Her mother wants the head of John the Baptist. So Salome demands his death and serves his head to her mother on a platter."

Lennon stilled, then slowly pivoted to face me. "If

the king owed me a favor, I wouldn't waste it on my mother. If she wants a favor from him, then she can shake her own ass in his direction. My ass, my favor." With that, she spun back to the shoes.

I cleared my throat. "That's fair."

"Damn right it is," she muttered.

After trying on a few pairs, she selected one to her satisfaction, and we headed for the register. She paused by the rack of coats on post-season sale.

"It gets cold at night. I wasn't really expecting that." She pulled one off the rack and held it up. "I didn't bring a coat or any kind of long sleeves except my hoodie."

"Some nights could get below freezing. We also take some rides to higher elevations. You will definitely want a coat for that."

Nodding absently, she ran her hand down the sleeve until she found the price tag dangling from the cuff. She chewed her lip, then shook her head, carefully placing the coat back on the rack. "I think I can get by with my hoodie. I mean, it's not *that* cold."

I squinted at the tag, brow furrowed. Money was tight for most of our guests—firefighters, EMTs, and most military didn't take home big paychecks, which was why we subsidized with donations and ranch work —but Lennon had never fit that mold. Everything about her screamed wealth. Her fancy designer sunglasses cost more than one of these clearance coats.

"The ranch will cover it," I said.

"Really?" Her lips parted in surprise, but then her eyes narrowed. "The ranch will cover it, or *you* will?"

I shrugged. "It's all the same."

Her expression hardened. "No, it's not. And no, thank you." She turned away, muttering, "Too good to be true. Men paying for shit is what got me here in the first place."

My stomach clenched. I didn't like the sound of that at all. What men? And what the hell did they do that brought her here? It was none of my business. I had told Holly that, and I stood by it. Everyone here had secrets. Things they had seen. Things they had done. If Lennon had been any other guest at this ranch, I wouldn't push. I would let her talk about it on her own terms. But I knew I wasn't going to do that. Not this time. Whatever had brought Lennon here, I intended to find out.

But I wasn't going to let her freeze to death while I did that.

"Then borrow one of mine. It might be loose in the shoulders, but you're tall. It should fit you well enough."

She eyed me like she thought it was a trap. "Really?"

"Sure."

"Okay." But she kept right on looking at me like she was waiting for the catch. "Thank you."

"It's not a problem."

We walked to the register and I bit my tongue against the urge to offer to pay for her boots. She wouldn't accept it, and nothing I had would fit her.

There had been a time when I'd had to accept charity from strangers, and no matter how kindly it was offered, it never ceased to sting a little. Maybe Lennon felt the same way, but I had a feeling it went deeper than that. It was more than pride with her. She doubted my motives.

Lennon handed over her credit card at the register. My jaw tightened as I realized there was no name on the card. It was one of those Visa gift cards that anyone could use. Maybe it was nothing. *Maybe.* But in my experience, little bits of nothing had a way of adding up to something.

Feeling my gaze on her, she glanced back at me, bouncing on her toes slightly like she was preparing to run—her fight or flight instinct kicking in. Looked like Lennon was a bolter. I focused my attention elsewhere to let her know I wasn't a threat. Because a hairpin trigger like that? It was learned.

I didn't know what brought a woman like Lennon Graves to a place like Mercy River Ranch. And I for damn sure didn't trust her.

But I fucking hated that she didn't trust me, either.

7

LENNON

THERE WAS SOMETHING NOT RIGHT ABOUT THIS PLACE.

First of all, there were an awful lot of men at this wellness retreat. Men, in my experience, defined "wellness" as well-fucked and well-fed. They did not participate in juice cleanses and sound baths—both of which had been promised on the website, although neither actually materialized.

Hell, I'd had to trick Benny into going to his annual prostate exam and afterward he pouted for a whole week. I had expected to be surrounded by women recovering from burnout and trying to lose five pounds. But unless they were all hanging out without me, I had the dubious honor of being the only female guest at Mercy River Ranch.

Secondly, those men were…something. I didn't know what that something was yet, but there was something binding them together that I couldn't quite put my finger on. They weren't friends—as far as I knew, all seven of them had arrived separately and hadn't known each other prior. They were all different ages, anywhere from Jarod, the baby of the group at twenty-three, to Caleb, who was fifty-seven. They didn't have similar backgrounds, education, or look the same.

But they all knew CPR.

I knew this because one night when they had all clustered together around one table at dinner, I overheard them discussing their go-to song for CPR.

Stayin' Alive by the Bee Gees was Caleb's favorite. "The classic."

Michael's song was Beyoncé's *Crazy in Love*.

Flowers by Miley Cyrus was Randy's choice. "Only God can judge me," he'd said when they laughed.

Aaron and Paul liked *Purple Rain* by Prince.

And Tyler and Scott relied on *Glory Days* by Bruce Springsteen.

It wasn't *that* weird to know CPR. But all seven of them not only knowing CPR, but performing it so often that they had a favorite song to help them keep the beat? That couldn't be a coincidence.

But the strangest thing about this place—and most relevant to the painful position I now found myself in—was that it was nothing like the website promised. When

I booked my cabin for June, I had been under the impression that my days would be spent pampering my mind and body with the kind of bougie shit I had come to associate with self-care: hot yoga in the mornings led by a bendy white woman, warm tea and organic vegetables for lunch followed by an afternoon nap and guided meditation, before closing out the day with a slow sunset hike on a gentle incline.

The website hadn't said a damn thing about a she-demon named Tamilee Jones masquerading as a physical therapist and personal trainer.

"Do you understand what failure means, Lennon?" Tamilee demanded, hands on her hips. She was Black woman with deep brown skin that didn't show a single line even though I suspected she was over fifty, blue eyeshadow up to her brow line and bright pink lips, standing at a mere five-foot-four, although her high-top hairstyle added another three inches.

I gave her a baleful glare despite the trickle of sweat that ran into my eyes and blurred my vision. "Yes. It means I can't."

"That's right. *Can't*. Not won't. As in, physically impossible. Now, is it physically impossible for you to lift those weights one more time?"

I wanted to say yes so damn badly. Because that next rep was going to hurt. I really didn't like to hurt. My idea of a good workout was super light weights and high reps that the instructor counted down for me, allowing me to zone out through the hard parts.

"Yeah, you have one more in you." She nodded firmly like there was no question of it. "You got this, baby."

Who knew a warm woman's voice calling me baby was all it took for me to summon superhuman strength and live up to my potential? Tamilee Jones should take her show on the road. Teach high school guidance counselors and mothers her ways. Maybe if I'd had someone like her telling me I could do it, maybe I would have actually believed it.

I hinged my elbows, curling the weights to my shoulders with a mighty grunt.

"Hell, yeah!" she hollered. "Now, see what happens when you try one more."

I gave her a baffled look but tried to tighten my biceps again. The weights jiggled, but I would have had to lift with momentum from my whole body to get them to the top of the rep. "I can't," I said.

"Exactly. You *can't*. Not without hurting yourself. That's failure. It's not your goal for every workout, but when you're finding your benchmarks, that's how you do it." Her bright pink lips tilted into a smile. "You did great, baby."

Feeling pretty damn proud of myself, I smiled back. "So we're done now?"

"We're done with arms. Now we move on to legs."

Goddammit.

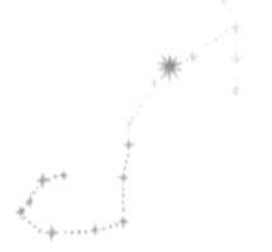

THE SILENCE WOKE me up again, as it had every morning this week. I didn't fight it. It was becoming my new normal, waking up before the sun to watch the stars fade into a purple dawn before I headed to the lodge to help Cecily and Amos make breakfast for the cowboys. It had stopped feeling like jet lag two days ago. Now it felt *good*—although I suspected that if anyone from my old life could see me now, they'd think I had lost my damn mind. *Blink once if you're having a mental breakdown, Lennon.*

Maybe I was.

But it didn't feel like a breakdown.

It felt like...like letting out a breath I hadn't known I was holding. All that tension I hadn't even been aware of slowing melting from my body with that one long exhale. A week ago, I wouldn't have said I was stressed— no more so than the average person, anyway. Maybe that was true, but it was also true that the average person was really fucking stressed.

There was just so *much*. Catastrophes around the world we couldn't do shit about. Catastrophes we *could* do something about, but that something felt so small that we rarely did even that. The daily grind of bills to pay, work to do, people to care for. A never-ending stream of things vying for our attention. I felt like I was constantly running as fast as I could, even though in actuality, all I was doing was standing still, staring at my phone.

There wasn't a single part of my body that didn't hold on to the effects of that, of treating every ding of my phone as life or death, wondering if that DM was going to be a floral arrangement inspired by one of my designs or a dick pic. My shoulders ached. My back spasmed. My stomach was constantly twisted in knots. And the funny thing was, I hadn't realized any of it.

I hadn't let myself *feel* any of it.

Until now.

A week without Wi-Fi—only using my phone to listen to audiobooks before I went to sleep and checking the burner phone once a day for an update from Hector—and I felt *everything*. It hurt, but a good kind of hurt. A tingly, achy feeling, like sticking your hand in hot water after you played outside in the snow without gloves. My body coming back to life.

The clouds hid the stars, but I didn't mind. The brewing storm had its own beauty. Wind whipped at my cheeks, and I tugged my hair loose from its bun so the wind could have its way with that, too. Maybe I really was smack in the middle of a mental breakdown, because I kicked off my Uggs so they would stay dry, tossed Jeremiah's borrowed coat onto the rocking chair, and left the safety of the porch.

The sky grew darker. I didn't hear thunder or see lightning, but I could sense a sudden shift in the air as the storm bore down on me. A cold drop of rain splashed against the crown of my head, followed seconds later by another one on my shoulder. *Here comes the storm.*

I closed my eyes and lifted my face to the rain.

8

JEREMIAH

FUCKING HELL.

Nothing could have prepared me for the sight of Lennon Graves out in the summer storm wearing nothing but skimpy shorts and a tank top, the outline of her body limned in gold from the light shining through her cabin window. She stood there with her face tilted to the sky as if she were offering herself to the gods. I took what they couldn't, my gaze eating up every part of her.

She knew I was there, even though she didn't look at me. I came this way at the same time every morning, doing a quick pass by the guest cabins to make sure all was well before heading to the pastures to bring in the horses. Ever since Lennon's first morning here, when she told me not to sneak up on girls in the dark, I had made sure she could hear me coming. She'd learned a lesson from our first encounter, too, and always had her coat on when I came through. Truthfully, every morning I told myself she wouldn't be out here, and every morning I hoped she'd prove me wrong, and she had.

But today...today I'd felt like a fool stomping along, knowing there wasn't a snowball's chance in hell of Lennon being out in this storm. With the rain coming down in heavy sheets, I hadn't even hoped for it.

Yet here she was. Her tanned skin was slick with rain. Rivers of it dripped from her raised chin and sluiced down her throat, following the ridge of her clavicle down to the full slopes of her breasts. I wanted to trace the path with my tongue, lick up every drop that disappeared into her deep cleavage.

No coat. Her shorts seemed to wither into nothing more than underwear, and the thin cotton of her tank top turned sheer. She wasn't wearing a bra. I could clearly see the dusky outline of her areolas and peaked nipples. My cock stirred because I had thoughts about licking those, too.

Thoughts I had no business having.

What the hell was wrong with me? She was a guest here. People came to Mercy River for healing, not depravity. I didn't trust her, and that was all the more reason to stop imagining the taste of her nipples in my mouth. A decent man would look away, but Gabriel could have blown his trumpet to summon us back to heaven, and I would still be standing here, staring at Lennon's breasts.

Fuck, they were magnificent.

"Lennon," I rasped, my throat the only dry thing left on the planet, which was fucking unfair given the circumstances.

I had felt attraction. Lust, even. But I had never known what it truly meant to *thirst* until now, and this woman was all that could quench it.

She looked at me then, blinking the raindrops from her eyes. "Hey." Her voice was barely audible over the soft roar of the rain pelting the dirt.

She ran her hands over her hair, past her ears, down her neck, squeezing the water from her skin as she went, and then left her hands there, cupping the sides of her throat. Her elbows pushed her breasts together.

Could a man die from this? It felt like I could die from this.

"Lennon." I exhaled her name nearly against her lips. When had I gotten so close? I had no recollection of crossing her yard, but I was already unzipping my trench coat, opening it wide, and wrapping her inside with me. The rain streaming down the brim of my hat would have hit her upturned face, so I took it off and held it over her head. "What are you doing out here in the storm, honey?"

Her gaze lifted to my hat and then slowly lowered to

my face with a baffled expression. She rested her hands on my chest, her fingers fiddling with the top button of my shirt. "I wanted…"

A raindrop fell from her nose to her bottom lip, and her tongue peeked out to swipe it up. My vision tunneled until that pink, plush mouth was all I could see. I might have made a sound, a quiet, needy groan. I hoped to everything holy she hadn't heard me.

She shivered. Her wet body had soaked through my flannel, but I tightened my fist on the placket of my trench coat and pulled her closer. Too close, maybe. With her hips flush to mine, she felt every hard inch of how she affected me.

Her eyes widened, but then her lips tilted into a wry smile. "I wanted to play in the rain. What about you? Why are you out here?" Her voice turned sultry as she leaned in. "Do you want to play with me, Jeremiah?"

Fuck yes, my dick screamed, which was why my dick wasn't in charge of me. What was more alarming was that every cell in my body agreed with it. My gut was normally reliable at keeping me out of trouble—and hell, I *knew* this woman was trouble—but right now it was flashing nothing but green lights.

Fuck it—

Her teeth chattered. My brain kicked on and I exhaled harshly. With my arm banded around her waist, I lifted her off her feet and walked us both onto her porch, with her muddy toes kicking me in the shins. "Inside. Now."

She laughed as I set her down. "All right, caveman. I need to shower before I head to the lodge to make your breakfast, anyway."

My breakfast—for me and a dozen other cowboys. But the way she said it made it feel more intimate. Like her effort was for me alone. Maybe I was a caveman because damn, that sounded good.

I waited for her to gather her shoes and coat. She sent me a look over her shoulder, like she was trying to figure out what I was still doing there.

"You look like you could use a hot shower yourself," she said.

I turned and walked away so I wouldn't take that as an invitation. The rain kept coming down as I stalked to the lodge, but I didn't feel a single drop of it. Holly was at the front desk when I pushed through the double doors.

She arched her eyebrows at me. "Coffee?"

"Shower," I said shortly and made for the stairs that lead to my living quarters on the top floor.

The moment the door clicked shut behind me, I pressed my hands to my face and hollered into them. It didn't do a damn thing to ease the frustration. I kicked off my boots and fought my way out of my overcoat like it was a wrestling match and I was losing. Agitation made me clumsy, and I slammed my shoulder into the doorjamb on my way to the bathroom.

Fucking hell. I didn't even know what temperature to set the shower. My skin was cold, but I felt like I was burning up inside. I flipped the knob to the middle, stripped off my flannel and jeans, and got in. The spray hit my skin and all I could think about was Lennon slick with rain. I slapped the knob, spinning it to as hot as it could go. Maybe it could scald the image of her from my brain.

Her wet mouth. The shape of her nipples. The glint in her eyes when she asked if I wanted to play. *Fuck— fuck.* I turned around so the spray hit me in the shoulder blades, then turned around again. If I stopped moving for even a second, I'd—

My hand gripped my cock before my brain could finish that thought. For a moment, I paused. Tried to talk myself out of it. It had been a long time since I'd done this—I couldn't even remember the last time I'd needed to. I'd always treated it like stress relief. Clear my head, settle my gut before a mission. Lust had never factored into it.

But this...I couldn't pretend this was about anything but *her*.

Fuck it. I was doing it anyway.

I let my hand move, let it slide up my shaft as I remembered her tongue licking the raindrop from her lip, let it pump a little faster as I imagined that tongue licking *me*. I didn't hold back my groan as I pictured her on her knees, looking up at me with those big doe eyes. Her breasts bare and bouncing as she worked me with that luscious mouth.

But I wouldn't come there. Not in her mouth. I wanted—fucking hell, what had this woman awakened in me with all her talk about facials? Tightening my grip, I tried to think of anything else. But I swiped my thumb over the tip, felt the moisture beading there, and couldn't stop.

I wanted to paint her with my cum. I wanted to watch it hit her puffy lips, her throat, her breasts. I wanted her to lick my cum from her lips like the raindrop, and then lick me clean, too.

My hand moved faster, my hips jerking. I came so fucking hard I splashed the tile with it. I fell forward on a roar, my hand slapping the wall. My chest heaved as I caught my breath from a full-body orgasm that had been unlike anything I'd ever experienced before in my life.

Slowly, my breathing steadied. My heartbeat slowed to its regular beat. The hot water felt good on my neck and shoulders, my back and its thick scars.

I flipped the faucet to cold.

9

LENNON

"Smells good, Graves." Mateo bumped my shoulder with his as he heaped his plate with food. "You made all this for us?"

"Amos made the eggs, and Cecily made the biscuits. I just did the bacon."

I didn't tell him that I had burned the first batch to an inedible degree while daydreaming about a certain cowboy wrapping me up in his coat. Amos would have banished me from his kitchen, but Cecily had reminded him that Miguel hadn't shown up for his shift today, so they were still short on help, and anyway, the pigs would be happy to eat the bacon. The idea of pigs eating their friends made my stomach turn, so I promised I'd eat the burnt bacon myself, even if it took all week.

Mateo took a bite, chewed, and then added two more pieces to his towering plate. "Perfect."

He pushed his glasses up his nose with his knuckle and grinned at me wide enough for his dimples to pop out. Then he took his plate and sat down on the stool leaning against the welcome desk, where Holly was already seated with her own full plate, and that weird chicken in her lap. There was something protective about the way they sat shoulder to knee. Who was protecting who, I wondered.

Of all the cowboys who weren't Jeremiah, Mateo was my favorite. He reminded me of a cross between a golden retriever and a border collie. Outgoing and energetic, a little goofy, hella smart. One of the nicest and friendliest people I'd ever met. Not that Jeremiah was rude or mean, because he wasn't—even though I had given him plenty of reasons to be.

Jeremiah was...contained. Reserved. Protective in a way that I should have found overbearing and annoying, but honestly? It felt *good*. No one had ever taken care of me like that before. No one had ever wrapped me in their own coat like my comfort might be more important than theirs. Certainly not my mother, who had always been the child in our relationship, or the men who had paid for my time. Not even Benny, who had been the best of them.

Which wasn't to say that Jeremiah was my favorite. He wasn't even in the same category as all the other cowboys in my mind. There was Jeremiah, and then there was everyone else.

"Thanks, Lennon." Liam raised his plate to me, then grabbed a biscuit.

"Yeah, thanks, Lennon." Seb was at my elbow with a plate of his own. "I'm starving."

"Amos and Cecily did most of it." I suspected they knew that, but I hated taking credit I didn't deserve. I craved head pats as much as any average girl who didn't get enough attention from her parents, but I liked to earn them.

"Yeah, but we pay them." Seb winked. I liked him, too, and I had a feeling a lot of girls felt the same way. It couldn't be more obvious if he'd had a neon sign flashing on his forehead: *Great fuck, terrible boyfriend.*

Fine by me. Men were more trouble than they were worth, and it was the biggest disappointment of my life that I remained attracted to them. The last thing I needed was a new boyfriend when I was still dealing with the fallout from the last one. A great fuck, though... I wouldn't say no to that. Depending on who was making the offer.

My gaze strayed to Jeremiah like it was pulled there by a magnet. I didn't try to kid myself about what that meant. I had made a promise to myself a long time ago, and I had kept it every day since. Everyone else might lie to me, but I never would.

I wanted him.

I wanted him, and unless he'd had a flashlight shoved down his pants during the storm this morning, he wanted me, too. Judging from the way he stood, arms crossed over his broad chest, a clipboard clenched in one hand, lips flattened to a grim line, he wasn't too happy about that. He hadn't looked at me once since I'd come in ten minutes ago to set up breakfast for them.

And he hadn't gone near the food.

My eyes narrowed. The cowboys we'd fed earlier had gobbled up the food like they hadn't eaten in a week. Ranch work led to big appetites. So Jeremiah standing there, refusing to take a single bite? Yeah, I took that personally.

"Are you hungry?" I asked. "I could fix you a plate."

He had been glaring at Seb next to me, but now he turned his face away so all I could see was his profile. His throat bobbed as he swallowed. He shook his head, heightened color cresting his cheekbone.

I couldn't resist poking at him, just a little. If he couldn't eat my food and fucking like it, then at least he could have the decency to meet my eyes. I wanted him to look at me like he had this morning, the way his blue-gray eyes were blazing hot and soft all at the same time.

Honey.

It wasn't the first time someone had called me that, but it was the first time it hadn't been condescending and so damn smug. The way Jeremiah said it, it flowed warm and sweet through my veins.

And now he wouldn't even look at me.

"You look flushed." I crossed the room to him. "Maybe you have a fever?"

I lifted my hand, but Jeremiah was faster. His hand snapped to my wrist like one of those old slap bracelets my mom kept from when she was a kid. *Shit.* I'd gotten what I wanted, made him look at me, but now that I had it, it felt like a lot more than I had bargained for.

For the breathless space of a heartbeat, I had the crazy notion that he was going to kiss me, right here in front of three cowboys, a cowgirl, and—for reasons that remained unclear to me—one very fluffy chicken. But of course he didn't.

Slowly, he lowered our hands and stepped back, his eyes still locked on mine. "Don't get too close. You might catch it."

Too late for that.

THE GUARDIAN

My hands shook as I gripped the steering wheel. That wasn't supposed to happen. He was supposed to turn the other way. The other way! I wanted him hurt, not dead.

Maybe he wasn't dead. I hoped he wasn't. I didn't mean for it to happen like this. I got out of my car on unsteady legs, looked both ways, then crossed the road. It was still dark out, and the rain was coming down something fierce. I shined my flashlight. He didn't go too far—not all the way to the bottom. A tree stopped his descent. I breathed a sigh of relief and then dashed back to my warm, dry car.

He was going to be fine. The universe was looking out for me. Maybe he'll have, like, a broken arm or something. That should keep him away for a few weeks.

Soaked to the bone, my teeth chattering, I cranked

the heat. Three miles down the road, I pulled over and reached for my phone. Hesitated. Can they trace the call back to me? I sucked my bottom lip between my teeth. Better not risk it.

I pulled back on the road, following the twisty Mercy River, but half a mile later I pulled over again. Fuck. I had to. I couldn't just leave him there.

"Nine-one-one, what's your emergency?" a woman's voice answered.

"I just saw someone drive over the cliff!" I made my voice high and panicked. "Hideaway Road."

I hung up before she could respond. Cell phone reception here sucked, so maybe she would think we had been disconnected. It was fine. Everyone knew the bend in Hideaway Road was dangerous. That would be the first place they would check. They'd find him and get him to a hospital. He was going to be fine.

Altruistic. That's what I was. Because honestly. Why would he *do* that? I mean, seriously. *There's no road there, dipshit!* If he had turned toward the fields like he was supposed to, we wouldn't be in this mess.

Shaking my head, I pulled back onto the road. Hopefully a patrol car or an ambulance would be cruising along here soon, and I needed to be far away when that happened. They wouldn't understand.

But Lennon would. She would totally get why I had to do it, but I couldn't tell her yet. It might scare her. She didn't know me like I knew her. That was the whole point, why I'd *had* to do it. She needed time to get to know me. And she'd need a job if she was going to make her move to Mercy River permanent.

I'd figured she'd want a job with animals—she'd always lamented that her landlord wouldn't let her have a pet—but I'd overheard her telling Mateo that she really liked working in the kitchen. So of course I made that happen for her. That's what guardian angels do.

And now that he was out of the way, she could stay at Mercy River as long as she wanted to.

One day, we would laugh about this.

My favorite song came on—another sign that I was on the right path. I turned it up over the roar of the rain and sang along.

10

LENNON

Mornings could be frigid and I was grateful I'd never know a winter here because I doubted I was cut out for that kind of suffering, but damn. *Damn.* A June afternoon in Wyoming might be my idea of heaven.

The air here was lighter somehow. Maybe it was the lack of humidity. I'd already used up the entire bottle of moisturizer I'd brought with me, but that was a small price to pay for being able to take a breath this deep. And that breath being full of wildflowers and ponderosa pine made it even better. I loved the city, and damn, how I missed it, but I liked this, too. It surprised me how much. The mountains, the trees, the vastness of the land and the sky... This place made my blood sing in a way I couldn't explain.

But right now it wasn't the mountains making my blood sing. It was the cowboys.

Shirtless, sweaty cowboys.

Even Holly had stripped down to a sports bra, but I was a lot less interested in that than the bear of a man passing out wooden mallets—the only one of the five of them who was wearing a shirt because god hated me, apparently. But at least his T-shirt was tight and light gray, which was the next best thing. He looked like a Viking with all that burnished gold hair and his thick muscles. I wanted to feel that mustache between my thighs.

I bit into the chocolate chip cookie I had snagged from the lobby and watched as they set up flags, poles, and wire wickets. It looked like croquet, but the space they were using was about half the size of a football field. The couple of times I'd played as a kid, the setup had taken maybe a quarter acre. Of course, there wasn't a lot of space to be had at the trailer park. Maybe this was normal.

I brushed the cookie crumbs from my hands and sauntered forward. "Can I play?"

"Fuck no," Jeremiah said at the same time Holly said, "Sure."

I split a glance between them. "So...yes?"

"No." Jeremiah's jaw tightened. "Guests don't play Blood Ball."

I watched Mateo push a wicket into the dirt. "I thought this was croquet."

"It's Blood Ball. You want to play croquet, you can use the equipment when we're done."

"Oh, let her play," Holly protested. "She'll be fine."

Something about the way she said that made me wonder if I would, in fact, be fine.

"I vote yes," Seb tossed in. I felt better about that.

Jeremiah pinched the bridge of his nose. "This isn't a democracy."

"The fuck it isn't." Seb turned to me. "The rules of the game are simple. Get from Pole A to Pole Z—that's the home pole—with more points than anyone else. We don't take turns. You just get your ball through the wickets and try to keep other players from doing the same. Each wicket is five points. Hitting another player's ball is ten points. Reaching Pole Z is worth twenty points. Making someone bleed is fifty points."

Ah. "So that's why it's called Blood Ball?"

"Nah. The name came first, the rules after." Seb grinned. "We call it Blood Ball because Holly said the five of us playing any game involving wooden balls and mallets, someone was going to bleed. She was right. It started as croquet, but none of us knew the rules and..." He smirked. "Things happened, as things do. So we figured we might as well award points for something that was going to happen anyway."

Well, that was foreboding.

I glanced at Holly, who stared back at me with a little smirk. "Having second thoughts?" she taunted.

My eyes narrowed. Yes, she was baiting me, but I was easily baited. "I'm playing."

Jeremiah made an annoyed sound. "Lennon—"

"What?" I snapped.

He ground his molars together. "Nothing," he gritted out.

"Great." I beamed at him. "Then I'm playing." I picked up the last mallet—green—and rolled the matching ball under my foot. "How does the game end? If no one is taking turns, how do we know when it's over?"

"The first player to reach the home pole ends the game," Seb said. "Yell *home* and the game stops. We look at the video to determine who won. Winner is the player with the most points, even if they never made it to Pole Z." Seb pointed across the field, to where a camera was set up on a tripod. "There's the camera. Don't knock it over. It's an automatic last place for fucking with the evidence, and you get latrine duty. Got it?"

I nodded. "Got it."

They lined up their balls at Pole A, so I did the same.

"Go!" Holly shouted, and then—

Chaos. Mallets, balls, bodies everywhere. Holy shit, I was going to get myself killed. I maneuvered my way to the outskirts of the field. No one noticed. They were too busy knocking each other down to pay any attention to what the weak little city girl was doing, and—

No one noticed.

A slow grin spread across my face.

I knew how to win.

11

JEREMIAH

It was a damn good thing I didn't need to have eyes on Lennon to know exactly where she was, because after what I had done in the shower this morning, I couldn't look her in the face.

She must have come to her senses and realized she didn't belong in this game because she hugged her corner for dear life. That suited me perfectly. With Lennon at my back, I could keep my attention focused on what really mattered.

Those fucking cowboys.

Running rescue missions for a decade had left me with certain skills. I knew how to account for multiple enemy combatants at once.

Holly was farthest away, on the other side of the

field, but that didn't make her safe. She was the fastest out of all of us, and deceptive in her tactics. She was also the most likely one of us to make Lennon bleed. It was a safe bet that Mateo, Liam, and Seb wouldn't do anything to truly hurt a guest, especially a woman. Holly had fewer qualms about that, and she'd had it in for Lennon from the moment she'd arrived. She wouldn't *really* hurt her, but she would absolutely scratch her up a bit.

Holly was dangerous, but she wasn't my top priority. Mateo would keep her in line. The two of them were more interested in besting each other than actually winning.

Liam...he liked to win, but he wouldn't see Lennon as a threat. He'd go after Mateo or Seb first. Eventually he'd come for me. Maybe he'd try to get the drop on Holly, but he wouldn't go straight for her because, unlike Seb, he wasn't big on suicide missions.

Seb was the one I needed to watch.

Would he hurt her? Fuck no.

Would he take advantage of the opportunity to get Lennon in his arms? Hell yes, he would.

And then...well, then I'd have to kill him.

"You gonna get in the game, Jay?" Seb jogged backwards in a circle around his ball, green eyes glinting, mallet across his shoulders. Fucking showboat.

"I'm in it," I growled.

Only it wasn't a fucking game to me.

His gaze flicked behind me and back again with an

annoying little smirk I wanted to punch right off his face. "Oh, yeah? Because from where I'm standing, it looks like you're more interested in playing bodyguard than Blood Ball."

I kept my eyes trained on him like I was completely oblivious to Liam sneaking up on my five o'clock. "Don't know what you're talking about, man."

Seb shot me a look of pure disbelief. "Don't you?"

Liam's yellow ball came to rest against mine with a quiet clink. Before Liam could stop me, I pressed my boot against my black ball, swung the mallet back, and hit my ball with a satisfying whack. The energy shot right through my ball and into his, sending it flying across the field. With a muttered curse, Liam went after it, middle finger raised as he ran past me.

Seb laughed, and his gaze landed over my shoulder again. The way his head tilted, I knew he wasn't looking at her face. My guess was she was bent over, lining her mallet up with her ball, perky ass in the air and those stupid fucking cutoff denim shorts riding up her long thighs.

"Hey, Lennon, baby, come over here and we can talk strategy," he called to her.

"What, so you can score an easy fifty points off the city girl?" she yelled back. "Do I look stupid to you, Seb?"

He was still laughing when I caught him by the waist and brought him to the ground, making sure he'd land on his knees. Knees were the easiest body parts to draw blood from, and I liked to win, too.

"Fifty points, asshole," I muttered as dark red swelled from right below his kneecap.

Seb grunted. "Is that your way of calling dibs?"

"You can't call dibs on a human being." We rolled to our feet, shaking off the fall. "I don't trust her, Seb."

"Shit, man. I don't trust half the women I fuck. Use protection and keep your mouth occupied with something that isn't talking. You'll be fine."

"That's your advice?" I shook my head. "Hell."

"It's good advice!" he protested.

"It's—oof!" I grunted as Seb tackled me. My forearm scraped against the dirt, and I winced. Glancing down, I saw long scratches flecked with red. It wasn't a lot, but it counted.

"Fifty points," Seb half laughed, half groaned. "And Mateo is coming for your girl."

I didn't need to see him. With my cheek pressed to the dirt, I could hear him. The ground vibrated as Mateo thundered closer.

Not yet.

Not yet.

Now.

I twisted, scissoring my legs so they caught Mateo by the ankles. His knee rammed my shoulder as he stumbled forward. With a holler, he fell across both of us.

We lay there in a grunting, tangled heap for only a

moment before Seb started shoving limbs aside. "I didn't deserve that, Jay."

"Yes, you fucking did," I muttered.

"For what? Having eyes?" Seb demanded, making Mateo snicker. "She's hot. What do you want from me?"

I want you to keep your fucking eyes closed around her. I choked back the words. Not because they weren't true. But if I said that out loud, I'd never hear the end of it. We were brothers, all of us: Seb, Liam, Mateo, Holly, and I. The blood that tied us together wasn't inherited— it was spilt, but that only made the bond stronger. And like any band of brothers, we tortured each other. That was how we showed love.

"You know Liam is going to take advantage of this moment, right?" Seb shoved me, then Mateo, as he tried to get up.

Mateo groaned through a laugh. "Or Holly."

I shot to my feet.

Fuck, that hurt.

I didn't have a second to worry about that, not with Liam and Holly bearing down on Lennon. The next several moments were full of even more pain. Bodies clashed together. Mallets swung at balls and ankles alike. Somewhere in the fray, I lost my own ball.

But I never lost Lennon.

She was there, behind me. I caught the movement of her hair in the periphery of my vision. Dark brown with gold mixed in that caught the sunlight. Her hair reminded me of dessert, the way shades of chocolate, caramel, and honey swirled together.

Focus, dumbass. This wasn't the time to get a craving for something sweet.

And then I heard it: Lennon's triumphant voice rising above the grunts and groans, crack of wood, and slap of flesh.

"Home!"

"ARE you going to do something about that, or am I?" Holly folded her arms over her chest and scowled at me. Her dark eyebrows pushed together over even darker eyes.

"Do something about what?" I asked, like Lennon wasn't doing some obnoxious victory dance, gyrating her hips like a complete dork, her green mallet held high above her head.

"I won! I won!" she sing-songed.

She had no right looking that fucking adorable.

There was no way in hell she had won, of course. I did not look forward to telling her that.

"Jay." Holly snapped her fingers rapidly in front of my face.

I reluctantly dragged my gaze away from Lennon. "What?"

"You know she didn't win! Make her stop."

"What do you care, Holly? In fact, Blood Ball is the only thing you *don't* care about winning."

Holly gave me a look that suggested she doubted my intelligence. "That's because I always *let* you win. You, or Liam, or Seb. Sometimes even Mateo, if I'm feeling generous."

That got my attention. I frowned down at her. "What do you mean, you *let* us win?"

She batted away my question with a flutter of her hand. "The important thing is, I did *not* let Lennon win. You wouldn't even let me get close to her. That's bullshit, Jay, and you know it. The game is very clear. It's every man for himself. Or herself."

"Yeah?" I arched my brows. "Then how do you explain Mateo running interference for you every chance he gets?"

"That's different." I snorted. "You *know* she didn't win. For starters, unless she tripped over her own feet, she didn't make anyone bleed—"

"She didn't trip," I ground out. I would have noticed.

"Secondly, she didn't win because there's *no fucking way*." She leaned in land jabbed me in the chest to punctuate each word. "No one's ever beaten one of us at Blood Ball before. Not even that SEAL from Lodestar Ranch."

"He was injured," I pointed out. "That probably slowed him down some."

"Is Lennon a SEAL?" Holly demanded, and then immediately answered her own question. "No. She is not. I don't think she's military at all. The truth is, we don't know what she did, where she's from, or why she's here."

My gaze flicked to Lennon, who was still doing that stupid dance. *Who are you?* I hated that I didn't know. But I hated even more that I cared so damn much.

"But we do know she didn't win Blood Ball. If you don't want to tell her, I will. In fact, I'd love to see the look on her face. A spoiled little city girl taking down a team of Tier 1 operators? I don't fucking think so."

"Aren't you from Seattle? That's a city, last time I checked."

She glared at me, and I sighed.

"Liam and Mateo are reviewing the video. There's no point in telling her she lost until we know who actually won," I said.

Holly's lower lip pushed out. "She's pissing me off, Jay."

"Live with it, Holly. She's not the only one who has a victory dance," I said pointedly. Holly wasn't known for being a gracious winner, either.

"Hey, guys?" Liam called quietly. "You need to see this."

Holly tossed her dark hair and flounced over with me following behind.

"What is it?" I asked, peering over Liam's shoulder as he pressed play on the camera.

"More importantly, who won?" Holly asked.

"That's the thing. Mateo and I watched twice, and we both counted the same." Liam cleared his throat. "Watch Lennon."

I watched. Pandemonium ensued, but Lennon paid us no mind. She stood perpendicular to the wicket closest to the home pole, one foot on either side. With a gentle tap, she sent her ball cleanly through the wicket. It stopped against the side of her foot. Then she tapped it back through again. Over and over and over. Five points each time.

Every time we made each other bleed, it cost us time. The fifty points we earned didn't stand a chance against her incessant five.

"No," Holly whispered, horrified. "*No.*"

When she was up by ten points, Lennon sent her ball flying into the home pole. Almost as though she had been aware of our scores the whole fucking time. "Home!" she hollered.

"Nooooo!" Holly wailed.

I straightened. My eyes met Lennon's six yards away. She bowed with a flourish of her mallet, and I couldn't help but chuckle.

Well, fuck me sideways. Lennon had won.

12

LENNON

I HAD BEEN AT MERCY RIVER RANCH FOR OVER A WEEK now and not once had I visited the spa. This was in part because, despite what the website had led me to believe, it wasn't *really* a spa, but more importantly, Tamilee Jones was one of the two massage therapists, and I wasn't sure I'd come out of it alive. But rising before dawn to cook for a few dozen cowboys and half a dozen more guests made me ache in muscles I hadn't known existed, so that afternoon I headed over.

The blonde woman behind the desk tossed aside her book the moment she saw me. "Lennon Graves! You're here!"

I froze in place. No one had recognized me since I'd left New York, but I'd hoped to keep it that way, at least until Benny's trial was over. The last time I'd heard from Hector was two days ago, when he'd told me the feds were deposing Benny's associates, and for me to stay out of sight.

"You know who I am?" I whispered. That wasn't good. People recognizing me meant I'd have to leave, and I didn't have anywhere to go.

Her laugh was big, coming from such a small person. "Of course I do. There are only five women who work at the ranch, and I'm one of them. You're not Holly and you're not Tamilee or Cecily, so unless you're the housekeeper they hired six months ago that I still haven't met, you must be the guest everyone's been talking about."

My shoulders had relaxed slightly as I realized she didn't recognize me from social media or the news, but at those words, they shot right back up to my ears. "People are talking about me?"

"Girl, yes." She laughed again. "Mercy River is a small town, and the ranch is an even smaller town. Entertainment is hard to come by. A pretty city girl like you getting our stoic cowboy all tied up in knots? Of course everyone is talking."

"I didn't do anything to Jeremiah," I protested.

Her lips curved slyly. "I didn't say it was Jeremiah."

Oh. Right. My mouth opened and closed like a hooked fish. A stupid, stupid fish.

She burst out laughing. I had a feeling laughter was

something she did a lot of. "I'm Emma Cole. What can I do for you, Lennon?"

"Um." I cleared my throat. "A massage, please. If you have anything open. I don't have an appointment."

"Hm." She consulted the computer. "Sure, I can fit you in."

"Great. Thank you." I hesitated. "It's not...Who with?"

"Me." She smirked. "Don't worry. I'm stronger than I look."

I eyed her doubtfully. She couldn't be more than five-three and her figure was delicate. But I preferred a lighter touch when it came to massage, anyway. Emma was exactly what I needed.

Ten minutes later, I remembered the phrase *Don't judge a book by its cover*. Emma might look like something I could fold up and put in my pocket, but the way she dug into the knots in my lower back was nothing short of fierce.

And the girl was a talker.

"I heard you won Blood Ball," she said as her elbow followed the line of my shoulder blade with ruthless precision.

"Guh," I grunted.

"That's amazing. No one has ever beaten them before. I mean, they don't usually let guests play because no one wants to see the ranch sued, but some of the ranch hands have given it a go. Two bruised ribs, one dislocated shoulder, and one broken ankle. Lots of blood."

"Mmph," I managed.

"Apparently no one got close enough to you to draw blood or even stop you from scoring."

That had been my whole strategy. I had known they didn't view me as a threat, and I had taken advantage of that. They were so busy knocking each other down that not one of them paid any attention to what I was up to. It wasn't a strategy I could pull off twice, but who cared? I had won.

"Seb said you have Jeremiah to thank for that." Her elbow paused. "Jeremiah," she repeated. "That's so funny. Every time I say his name, your muscles tense. Jeremiah." My shoulder twitched, and she laughed. "Oh, girl. Looks like the stoic cowboy has the city girl in knots, too."

There was no point in denying it. My body had betrayed me.

"He protected you, you know." Emma's hands glided up my back, her thumbs following the tight muscles next to my spine. "I worked on Seb yesterday and he told me all about it. It wasn't until they watched the video that they figured it out. Do you know that man didn't hit his own ball through a wicket a single time? He was too busy knocking anyone down who came too close to you."

Jeremiah had protected me? That hadn't occurred to

me. I'd kept a tally in my head of everyone's points to make sure I didn't end the game when I was down. When I knocked my ball into the home pole, ending the game, it put me in first place by a mere ten points. I'd known what all their scores were, but I hadn't given any thought to why they played the way they did.

Why would he do that? I wasn't in any real danger. Liam, Seb, and Mateo wouldn't have knocked me down. Even Holly would have gone easy on me. Maybe she would have drawn a little blood, but nothing that would require a hospital visit.

"You should come out with us tonight," Emma said. "Me, my sister Grace, Tamilee, and Cecily. We're going to Sundown. It's nothing fancy, but it's always a good time."

I considered. Hector had told me to lie low, but a dive bar in a town boasting a population of four hundred was still lying low, right? No one in Mercy River cared about some New York City millionaire getting arrested for tax evasion, even if that millionaire had criminal ties. Anyway, it had been a while since I'd had girl time.

But what was the point in making friends when I'd be gone in six weeks? On the other hand, friendship didn't have to sprout roots. Some people were meant to be in your life for only a short time. That happened to be all my relationships, so why should Cecily and Emma be any different?

"Sure. I'd love to."

I didn't ask if the cowboys tagged along.

But I wanted to.

WITH THE SUN low in the sky, turning the mountains to fire, I found myself at a saloon called Sundown with a shot of tequila in one hand and a wedge of lime in the other.

"To our ancestors," Cecily said, raising her shot glass. "May they look the other way tonight."

"Lord, no, I'm not drinking to that," Tamilee protested. "In this honky-tonk? I don't think so. My ancestors better have their eyelids peeled back and their prayers ready. I did not survive *Don't Ask, Don't Tell* in the Marines to be taken down now."

"What? There's no way you're old enough for that." My eyes scanned her uncreased face. "I've been in Wyoming all of a week and a half, and my skin already feels like a dried-out mummy. I've aged ten years. What moisturizer do you use? Tretinoin?"

Tamilee patted my hand. "It's not the moisturizer, baby. It's the melanin. The same reason I'm not toasting to my ancestors closing their eyes."

Emma laughed. "I don't know how much trouble we

can get into anyway with every one of our bosses sitting in that booth over there."

For the thirteenth time since I had walked through the door, my gaze slid to where Jeremiah had claimed the outer seat of the booth. Seb was next to him, with Holly and Mateo sitting across from them. Four beers were on the table, but I hadn't seen Jeremiah take a single sip of his.

"Liam's not with them," Grace Sherwood noted. Grace was Emma's older sister, and they had the same white-blonde hair, but her eyes were blue, not green. She didn't work at the ranch, but her fiancé, Alex, was a ranch hand there. Grace taught fifth grade at the local elementary school. "Babysitting duty?"

Emma nodded with a little laugh. "Blair is probably painting his nails as we speak."

"Um, excuse me, hello?" Cecily wiggled her fingers at the shot glass she still held up high. "Are you all really going to leave me hanging like this? We still have salt on our arms."

Laughing, Grace clinked her glass to Cecily's. "To girlfriends and cheap drinks."

"Now, *that* I'll drink to." Tamilee raised her glass. "To girlfriends and cheap drinks."

"To girlfriends and cheap drinks!" I chorused with Emma, both of us tapping our glasses with the others.

We licked the salt off our wrists, downed the tequila, bit the limes, then slammed our glasses on the wooden bar top. Warmth shuddered through me, leaving me a little looser in its wake. I wasn't a big drinker, so when I did imbibe, it packed a punch.

"So, you were a Marine?" I asked Tamilee. I loved getting to know people even when I didn't intend to know them for more than a night. People and their stories fascinated me. I recalled the "About Us" page on the ranch website, and how they had all served in the military.

Tamilee nodded. "That's right. They paid for college and my DPT to be a physical therapist."

"And the Marines is how you met Jeremiah and the others? I mean—" I bit my lime again. "I mean Seb, Liam, Mateo, and Holly?"

"Oh, no. I didn't meet that lot until I came to Mercy River. It was Daniel Cole, Liam's younger brother. I was his physical therapist when he was injured on his first tour. Daniel is the one who brought all of us here. He's the linchpin."

"My husband," Emma added quietly, and I blinked in surprise. I hadn't realized she was Liam's sister-in-law. "Blair's dad."

Tamilee squeezed her hand. "That's right."

There was no wedding ring on her finger. Emma saw me look and gave me a tight, sad smile. "Widow."

"I'm sorry," I said. The words weren't enough, but they were all I had.

She nodded, her green eyes shiny. "Thank you," she

said. "It was years ago, but I still cry. I cry about everything."

Tamilee squeezed her hand again. "He was a good man. And, as I said, the linchpin of the group. He and Liam grew up here, you know. This was their family's ranch for generations, but a few hard years back to back, and they had to sell. Daniel had the idea of them all investing and being part-owners and opening up the ranch to paying guests."

"I didn't know that," Cecily said. "I mean, I knew Liam's brother died in a car accident some years before I came here, but I didn't know the ranch was his idea."

"There's a memorial page about him on the website," Tamilee said, and I frowned because somehow I had missed that. I thought I had looked at everything on the website before booking my cabin for two months, but then again, with my life in shambles, I probably missed a lot of things.

"They don't talk much about Daniel," Emma said softly. "Not with guests or staff, anyway. They're a pretty insular group, the five of them. And I think it's still a painful subject for all of us." She ran her fingers through her hair, fluffing it up with a little shake. "Anyway. Can we...I don't know. Talk about something else? Please?"

Grace gave her sister a side hug, then signaled Tonya, the bartender. "On it."

"Another round?" Tonya asked, palms braced on the bar.

"Hell, yes!" Cecily exclaimed.

"Wait, who's driving?" I blurted out. Grace had met us here, and Cecily had given me and Emma a ride. Tamilee had insisted on driving herself so she could leave on her own schedule, claiming her two decades on us meant she had a bedtime two hours earlier.

"Don't worry. I'm switching to water now," Emma said. "Can't let Blair see me sloppy. Between me and Jeremiah, we'll get everyone home safe and sound."

At the mention of his name, my gaze slid his way again. And then it stayed there, lingering on the way the brown beer bottle was nearly completely hidden from view as he rolled it between his large palms.

There was something about his hands that fascinated me. The size, for one. I didn't have to wonder if the size of his hands might portend the size of other delicious things because I'd already felt the proof of that pressed against my rain-soaked body. But they looked so damn *capable*. That large knot of muscle between his thumb and forefinger. Those long, blunt fingers that looked both nimble and strong made me think of all kinds of ways to put them to good use.

Watching Jeremiah engulf the bottle with one hand, his index finger hooked around the neck, was better than a porno. I wanted those hands on me.

"Jeremiah is driving?" My voice sounded far away to my own ears. Every cell in my body was leaning toward him. I hadn't seen him since Blood Ball yesterday—

when he'd used his body to protect mine, according to Emma. I still didn't know what to think about that.

"He never has more than a beer when we're out," Emma said. "Always insists on being the designated driver." She shook her head, laughing. "He trusts them with his life, but not with driving, apparently."

Cecily nodded. "Control freak."

"We don't call him Dad for nothing." Tamilee raised her glass, then tipped it to her ruby lips, swallowing it down in one gulp. "*Whew*. Now I'm switching to soda. Hangovers are nasty at my age."

"He's protective." Emma tilted her chin to me with a sly little smirk. "Right, Lennon?"

I yanked my gaze from Jeremiah with a sputtering cough. "Um, what?"

"What?" Cecily echoed, splitting a curious look between us.

Emma grinned. "Our girl Lennon won Blood Ball yesterday."

There was a moment of stunned silence. The bar hummed around us, low murmurs of conversation, country music on the overhead speakers, the tinkling of ice dropped in glasses.

Grace hooted. "Well, fucking cheers to that! Hell, yeah, Lennon! This round is on me." She wrapped her arms around my shoulders and half-squeezed, half-shook me.

I laughed. "No more shots! I won't be able to walk out of here."

"Beer, then?" Grace asked. When I nodded, she signaled Tonya.

"But what does Jeremiah have to do with anything?" Cecily pressed.

"He wouldn't let anyone get near her." Emma smirked again. "Lennon is probably the first person in the history of Blood Ball to not actually bleed."

Tamilee took a long sip of water, then delicately dabbed a napkin to her lips. Her lipstick hadn't budged. "Of course Jeremiah protected you. I'm only surprised he let you play at all. Guests don't play Blood Ball. That would be a lawsuit waiting to happen."

"He didn't have a choice," I admitted. When they all looked at me with raised eyebrows, I threw up my hands. "What? Holly practically dared me. What was I supposed to do? Walk away?"

Tamilee hooted. "Oh, baby. It's a good thing you're pretty."

I flinched. *Are you stupid, Lennon? Or just lazy?* The words still echoed in my head years after they'd been spoken. Sometimes it was my mom. Sometimes a teacher. Sometimes another kid. They all thought the same thing. Either I wasn't trying because I was lazy, or I *was* trying and I screwed up because I was stupid.

But Tamilee didn't know me well enough to hit that

sore spot on purpose, and I wasn't going to bring down the vibe of girls' night by telling her. I didn't beg for compliments from anyone, and I didn't need Tamilee to tell me she didn't *really* think I was dumb.

Or maybe I was afraid she'd confirm it.

Tonya set a bottle in front of me. I nodded my thanks and pulled it closer. "Holly gets under my skin," I muttered into my beer.

Tamilee shook her head. "Holly never takes an inch if she can steal a mile. If you keep letting her wiggle in there, one of these days she's going to show up in a full Lennon skin suit. You don't want that."

I wrinkled my nose at the mental image. "Ew."

They all loved Holly, though. I didn't get it, but they did. I glanced at Jeremiah's booth again because I couldn't help myself and nearly fell off my barstool at the sight of his face in Holly's hands as she leaned across the table to him.

"Is there...is there something going on with Holly and Jeremiah?" I stuttered.

"What? Holly and *Jeremiah*?" Emma burst out laughing with her head thrown back like it was the funniest thing she had ever heard. "Girl, no. Jeremiah isn't messy like that. Hell, I don't think I've ever seen him with a woman who wasn't an employee or a friend. Whatever he gets up to, he keeps that shit locked down tight."

Then why was Holly's face so close to his? Not that I cared. But seriously. Their mouths were almost touching. It was unsanitary, that's what it was.

I drained my beer. "I need some air."

13

JEREMIAH

"IF YOU DON'T STOP STARING AT HER, I'M GOING TO PLUCK your eyeballs out." Holly's fingernails scraped against my five o'clock shadow. "You're making me nauseous."

"How can I be looking at anyone but you when you're two inches from my nose and blocking everything with your enormous head, Holly?"

Almost everything. In my peripheral vision, I saw a blur of dessert-hued hair as Lennon twirled off her stool. She was heading for the exit—alone.

I covered Holly's hands with my own and pried them from my face. "I'll be back."

I slipped out the door, ignoring Holly's dramatic sigh behind me. There were bears out there. Probably not right by the door, but somewhere nearby. At the very least, there were raccoons. Raccoons didn't used to be a problem in Wyoming, but then the rich people came and somehow they brought the raccoons with them. And now Lennon was outside all alone with the raccoons.

I pushed through the heavy wooden doors and tripped right over Lennon. With a startled yelp, she drove her elbow straight into my ribs.

"Fuck!" I gasped. I doubled over as I struggled to inhale a full breath.

She did a double take over her shoulder, then whirled to face me. "What did I tell you about sneaking up on women in the dark, Jeremiah?" she demanded. She gave my shoulder a not-very-gentle shove. "What. Did. I. Tell. You."

"Bad," I wheezed.

"That's right. *Bad*. The opposite of good. And now look at yourself."

Why would I look at myself when I could look at her? So I stared at her while I tried to catch my breath. She shook her head as if she were disappointed in me. Her diamond earring sparkled in the flicker of the fake-flame lamps that hung on either side of the door.

She planted her fists on her hips. "What do you have to say for yourself?"

I held up a finger to indicate that I still needed a

moment. She waited. I straightened and bent to the side, stretching out the kink in my ribs from her damned elbow.

"Well?" she demanded.

"You're missing an earring," I said.

She blinked at me like it took her a moment to comprehend the words, and then her hands flew to her earlobes to verify. Her face fell. "Shit." She looked at her feet as if she expected to find her earring there. It wasn't. "Shit."

"Expensive?" I asked.

"Yeah." She squeezed her eyes shut, sighing. "What was I thinking wearing them out here? But I never take them off." Her eyes popped open. "It must have happened during Blood Ball." She groaned. "I'll never find it."

"I'll take a look tomorrow."

She laughed. "For a tiny diamond in a field? Okay. Good luck."

I rubbed my jaw and shrugged. "I'm pretty good at finding things."

People, mostly. Information, too. That was what I had done in my prior life. Search and rescue operations for people we couldn't afford to lose. I had to bite back the urge to tell her that I had a one hundred percent success rate. What the hell was that about? Bragging had always made me uncomfortable. What did I care about impressing Lennon?

But I did care.

"What are you doing out here, Lennon?" I asked.

"Getting some air. Looking for stars. Alas." She gestured to the dark, cloudy sky. "What about you?"

"Same. Air. Stars."

Her head tilted as she considered me. "I don't think so."

"You don't?"

"No." She shook her head. "You're always around. Keeping me warm. Scaring off assholes. Protecting me in games I have no business playing. So, no, Jeremiah. I don't think you're out here counting stars. I think you're here for me." She swayed closer. Her eyes moved over my face. "Are you going to deny that?"

I shook my head. My heart thumped so hard in my chest I wondered if she could feel the vibrations of it like an earthquake.

She rolled up on her toes. Pressed her lips to mine. The world stilled. It was a shock, her soft, warm mouth. The closeness. The *feel.* She pulled back before I had fully recovered from it.

I gave her an incredulous look as she rolled back down.

Like hell.

I followed her down until my mouth found hers again. My right hand cupped the back of her head, my left arm banded around her waist, and I bent her back, keeping our bodies tight together. She flung her arms around my neck and fucking *smiled* against my mouth.

"Finally," she murmured.

That was all I needed to lick my way in. And there was that thirst again, crackling through my veins like wildfire, burning everything in its wake—reason, sanity, morality—until all that was left of me was this thirst.

She came with me when I straightened and wrapped her legs around my waist. She tasted sweet like tequila, and I was dizzy with thirst. I tilted her back against the wall. Leaned into her. The sudden rough contact of being pelvis to pelvis with her knocked the breath out of me, and we groaned into each other's mouths.

And then her lips latched onto my tongue and she sucked. I felt it everywhere. My tongue. My chest. My dick. Everything ached. Everything craved.

The sound I made wasn't fully human. I wrenched my mouth from hers and dropped my forehead to the wall, panting. It didn't feel good, the rough wood biting into my skin. I pushed harder.

Slowly I became aware of soft fingers sifting through my hair, tugging gently. I lifted my head and looked at her. Sweet brown eyes with those pretty green rings met mine. Her lips, puffy and pink from kissing, shifted from a smile to a smirk.

"So, you're saying it's a bad idea to fuck against the saloon wall where everyone can see us?" she teased drily.

I couldn't help the hoarse laugh that escaped me. The things this woman said. I never expected it. "Probably. Yeah."

"Yeah," she echoed. "Well, that's a damn shame."

She unhooked her legs from my waist and I put her on her feet. My brain knew we couldn't fuck against the wall, but my body was raising excellent points. I couldn't seem to stop touching her hair, twisting it in my fingers.

A throat clearing behind us had us both freezing in place, staring at each other with wide eyes. Slowly we turned to face Cecily.

"Hope I'm not interrupting anything," she deadpanned.

"Nope," Lennon said breezily. "Just looking at the stars."

Cecily looked up. The sky was nothing but clouds. She raised her eyebrows at us. "Sure. Anyway, people are starting to head out. Grace is going home with Emma and crashing there. Lennon, you and I are with Tamilee."

Lennon took a step forward, but I pulled her back by a belt loop. "I'll take Lennon. We're going to the same place, anyway."

Cecily made a huff of disbelief under her breath. "Don't take this personally, boss, but I need to hear Lennon say she's okay with that. Girl code."

Girl code? Because—shit. I had just implied that Lennon was spending the night with me. "I mean,

Mateo, Holly, Lennon, and I are all going to the same place." Great, now it sounded like an orgy. "The ranch," I clarified. "Not my bedroom."

Lennon snickered. Heat rose up my neck.

"Sure. Whatever." Cecily crossed her arms, chin jutting stubbornly. "Still need to hear it from Lennon."

"I'm fine, Cecily," Lennon said on a choked laugh. "Jeremiah can drive me home. Thank you."

If Mateo had thoughts about me dropping him and Holly off at their cabins before Lennon, he kept them to himself. Holly did not. She was still walking up the path to her front door when my phone buzzed with her text.

HOLLY

I don't trust her.

ME

You don't trust anyone.

HOLLY

That's not true. I trust Mother Clucker.

ME

This might come as a shock to you, but Mother Clucker is not a person. She's a chicken.

Holly unlocked the door and flipped on the light, illuminating the middle finger she raised at me.

"That's an odd way to thank you for the ride home," Lennon remarked.

"Yeah, well, Holly's a little odd." I shifted into drive and circled back onto the dirt road to the guest cabins. "But her heart's in the right place."

Lennon bugged her eyes out in mock disbelief, one hand slapping delicately to her chest. "Holly has a heart?"

I chuckled. "She does, something you'd find out pretty damn quick if you hurt someone she loves." I reflected. "Or Mother Clucker."

She twisted in her seat to face me. "Okay, what is the deal with that? Why a chicken?"

"Ask her yourself."

Lennon pulled back, wrinkling her nose. "I'll pass."

"Suit yourself." I glanced sideways at her. "You know the reason you two don't get along is because you're too much alike, right? If you really got to know each other, you'd be inseparable."

"That is a terrible thing to say." She flicked my thigh, making me laugh. "Why do you care if Holly and I are friends, anyway? I'm only here until the end of July."

I didn't want to think about that. Not her leaving, and definitely not why it might mean something to me for her to get along with people I cared about. "Just trying to prevent carnage, that's all."

"You know Holly started it, right? I have been perfectly pleasant."

"Holly doesn't warm up to anyone easily." *Especially not people she doesn't trust.* I pulled up to her cabin and cut the engine. "I'll walk you to your door."

"It's ten steps."

"I'll walk you to your door."

She was halfway out of the truck when she paused to smirk at me over her shoulder. "Are you going to give me a gentlemanly goodnight kiss?"

I shot her a look as I unbuckled, maintaining eye contact as I left the truck and came around to her door. "No."

"No?" Surprise and disappointment flashed in her dark eyes.

I took her hand to help her down. "No. I'm not going to give you a gentlemanly kiss goodnight because I can't be a gentleman with you right now. If I start kissing you, I'm not going to stop."

Her face tilted closer to mine. "You could come in."

Fuck, I wanted to. Saying no hadn't ever been a problem for me and I didn't understand why it was now. *Yes* should feel like love. Safe and manageable. There was nothing manageable about what I wanted to do with Lennon. It was wild and ferocious.

My gaze dipped to her mouth, and I groaned. "I think you might be drunk, honey."

"Not drunk. Tipsy. Still fully able to consent to this." She nipped at my jaw. "If you want to."

"I want to." Fuck, did I ever. My hands flexed on her hips. "But I can't."

With a soft laugh, she ducked under my arm and headed for her door. "All right, Boy Scout."

I shoved my hands into my pockets so I wouldn't reach for her and followed her to her door.

She glanced back at me as she dug her key out of her bag. "That's the weird thing about this place, you know. Everyone here is a Boy Scout."

Her smile was fuzzy around the edges. Definitely tipsy. She swayed slightly, and I yanked my hands out of my pockets in time to steady her. Touching her was dangerous, but I couldn't let her fall either. "What do you mean?"

"I mean..." She whipped the key out of her bag with a flourish, like she expected applause. "I mean, *everyone* knows CPR. Not just the people who work here. The guests know CPR, too. That's a Boy Scout thing, right?"

I stilled. "You don't know CPR?"

"*No*, I don't know *CPR*." She blew a raspberry. "That's ridiculous. Where would I learn CPR?"

I stared down at her. She stared back, her doe eyes big and deceptively guileless, like maybe she really didn't understand what she was telling me. I took the key from her, unlocked the door, and nudged her inside. "Get some rest, Lennon."

I drove back to the lodge with my dick aching and my head a goddamn mess. I didn't know what the hell I was doing with this woman, but one thing I knew for damn sure. You didn't come out of the military without knowing CPR. The same applied to first responders.

Lennon Graves had been lying since the first day she came to Mercy River Ranch.

14

LENNON

For the first time since I'd arrived at Mercy River, the sun managed to beat me to rising. Staying out past nine o'clock might have had something to do with it.

That, and the horny, frustrated thoughts that kept me tossing and turning for another hour after I turned off my audiobook.

But then I'd slept and slept well. I woke up in an insanely good mood.

He kissed me.

The thought popped into my head with a giddy giggle before I'd even opened my eyes. I rolled onto my stomach and screamed into my pillow, kicking my feet under the covers.

He kissed me.

I wanted to dance around the room, singing songs to squirrels like a Disney princess or something. Because that kiss...that was some fairytale shit.

I hadn't even known kissing could feel like that. Sure, I'd seen *The Princess Bride*. I'd read books. I'd even heard people talk about it in real life. But I'd always figured they were...I don't know...making shit up. You couldn't *really* lose your mind with the need to rip someone's clothes off and pull them inside you *right fucking now* just from a kiss.

You could, it turned out.

I could.

That was a wholly new experience for me. I'd always enjoyed sex. I liked the men I was with, even if my favorite thing about them was their bank account. Sex had felt good. Kissing was perfunctory but enjoyable. It hadn't occurred to me that I was missing out on anything.

But now I knew. I was missing out on Jeremiah.

It was like living in Alaska your whole life, thinking you knew how summer felt, and then visiting Florida in July.

A fucking epiphany, that's what his kiss was.

I threw back the covers and hopped out of bed. It was Amos and Cecily's day off, which made it mine, too —a weird way to think about it when the ranch wasn't paying me to cook—and Emma had invited me over for lunch with Grace and Blair.

But that was a few hours away. Maybe I'd shower, eat breakfast at the lodge, and then go find Jeremiah for a riding lesson. Get him to teach me cowgirl shit. Real cowgirl shit, not how to save a cowboy—although that was an appealing way to spend the morning. But I'd been at the ranch for nearly two weeks and had yet to spend even a second on the back of a horse. Actually, I'd never been on a horse before. It looked like fun, though. I wanted to give it a try.

The buzz of my phone startled me. I'd turned it off every night after listening to an audiobook and stuck it in the nightstand drawer so I wouldn't think about it. Hector didn't want me on social media until Benny's mess was over, but I knew if my phone was on or within reach I wouldn't be able to resist scrolling. Last night I'd forgotten to turn it off.

I glanced down at my phone. *Mom.* Heaving a sigh, I answered, putting her on speaker. "Hi, Mom. What are you doing up this early?"

"Early?" Mom's voice was raspy from decades of smoking. "It's nine a.m. Some of us have respectable jobs, Lennon."

Right. There was a two-hour time difference between Virginia and Wyoming. I ignored the dig about my profession and said, "How are you?"

The real question was *what do you want?* But I knew

she'd get to that eventually. She always did. She liked to work up to it first. Give me a sob story I couldn't say no to.

"Someone called for you," she said, surprising me.

"What do you mean?" I asked.

She huffed, as if I were being purposefully dense. "I mean, someone called *my* phone to ask if you were around."

I frowned. "Around...Virginia?"

"Yes, Lennon. Obviously." I heard the metallic flick of her lighter and then a deep inhale. "People are worried about you."

"What people? Who's worried about me?" I demanded. Benny knew where I was, and no one else would care. I wasn't a loner, but I had acquaintances, not friendships. People I went to Pilates with or brunch. Honestly, my social media followers were more likely to notice my absence than anyone in my offline life, which was why I had pre-scheduled posts for the month.

This had to be about Benny. And right now, anything about Benny that didn't come straight from Hector wasn't good.

Mom exhaled. I imagined white smoke streaming from her lips. It was something I'd seen so many times, I almost felt nostalgic for it. It was so familiar. Comforting, even.

"The man who called. Keep up, Lennon. Honestly, talking to you is an uphill battle," she snapped.

That was familiar, too. But a lot less comforting.

"Okay, Mom. Did he leave a name or a phone number where I can reach him? Can you tell me exactly what he said?"

"Hm. You know, he didn't leave a name. That's odd. Maybe I missed it. I wasn't feeling well when he called, so it was hard to concentrate—"

"Mom." I rubbed my temple. "What did he say?"

"Just that no one has heard from you in almost a month and they're all worried you might be in trouble or something. He gave me his number so I could call him in case you turned up."

I frowned. That was odd. "He wants you to call him? Not me?"

"That's what he said. He was afraid you'd be mad at people checking up on you. Miss Independent." She cackled. "That's you, all right. Always too big for your britches. Can never admit when you bit off more than you could chew."

My jaw clenched. "Did he say anything else?" I ground out.

"No, that was it. So, what's going on? Where are you? Are you in trouble?" The genuine concern in her voice eased some of the tension in my jaw.

"I'm fine, Mom. Just taking a vacation, that's all."

"Ohhh, a vacation," she sing-songed. "Must be nice."

My teeth clacked together again. "It *is* nice," I said defiantly.

"Well, I'm glad you're not in trouble. I thought you might be, because he sounded like a mobster."

I rolled my eyes. "And what does a mobster sound like, Mom?"

"You know. That New Jersey accent." Another long exhale of smoke. "Italian."

"Well, that's not offensive at all," I muttered.

"Oh, don't be so high and mighty. Stereotypes are stereotypes for a reason."

I kept my mouth shut about stones and glass trailer houses, and I didn't bother to explain that technically, the mafia was a Sicilian thing. That would only give her the opportunity to insult Sicilians.

"Well, thanks for passing on the message, Mom. If he calls again, tell him I'm in the Finger Lakes."

"I'll do that." She dragged on her cigarette. "You know, I had to take a sick day because of his phone call. I was already feeling off, and then he called and got me all worried about you. If I don't work, I don't get paid, you know."

And there it was. Every phone call came with a price. "I'll wire you money."

I hung up, my stomach twisting, and immediately called Hector. "What the hell is going on? Is Benny okay? People are calling my mom looking for me. My *mom*, Hector," I hissed. "You tell them that if they go anywhere near her, I'll—"

"Calm down, honey." I had always hated being

called that, but I hated it even more now that I knew how good it sounded coming from Jeremiah's lips. "Your mom is fine. It was just the feds trying to get information, because Benny's not giving them nothin'. They thought he'd plead out and give them the names they really want, but Benny's not a snitch. Stay low, do what I told you, and everything will be all right."

"Okay."

I believed him, but I didn't trust him, and I couldn't shake the feeling that something was wrong.

"Wow, you're pretty." A girl I presumed to be Blair, Emma's thirteen-year-old daughter, scrutinized my face with eyes the same pretty green as her mom's before hollering over her shoulder, "Mom! Your friend is here! Can I do your makeup?" she asked as she turned back to me.

"Um, sure?" I stepped inside.

"Right now?" she pressed.

"No, not right now," Grace answered for me. She nudged her niece aside. "Let Lennon get some food first." She gave me a hug, just like she did when we med for the first time last night, and then pushed me in the direction of the kitchen. I had never been a hugger, but I didn't mind when it was Grace. "Emma is making chicken salad sandwiches."

I glanced around as I followed Grace to the kitchen. Emma and Blair didn't live at the ranch. They were on the outskirts of town, in a sweet one-story bungalow with gabled windows and cedar-shingled siding. There was a baby grand piano in the living room and family photographs everywhere I looked. My gaze snagged on a photo of Emma holding baby Blair while a man who looked a lot like Liam kissed her forehead. That had to be Daniel.

Emma was chopping celery when we entered the kitchen. "Hey! You made it!"

"Thanks for inviting me." I glanced around the small, cozy kitchen. "What can I do to help?"

Emma waved a hand. "Nothing. Are you kidding me? You cook breakfast for us every day. I'm not letting you make us lunch. That would be like you asking me for a free massage. Only family members get free labor."

I laughed. "I would love a free massage. Got any brothers? I'll marry in."

Emma snorted. "Nope. Grace and I are all our parents were willing to have. Though I do have a brother-in-law who happens to be single, if you're interested." She went back to chopping celery. "You know, he never takes advantage of the family discount. He never comes to the wellness center when I'm working, either. Maybe he hates massages."

Grace rolled her eyes. "Liam hates anything that requires him to relax and be less of a grumpy bastard. But it doesn't matter because Lennon has her eye on a different cowboy."

"I...what?" I sputtered.

"Ooo, that's right!" Emma dumped the celery into the bowl of shredded chicken, wiped her hands on her pants, and reached for the cupboard. "We need to talk about that. But first, can I offer you something to drink? We have iced tea, water, and Coke."

Noting the pitcher already on the counter, I said, "Iced tea would be great, thank you."

Grace poured, and we sat on the stools tucked under the counter. Emma grabbed her cutting board, the knife, and a bag of red grapes and set up facing us. They looked at me expectantly.

"Um," I said, my gaze darting from Emma to Grace and back again.

"Not to be all high school about it, but Cecily said she saw you and Jeremiah all wrapped up in each other outside Sundown." Emma sliced grapes in half as she talked. "Is that true?"

"We might have kissed," I admitted.

Emma set down the knife and stared at me with a dumbfounded expression. "Wow."

"Wow," Grace echoed, shaking her head.

"Wow," Blair said behind us. When we looked at her, she shrugged. "I've never seen Jay show any interest in a girl before. Or a man." She plucked a grape from the bunch and popped it into her mouth. "I was starting to think he was a eunuch."

The memory of him hard between my legs as he pressed me to the wall came flooding back. "Definitely not a eunuch," I muttered.

Emma pointed her knife at me. "I'm going to need to know how you know that." She pointed the knife at her daughter. "And I need you to tell me how you know that word."

"What, eunuch?" Blair asked, helping herself to another grape. "It was in *Dogma*. That's a movie from the nineteen hundreds. My friends and I are really into vintage stuff right now."

"Careful, kid," Emma warned, but her lips twitched with laughter. "I was born in the nineties."

Blair smirked, completely unrepentant. "Yeah, Mom. You're vintage."

"That's it! You're grounded for a thousand years."

Blair snorted and grabbed one last grape. "How about instead, I go to my room so you can talk all about how Jay isn't a eunuch because I really don't want to be here for that. Call me when lunch is ready. Byeeeee." She twirled out of the room, leaving us laughing behind her.

"Nothing like a thirteen-year-old girl to keep you humble," Emma said. "Now. About that kiss. I'm thinking it was a really good one if it told you Jeremiah isn't a eunuch."

I took a nonchalant sip of my iced tea. "It was all right."

"All right?" Grace smacked my arm playfully. "Then why do you have the goofy grin on your face?"

"Fine, fine." I nibbled my lip. This was uncharted territory for me. I didn't gossip with girlfriends about my love life, and I shut it down quick any time one of my subs asked something too personal. In fact, I steered clear of talking about myself at all. Most people didn't even notice. People loved to talk about themselves.

But Emma and Grace were staring at me, waiting for my answer. They weren't going to let me off the hook.

"It was the best kiss of my life," I admitted. "But that's all it was. A vacation fling."

PRETTY GREEN EYES hovered an inch from mine. I sat on the floor with my back propped against the couch. Blair knelt next to me, scrutinizing every inch of my face.

"You have, like, zero pores," she announced. She rocked back on her heels. "That's kind of boring."

"Sorry," I laughed.

Blair tilted her head, still studying me. Suddenly her eyes lit up. "Hey, can I make you ugly?"

I blinked rapidly. "What?"

"Like, old."

"I think you mean vintage," Emma said drily. She was curled up on the far end of the couch, watching us as she knitted a blanket.

Blair was already rummaging through her makeup kit. "It would be good practice. I'm already great at making people pretty. And sometimes my friends let me do their makeup for Halloween. But they all want to be pretty things, like elves and fairies. No one ever lets me make them ugly. I practice on myself sometimes, though. I've got some liquid latex that's great for making lines and wrinkles."

I shrugged. "Sure, why not." I eyed her kit. "All your stuff is clean and sanitized, right?"

Blair nodded solemnly. "I gave Uncle Liam pink eye once, and he was *mad*. I'm really careful now. Anyway, next year I'll be fourteen and I'm going to start charging people to do their makeup for, like, prom and weddings. No one will hire me if I'm gross."

"Very true." I leaned back and closed my eyes while she dabbed moisturizer onto my cheeks, forehead, and chin. "I respect the hustle."

"Hang on, I'm going to go get my spa headband to keep your hair out of my way." Blair jumped to her feet and dashed to the stairs.

"Hey, toss me that mascara, will you, Lennon?" Grace asked from her chair across the room. "I need to take a photo so I know what to buy. It's really good."

I looked down at the pile of tubes. At least two looked to be mascara. I held one up, glancing at the label. "This one? Lux?"

Grace shook her head. "No, it was something XL. I can't remember the brand, but I remember that."

Emma leaned forward and peered over my shoulder. "That's it. See? XL." She tapped the letters.

I blinked and looked again. "Oh. I don't know why I thought it said Lux. Letters moving around on me again, I guess." I tossed Grace the tube.

She caught it with both hands and sent me a curious look. "Dyslexia?"

I forced a light laugh. "No, I just suck at reading." *Are you lazy, Lennon? Or just stupid?* I pushed the voices down and kept smiling.

"Because letters move around?" Grace snapped a photo of the mascara with her phone and then tossed it back to me. "And maybe your brain hallucinates letters and words that aren't there, filling in the gaps to make sense of it?"

Like changing XL to Lux. I stared at the tube in my hands. "Sometimes," I said.

She nodded. "I've had a few students with dyslexia. That's how they describe it."

"Or maybe I'm just stupid."

I meant it as a self-deprecating joke, but Grace shot up from her chair and stormed toward me. She squatted down, putting us eye to eye. "We don't use that word. You are not stupid. There are learning difficulties, and there is willfully ignorant. Stupid doesn't exist."

My eyes burned. "There are people who have known me my whole life who would disagree."

"Then tell them to call me." Grace's face turned red with fury.

"Do it," Emma said. "She's vicious."

Grace patted my knee. "You should get tested for dyslexia. It's missed a lot in kids. Plenty of people don't get diagnosed until adulthood."

I chewed my lip. "Can they fix it?"

"No, it doesn't work like that. But specialists can help you find ways to manage the challenges."

Blair came bounding back into the room with a white terry headband in one hand and her phone in the other. "Uncle Liam wants to know why no one is picking up their phone."

Grace smirked at her sister. "He means you."

Emma rolled to her feet. "I left my phone in the kitchen. What's going on?"

"Dunno," Blair said. "Something about Jeremiah leaving with Grandpa."

My body jolted at the sound of his name. Jeremiah hadn't been at the lodge this morning, or at the stables. I had assumed he was...I don't know, doing cowboy shit with cows or something...but from the anxious look on Emma's face, something else was going on.

"He's with Dad?" Emma's brow pinched. She exchanged a look with her sister before bolting to the kitchen.

"What?" I scrambled to my feet. "What's going on?"

"Nothing good if he's with our dad," Grace said. "Dad is the sheriff."

15

JEREMIAH

"Got a minute?"

I looked up from the photo of Lennon in a purple pantsuit, sitting on a desk with one long leg crossed over the other, to find Sheriff Sherwood leaning in my office doorway. Since that was never a good thing, I shut my laptop. "I can spare some time. What can I do for you?"

Sherwood stepped inside and shut the door behind him. "Miguel López. He works here?"

"He's in the kitchen most mornings," I allowed.

Nodding, Sherwood took a seat across from me and crossed his ankle over his knee. He pulled a pen and spiral notepad from his breast pocket and flipped to a blank page. "When was the last time you saw him?"

I laughed and leaned back in my chair. "Now, Sheriff, you know that's not how this relationship works. Miguel is a good kid. So how about you tell me what this is all about, and I'll determine what information is pertinent?"

Sherwood's jaw worked. A man like him didn't cede control easily. But we had history, and that history was a point in my favor. He trusted me. I was still making up my mind about him.

"Miguel is in the hospital," the sheriff said finally. "Car accident. He missed the curve where Hideaway Road follows the river—you know the one—and went right over the edge. He was pretty disoriented when they brought him in We're trying to put together a timeline of what happened."

"Shit. Is he going to be all right?"

"The doctors expect him to make a full recovery. But I won't lie, the kid is in rough shape. Broken clavicle, broken ribs, broken ankle. Concussion. He dragged himself up the embankment to flag down help. He doesn't know how long he was out there. Thinks maybe a full day and night."

"Fuck," I muttered, tugging at my hair. "Miguel was in Mexico for a week visiting family. He was supposed to be back Monday, but he never showed up for work."

Two full days ago. Two days and two nights. Shit. I should have called to check on him. It wasn't like me to let one of mine slip through the cracks like that. I had let myself get distracted, my head muddled over Lennon, and Miguel had paid the price for that.

"Talk to Amos Tallbull. He runs the kitchen and handles the staff schedule. He might know something I don't." The words tasted rancid in my mouth. *I should have known something.* My employee, my responsibility. Two fucking days on the side of a hill with broken bones? Fuck.

Sherwood jotted down the note. "Cecily Shepherd works in the kitchen, too? She's the one who found him this morning. Said it was her day off and she was worried about him because it wasn't like him not to call—"

"It's not," I confirmed. "Like I said, he's a good kid. Clean driving record. But you know that bend. This isn't the first accident there."

Sherwood grunted noncommittally.

I studied him. "You don't think this was an accident." It wasn't a question.

Sherwood twirled his pen between his fingers. "Miguel says there was another car that forced him off the road. He remembers bright lights coming out of nowhere and he swerved. We got a call that morning from a driver claiming she saw a car go over the edge. Sent out a patrol car but didn't see anything. Miguel was down there the whole time." He rubbed his index finger over his bottom lip, brows pinched. "Something isn't adding up. You want to come take a look at the scene?"

"I'm not a cop. I doubt I'd have much to add."

"We'll see." He tucked his notepad back into his pocket and rolled to his feet. "You have an interesting way of finding things that don't want to be found."

HIDEAWAY ROAD HAD COME by its name honestly—through dishonest people. Two hundred years ago, Mercy River wasn't much more than a train station, trading post, and hotel with rooms by the hour. Hideaway Road back then was an elk migration trail used by Mercy River's less savory citizens to hide out after relieving weary travelers of their valuables.

The road was paved now, but it could still be treacherous, particularly where it curved around the river. Yellow signs warned drivers to take the bend at thirty-five miles per hour. Three drivers in the last ten years had ignored that warning—twice with drunk drivers, and once with a showoff teenager—and with no guardrail to catch them, they went right over the edge. All three had died.

The county responded by putting up another sign.

Miguel's truck was fifty feet down the embankment. He had gone rear first over the edge and collided with a tree, which had probably saved his life, even as it had broken his bones and left him with a concussion. The airbag had deployed, and the seatbelt had kept him from flying through the windshield.

"You can see from the tire tracks here that Miguel hit the brakes. The front tires locked up and the back tires kept spinning, sending him into a skid. Went tail first." Sherwood pointed to the deep black marks in the gray asphalt.

"So he must have been going faster than thirty-five," I noted.

"Most locals do. You take this road long enough, you tend to get comfortable with it. You'll see."

I had been in Mercy River for eight years now, but to people who had been here for two or three generations, I was still a newcomer.

"He was heading to the ranch?" I asked, ignoring his dig.

Sherwood nodded. "That's what he told us."

"It was dark. They start cooking at four-thirty, feeding the ranch hands first, then the lodge staff, then the guests. He drives in Monday mornings, stays the week at the bunkhouse, then drives back home to his folks' house on Friday." I rubbed my chin. "He said the bright light came out of nowhere?"

"That's right."

I considered. The drop-off to the river was on one side of the road, and the other side was a copse of trees that bordered pastureland. But standing here, where

Miguel's truck left the road, I could see cars along the road beyond the bend. "Miguel should have seen the headlights coming."

"Maybe he dozed off, and the headlights woke him up." But I knew the sheriff doubted his own hypothesis, or he wouldn't have brought me out here.

I frowned. What were we missing? *Monday morning.* "It was raining. Miguel wouldn't have fallen asleep at the wheel. Not in a storm like that. He would have been paying attention." I looked past the bend again. "Visibility would have been worse, though."

"So, an accident."

"Then why didn't the other car stop? Why didn't someone call for help?"

Sherwood shrugged. "Drunk. High. Scared. Asshole. Pick your motive, and I've seen it. You know as well as I do that there are all kinds of people in this world, and even good people make shitty choices from time to time."

If Sherwood had known exactly how that statement applied to me, he wouldn't be standing next to me now, debating the finer points of humanity as it applied to a crime scene. He'd arrest me.

I said nothing as I surveyed the stretch of road. "No skid marks from the other driver? He didn't even try to brake?" Asshole.

Two short, dark marks caught my eye by the edge of

the road. They couldn't have been more than a yard in length. I squatted down to get a closer look.

Sherwood folded his arms. "I saw that, too. Probably from a different incident. The angle is all wrong for it to have been another driver coming around the bend."

I turned my head, following the angle. If the vehicle that made this mark had kept going in a straight line, it would have gone straight into the oncoming lane at the top of the bend and then over the edge.

I looked the other way, toward the trees. The vehicle that left those marks would have come from there, which didn't make a whole lot of sense.

But neither did the broken grass and weeds, in two sections six feet apart.

I straightened. "A vehicle was parked there under the trees. Can't say for sure that it was there Monday morning, but it couldn't have been too long ago."

Sherwood came to stand next to me. His expression didn't change as he stared at the faint marks with his hands on his hips. "Dammit," he swore softly. "Someone was waiting for him. Someone who knew he'd be coming this way at this time."

"That's a big jump from some broken weeds." But my gut was telling me the same thing. Someone had been waiting for him that stormy morning. This wasn't an accident.

With a sigh, Sherwood pulled out his notepad and pen again. "All right. I'll have to wait until Miguel is out of surgery to ask him questions, but I can start with you right now. Have you noticed anything out of the ordinary lately? With Miguel, or at the ranch?"

Lennon.

It had only taken fifteen minutes to verify what my gut had been telling me all along: Lennon Graves had no business being at Mercy River Ranch. No *good* business, anyway. Shady business? Yeah, I could see more than one pathway that might have led her straight to our doorstep.

She wasn't military or a first responder. She was a cam girl.

Her account had been paused a couple days before she landed in Wyoming and she hadn't streamed since. But there were still photos of her up. Lingerie and a pot roast. Lingerie and a bouquet of flowers. Even with the black lace mask and blue contact lenses, I recognized her mouth and the shape of her jaw. It was her.

I hadn't had time for more than a cursory glance into her subscribers before the sheriff showed up in my office. Going any deeper would require Mateo's skills. Maybe he could determine if one of her subs had a link to the ranch.

But what the hell would any of this have to do with Miguel? I knew for damn sure Lennon was nowhere near this road Monday morning. The image of her was seared into my brain.

Even if I hadn't been her alibi, I knew in my gut she

wouldn't knowingly have hurt another person. Not like that.

Maybe it was nothing more than a coincidence that Lennon was here at Mercy River under false pretenses at the same time Miguel was forced off the road.

But in my experience, too many coincidences weren't a coincidence at all.

It was a trap.

THE GUARDIAN

Everyone was talking about it. Literally EVERYONE. If I heard one more word about Lennon and Jeremiah kissing outside Sundowner, I cannot be held responsible for my actions.

But at least they found Miguel. That's good. I knew he'd be fine. I just hadn't counted on the utter incompetence of everyone around me. I told them where to find him! Did they even bother to check? I doubted it. If you want something done, you had to do it yourself.

My mood sucked today. The old darkness threatened to pull me under. I haven't felt this way since Lennon arrived at the ranch. She's been the sunshine that let me blossom after a rough storm. But today I was shrinking in on myself again. My belly hurt.

Self-care. That was what I needed. An afternoon in bed with Skittles and Diet Coke, rewatching Lennon's videos. We're not supposed to record her or screenshot —it was against the terms of service—but I wasn't not like her other viewers. I wouldn't trust a single one of them as far as I could throw them. But I was different. I didn't want to dox her or get myself off. There was something soothing about her. Her voice made me feel like everything was going to be okay. That *I* was going to be okay.

Maybe because when I was in the hospital, she told me I'd be okay, and she was right. That was how we'd first found each other. My asshole nurse had thought I was asleep. He'd parked his ass right on the edge of my bed to watch her live video.

Fucking pervert.

I hadn't been asleep. I'd watched the whole thing over his shoulder. Lennon had been dressed in a men's white button-down which she'd tied in a knot at her waist to show her navel, a cherry red bra that matched her lipstick, a tiny pair of denim shorts that were so tight I feared for her clitoris, and a pair of wedge sandals. Her hair was up in some 1950s style and she wore a black lace mask over the top two thirds of her face. Bright blue eyes—which I now knew were colored contacts.

She arranged flowers into a bouquet as she talked to her viewers. She had a wicked sense of humor and I'd had to bite my lip more than once to keep from chortling out loud. But mostly what I noticed was how kind she was. She genuinely cared about these troglodytes watching her.

There was a little box at the top right corner that kept track of how much money people were tipping her. When it hit a certain amount, she took off her top. Money kept coming in, and she took off her shorts, leaving her in the red bra and matching thong. I didn't know if she took off anything else, because that's when the nurse took his phone with him into the bathroom. I could hear him beating himself off.

Men. The fucking *worst*.

Something about her stuck with me. Not the nudity, although it was hard to believe a person that beautiful could actually exist in the world. The kindness. The humor. My world had turned gray, and she was the sun peaking through.

So I found her on the site, subscribed to her channel, and the next day she made a special point of thanking me for joining. She could only see my user name, of course, so she had no idea it was *me*. She probably thought I was just another man, although now I knew she had female viewers too. When I thanked her for entertaining me through my hospital stay, she asked for the room number.

"You're going to be okay," she told me. "It's going to get better for you. I can feel it."

The next day, a bouquet of pink peonies were delivered. It had to be her.

It sure as hell wasn't the ex-boyfriend who put me here.

I settled in with my candy, soda, and Lennon. It was one of my favorite videos because I was the first one on her channel, so I had her all to myself for five whole minutes before anyone else joined. She talked to me like I mattered, looking into the camera like she's looking into my eyes. She laughed at the joke I typed into the chat box.

Watching her calmed me down. My universe was centered again. The scar doidn't feel so tight anymore.

Jeremiah was nothing more than a pleasant distraction. A fling. Can I really blame her, when she spent the last nine months with that old rich guy who probably couldn't get it up for more than two minutes at a time? Sex was a natural, primal urge. She'll fuck him and move on.

What we had was stronger than sex. Stronger than romantic love. Those kinds of feelings wither and die. Friendship was forever.

It could be worse. Lennon had terrible taste in men —her one flaw. Thankfully, I was here to help her. But Jeremiah wasn't so bad, for a cowboy. I had always liked him.

It would be a shame if I had to hurt him.

16

LENNON

THE STARS HAD FADED INTO THE PURPLE-GRAY DAWN BY the time Jeremiah ventured to my cabin. I had lingered longer this morning, hoping he'd show but bracing myself for disappointment. It had been quite the mind-fuck yesterday to wake up giddy over this man only for those feelings to slowly fizzle away as the hours crept by with no sign of him.

Whatever business he'd had with the sheriff, it hadn't taken all day. He'd been back by late afternoon. He could have found me feeding the goats with the other ranch guests, but he hadn't. He could have found me in the dining hall at dinner, but he hadn't. He could have swung by my cabin after nightfall. I'd left the lamp on so he'd know I was awake if he happened to come my way. But he hadn't.

Men came in all sizes, shapes, and attitudes, but this much had always held true: they didn't do shit they didn't want to do. If Jeremiah had wanted to, he would have. Clearly, he didn't want to.

But I stood under the cold, dark sky anyway, because *I* wanted to. Because that kiss wasn't enough. I wanted more.

And now here he was, and my heart gave a little jump of hope that he wanted more, too.

He stopped when he saw me. "Hey."

My lips parted, but no sound came out. Literally no sound at all. I couldn't push a single syllable out through the sudden dryness of my mouth. I cleared my throat and swallowed. "Hey."

He crossed the yard. My heart picked up speed with every step that brought him closer to me.

Shit. *Shit.*

I couldn't remember the last time I'd had an actual crush on a man. But that was exactly what this was. Rapid heartbeat. Sweaty palms. Giggling and kicking my feet. I was crushing harder than a fourteen-year-old girl meeting her best friend's older brother.

How fucking embarrassing.

"I thought you were avoiding me," I blurted out.

His head tilted as he studied me in the dawning light. "What made you think that?"

"Oh, I don't know. Maybe the fact that you *were* avoiding me?" I teased.

I figured he'd deny it, maybe smooth over the awkward moment I had created with a pretty compliment and then let me down easy.

But he chuckled softly under his breath. "All right. But in my defense, I didn't know what to say."

"*Hey* seemed to work pretty well," I pointed out.

His lips quirked under his mustache. "True. Maybe I'll try it again sometime."

I was wearing his coat unzipped—it was warmer this morning—and he grabbed the placket and tugged me closer.

"You don't have your earrings in," he remarked as he locked the hems together and slowly zipped me up. Oh, god. There was that awful, embarrassing, fluttery feeling in my chest again. "Did you find the missing one?"

"I looked around the cabin in case it fell out when I was changing or something, but no luck. It could be anywhere. I think it's a lost cause."

He checked his watch. "I have a few minutes. I'll see if I can find it."

"Right now?" My eyebrows pinched. The sky was streaked with pink and gold, but the sun hadn't crested the mountain ridge yet. "It's barely light outside."

"I'll find it." He wrapped his arms around my waist, and before I knew what was happening, he'd lifted me off my feet and marched up the path with me. "I have a theory."

"What's that?" I asked breathlessly, arms looped around his neck, because where else would they go? My mouth hovered near his temple. The strangest urge came over me to kiss him there, on that cluster of golden-brown freckles along his hairline. My stomach felt all swoopy even thinking about it.

God, crushes were dumb.

"Monday morning. The rainstorm." He set me down, then took a step back. "You were standing right here, where I am now. I think that's when you lost it." He pulled a headlamp from his coat pocket, flipped it on with his thumb, and handed it to me before dropping into a squat. "Move the light around. See if you can pick up something shiny."

I let the light follow his hands as he brushed them over the dirt and short grass. "Why do you think I lost it in the rain?"

"You did this thing with your hands. Dragged them over your hair and face like you were trying to squeegee the water off you." He shifted further onto the grass, off the dirt path. "It would have bounced, but not far," he muttered to himself.

I squatted next to him to get closer with the light. "I don't remember that."

"I do."

His gaze flicked to my face, then to my chest. He

couldn't see my shape hidden beneath his coat, but the sudden pink on his cheekbones made me feel like he could. I didn't hate it. If I hadn't been buried in his coat, I would have been squeezing my boobs together, propping them up to give him a better view.

A rainbow reflected on his black coat, and I gasped. "Wait—I think—" I wiggled the light, and the rainbow danced.

"Got it." He plucked the earring from the grass, holding it up between his thumb and forefinger.

I gaped at it. "Holy shit. I can't believe you found it. That's incredible."

"Things have a way of coming unhidden, if you know where to shine the light." He turned the earring over in his hand, studying it. His jaw clenched. "The sheriff—" He broke off, frowning.

The sheriff? Why had he brought that up now? My throat squeezed. Outside of vaguely hoping everything was all right, I hadn't given a second thought to why the sheriff had needed Jeremiah. It wasn't any of my business—but what if it was? If the FBI knew I was here, they'd want local law enforcement's cooperation, wouldn't they? Maybe? I didn't know how any of that worked.

"Was it about me?" I blurted out.

There was no surprise in his expression at the question, just a calm sort of focus. "Is there a reason the sheriff would be asking about you?"

My laugh sounded fake to my own ears. "I can't think of any crimes I've committed lately." Running away before they could ask me about crimes other people had committed wasn't a crime in and of itself, right? I sure hoped not.

He regarded me quietly, not rushing to more questions. Giving me time to expound on my answer. I shifted nervously. Those blue-gray eyes were as good as a shot of truth serum in my veins. Any second now, I was going to vomit out the whole story.

"Here's your earring." He dropped it into my hand.

"Thanks," I rasped, my throat dry.

He turned to go, then paused. "You want to go for a ride this afternoon?"

I blinked, surprised. "Yes. But I've never ridden a horse before."

"That's okay. I'll give you a lesson."

I watched him go, feeling excited and uneasy at the same time, and then ran inside to get dressed. Hopefully, Cecily and Amos wouldn't care that I was late. It wasn't like I was getting paid, but they were counting on me. I hated letting anyone down, but especially Cecily. The way she'd made sure I felt safe with Jeremiah before leaving the bar had been so sweet.

It wasn't until I was pulling on my boots that I realized Jeremiah had never told me what the sheriff wanted.

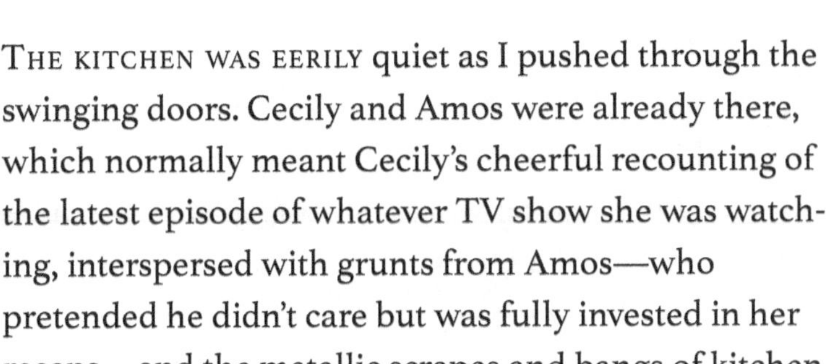

THE KITCHEN WAS EERILY quiet as I pushed through the swinging doors. Cecily and Amos were already there, which normally meant Cecily's cheerful recounting of the latest episode of whatever TV show she was watching, interspersed with grunts from Amos—who pretended he didn't care but was fully invested in her recaps—and the metallic scrapes and bangs of kitchen work.

I had always been good at reading a room, and right now the room was telling me something was very wrong before I even opened the door.

"What's going on?" I asked, my gaze darting between Amos and Cecily.

"Lennon!" Cecily spun away from the prep table and threw her arms around my neck, sniffling back tears.

"Whoa." My wide eyes met Amos's over her shoulder. "What happened?"

His mouth flattened into a grim line. "Miguel—he was supposed to work Monday but didn't show up." I nodded. "He was in an accident. Cecily found him yesterday morning. Barely alive. Poor kid."

"Oh my god." I rubbed Cecily's shoulder blades. That must have been why the sheriff was with Jeremiah. It was about Miguel, not me. Guilt chased the relief away. *Not everything is about you, Lennon. Don't be so self-ish.* No wonder Jeremiah had looked at me like I had disappointed him. "Is he going to be all right?"

"They say so. His parents are at the hospital with him, and they'll keep us informed," Amos said.

Cecily pulled back, her eyes red-rimmed and glassy. "It wasn't like him to miss work and not call. He's been here three years and only missed work one day when he was sick, and he called, you know? He doesn't ever just not show up. I knew something was wrong." Amos handed her a paper towel and she wiped her nose. "I should have checked on him sooner. That's what you do for friends. You don't leave them for dead by the side of the road. Who would do something like that?"

It must have been horrifying for her to find him the way she did. I didn't know Cecily well enough to have the perfect words to make her feel better, so imperfect words would have to do. "You did everything you could, Cecily. I know it's easy to get dragged down by the weight of all the things we should have done, but think of what you actually *did.* You spent your day off looking for him. You got him help. He would have died without you."

Her head bobbed rapidly as she moved the paper towel through her fingers, looking for a dry spot. "I didn't let him die. He's going to be okay."

"Gotta get to cooking now. Whole lot of hungry cowboys and guests wanting breakfast." Amos's voice was as gruff as ever, but he dropped a large hand on Cecily's shoulder and squeezed. "You need to sit this one out?"

"No." Cecily shook her head. "I can do this. Miguel would smack me upside the head if I sat around crying over him, especially now that he's going to be all right." She wiped her nose again and looked up at me. "Maybe we could go visit him in the hospital this afternoon? Could you drive me?"

Before I could answer, Amos said, "I talked to his dad this morning. He's out of surgery, but they're not allowing visitors who aren't family yet."

Cecily's shoulders drooped. "Oh. Okay."

"Jeremiah is giving me a riding lesson this afternoon," I volunteered. "If he has any updates on Miguel, I'll pass them on. Give me your phone number."

"You're going riding with Jeremiah? Just the two of you?" Her brows furrowed. "He doesn't usually do that. But that's good. He was with Sheriff Sherwood yesterday, after the sheriff took my statement. I want to know what the sheriff plans on doing about this."

She looked heartbreakingly young. Her shiny eyes tugged at my protective instincts. I wanted to tell her that everything would be all right.

But I couldn't shake the feeling that trouble had followed me here.

17

JEREMIAH

MOST PEOPLE WHO CAME TO MERCY RIVER RANCH considered horses to be an asset. Cattle were our business, but horses were our heart. I had witnessed it time and time again, the way a horse could heal a wounded soul.

Judging by the way Lennon backed up with a surprised gasp when Indigo sniffed her, she did not agree. I bit back a smile.

"This is Indigo. He likes city slickers." I held the black gelding's reins loosely in one hand while Lennon gave us both a dubious look.

"*How* does he like city slickers?" she asked suspiciously. "Served with a side of oats for breakfast?"

I chuckled. "I know he looks like a demon, but I

promise you're safe with him. This boy is bombproof. Aren't you, boy?" I gave him a solid pat on his neck, and he turned to look at me. "Nothing fazes him."

"He's not the one I'm worried about," she muttered, but she stretched tentative fingers toward his nose and rubbed gently with the back of her knuckles. "He's soft," she said begrudgingly. She shifted closer.

"Horses can sense a person's emotions," I told her. "They're prey animals, so they're wired to stay alert for signs of danger. That means if you're a nervous rider, your horse is going to pick up on that and start acting out. But Indigo here, he stays calm no matter how silly his rider is. That's what makes him good for greenhorns."

"Is he slow?" Lennon asked hopefully.

"As slow as you tell him to be," I evaded.

Indigo was one of the smartest, most intuitive horses I'd ever had the pleasure of riding, but slow wasn't his preferred speed. That wasn't necessarily a bad thing, though. I'd learned the hard way that a lazy horse and an inexperienced rider were a match made in hell. Once a lazy horse realized his rider didn't know shit, he'd take advantage of that and graze away, no matter how much his rider kicked.

A horse like Indigo, who liked to stretch his legs and didn't care too much if his rider bounced like a sack of potatoes on his back, was a much better fit for a new rider.

"Ready to ride?" I asked.

Her brown eyes widened. "But I don't know how."

"It's not the kind of thing you learn on the ground, honey." I placed the reins in her left hand. "Face the horse, left hand on the saddle horn but don't drop the reins, right hand on the cantle—that's the back of the saddle. Yes, right there, you've got it. Left foot in the stirrup. Now step up and swing your right leg over his back."

"I don't know if I can do this."

But even as she spoke, she gave an experimental hop and then went for it for real. It wasn't graceful, but she was in the saddle. That was one of the things I liked about Lennon. Even when she doubted success, she was always game to try. She gave it her all.

I fixed the length of her left stirrup, then rounded Indigo's head to lengthen her right stirrup so they matched. Moving back to the left side, I checked the girth one last time to make sure it was tight enough.

I gave her a quick lesson on the basics, showing her how to hold her reins with her left hand and to steer by gently placing the reins on the right side of Indigo's neck to turn left, and on the left side to turn right. When the stiffness in Lennon's shoulders melted a bit and her right hand relaxed its death grip on the horn, I swung up on Ruby, a pretty chestnut mare with a fondness for open spaces, Indigo, and sneaking up on unsuspecting folks with a sharp whinny that could raise the dead.

"See those trees over there?" I pointed, and she nodded. "There's a meadow right beyond them. That's where we're going."

Her hand tightened on the horn again. "We're not staying here in the ring?"

"Wildflowers are blooming. There's no better way to see them than hiking or on horseback."

The truth was, Lennon and I were overdue for a conversation, and that conversation needed to be had away from certain nosy cowboys. After digging through her past yesterday, I intended to confront her with it. Drag a confession out of her and then send her packing.

This morning I had the opportunity to do just that, and what had I done instead? My brain had short-circuited at the sight of her wearing my coat unzipped and nothing but those tiny shorts and camisole underneath. How was I supposed to have that conversation with her when her peaked nipples were taunting me like that? I'd zipped her up in my coat so I wouldn't pounce on her like a rabid dog.

And then I'd offered to find her earring.

And *then* I'd asked her to come riding with me.

If I hadn't gotten the hell out of there, I probably would have found a way to kiss her again. Gotten her out of my coat and into her bed.

And that was a real fucking problem.

"IT'S SO BEAUTIFUL HERE." Lennon lifted a hand to her forehead to shield her eyes from the brilliant afternoon sunlight and gazed at the field of wildflowers that stretched all the way to the mountains. "The sky goes on forever. I guess that's why you all wear cowboy hats, huh?"

"Here, take mine." I turned Ruby to pull up next to Indigo, removed my tan Stetson, and plopped it on her head. It sank low on her forehead.

Laughing, she pushed it higher. "It's a little big. But thank you."

She nudged Indigo with her heels, hips swaying to the horse's movements. *Wear the hat, ride the cowboy.* It was a favorite saying around here during tourist season, when women on vacation were looking for a cowboy adventure. Watching Lennon's hips roll, her dessert-colored hair tumbling down her back under my hat, I saw the appeal. I could imagine. Lennon above me, my hands on her hips, her breasts—

Fuck. I had gone from half hard to fully hard in ten seconds like a teenage boy who hadn't learned to control himself yet.

With a muttered curse, I rose in my stirrups and surreptitiously adjusted myself, hoping to hell she didn't choose this moment to look back at me. *Eyes forward, honey. Pay no attention to the blue-balled dumbass behind you.*

She halted again, looking down at the yellow flowers. "Dandelions, right?" She fished her phone out of her bra for the third time, tapped the screen to open the app she'd been using to identify wildflowers, and aimed the camera at the flower. "No, it's pale ago...ago..." She frowned over the unfamiliar word. "It's fake dandelion." She laughed, looking at me over her shoulder just as I eased back into the saddle. "They're pretty, though. Even if they are little fraudsters."

Just like someone else I know.

The meadow was thick with early summer flowers. Indian paintbrush in red, orange, and pink were interspersed with yellow fake dandelions and white daisies. Lennon had been snapping pictures left and right.

"It's tempting to pick a bunch for your cabin, isn't it?" I hinted. "I bet they'd look pretty in a vase on your nightstand."

She didn't take the bait. "I think they're prettiest right where they are. If everyone picked themselves a bouquet of wildflowers, there wouldn't be any left."

I ground my teeth in frustration. I had given her a couple of opportunities to tell me the truth, and she'd sailed past all of them without batting a guilty eye.

"Have you been riding horses your whole life?" she asked, changing the subject.

She did that a lot, I'd noticed. Turned the subject back to me when it edged too close to something personal for her. Usually she paired that with a compliment. I never trusted flattery, but the way Lennon seemed both sincere and genuinely curious, it didn't feel like she was blowing smoke up my ass. Which probably meant that I was more susceptible to a pretty girl showing an interest in me than I cared to admit.

I let the silence stretch a moment instead of answering right away, so she paused a moment, studying me, and then continued, "You look like you were born in the saddle. I can't imagine you bouncing around like a sack of potatoes."

"Everyone's a beginner at some point," I said.

A flicker of disappointment crossed her face. I hadn't answered her question. Hadn't given her any more than she'd given me. Maybe that was the problem. Lennon was locked down tighter than Fort Knox, but I wasn't much better. If I wanted her to open up, I had to go first. Trust went both ways and I hadn't earned hers yet.

"I grew up on a compound. Several families shared the labor of working the farms. We had horses, mostly for working fields or pulling carts. We didn't ride and, looking back, I'm glad I didn't learn until I came to Mercy River." I rubbed my thumb over the soft leather of the reins. How deep into this was I willing to go to get answers? How much of myself was I willing to bare? "The Bible told us that man was to have dominion over the beasts of the field and the fowls of the air. How I was raised..." I worked my thumb harder over the leather. I hated talking about this shit. "They didn't interpret it in a gentle way."

"Amish?" she asked with a tilt of her head.

"Polygamists."

Her mouth fell open in surprise. She blinked rapidly. "Like...free love? Hippies?"

I barked a laugh. "There was nothing free about it. The compound was a religious cult, a Mormon offshoot that still followed the old doctrines. They believed their leader was the one true prophet of God, as his father had been before him, and his father's father, and so on for over a hundred years, when God had told them to shun the modern world and associate only with each other. Only the highest church leaders had cars or phones. No television or radio. No jeans or skirts above the ankle for women. We dressed like it was still 1880." I paused. "We were homeschooled until we were thirteen. Basic math, reading and writing, and the scriptures. Nothing about science or history. I had never heard of dinosaurs. Or Canada."

"How is that even possible?" She shook her head like she couldn't fathom it. "And then you joined the military? That must have been such a shock."

"By then I had already been out for a few years. The structure and discipline that the military offered was actually a relief. It felt familiar."

"So your parents left the compound? Your family isn't there anymore?"

I paused. This was the ugly part. "My parents are still there. I didn't leave willingly. I was banished at fourteen." *You have sinned, Jeremiah. You are hereby banished for your earthly life, so that your stain does not besmirch us all.* I could still see my father's face as he spoke the words. "My father dropped me off at a church in a town three hours from home in the middle of the night and told me someone would get me in the morning."

"Banished. At fourteen." Her eyes pleaded softly, like she was hoping I'd take it back. "You were only a child."

"At fourteen, I was considered a man. That was the problem. According to church doctrine, polygamy was a requirement to enter heaven. But the compound was insular. Few left, and no one new came in. Hard to promise every man three wives when the birthrate is pretty close to a fifty-fifty split between the sexes. They had to thin the herd." I lifted a shoulder.

"So, what, they could keep all the women to themselves? That's disgusting."

"According to my father, the reason for my banishment was that I committed the sin of masturbation. I think that was bullshit, though. It only happened once, nearly a year before they sent me away." I still had the scars from that lesson.

My breath hitched. Why had I told her that? I had never shared it with anyone, not even my foster parents.

The shame of it weighed on me even now, even knowing that the shame shouldn't have been mine to bear.

Her hand tightened on the reins enough that Indigo tossed his head in annoyance. "Loosen your hold on him," I told her. "He can feel all your emotions."

"Oh." She relaxed her hand and gave him a brisk pat on the neck. "Sorry, big guy. I'm just so *mad*. I don't know which is worse, tossing you out because you were their competition, or banishing you for masturbation. Honestly," she huffed, her eyes narrowed to furious slits. "I'd like to smack them in their sanctimonious faces with a purple dildo."

That startled a laugh right out of me. "Why purple?"

"For whatever reason, most sex toys seem to be purple. And it's my favorite color." Her gaze shifted from me to the mountains and back again. It wasn't hard to meet her eyes. She made it easy for me. There wasn't a lick of judgment there. "Can I take your picture?"

"What?" I startled, straightening in the saddle. "Why?"

"Why?" she repeated, laughing. "*Why?* Look around you, Jeremiah. The flowers, the mountains, the blue Wyoming sky. And you in the middle of it all, looking like the whole reason anyone crossed the Mississippi River in the first place."

I didn't know what to do with my hands when she said shit like that. I didn't know what to do with my face when she looked at me like she was remembering what my mouth felt like.

"It's not hard to cross the river, Lennon. There are bridges now, you know."

"Just sit there and look pretty, cowboy. Here, you need your hat for the photo." She circled Indigo closer. And then she paused with her hand on my hat and looked at me. "I don't take it lightly, what you shared with me. I know I sounded flippant. I don't mean to. I don't really know what to say to all this, except...well, I think you're incredible, Jeremiah."

In the split second between her removing the hat from her head and putting it on mine, I suddenly knew exactly what to do with my hands and face. I cupped her soft cheek in my palm and covered that smirking mouth with mine. A sweet kiss, nothing like what we did outside Sundown. This wasn't fire and thirst. It was milk and honey. And that made it all the more dangerous, because I didn't feel it in my cock.

I felt it in my chest.

"What was that for?" Her dark eyes scanned my face, the pretty green around her pupils shining like meadow grass. She looked at me like that, and I couldn't do anything but give her the truth.

"Flowers, mountains, sky, and you in the middle of it all, looking like the reason for everything."

Her lips parted in surprise. There was something vulnerable in her expression, but in the next second she leaned back, the mouth that had softened against mine once again twisted into a jaded smirk.

"Damn, that's a good line, cowboy." She nudged Indigo forward and called over her shoulder, "Stay there. I want the mountains to be the backdrop behind you." Lennon halted Indigo several yards away and held up her phone. "Okay, look pensive and masculine. Shouldn't be too hard for you."

Her shields were back up.

Maybe I was asking for too much. I had told her what had happened *to* me, but I hadn't told her what I'd *done*.

I hadn't told her about Hannah.

18

LENNON

NOT EVEN MY AUDIOBOOK COULD DROWN OUT THE thoughts in my head as I tried to soothe myself to sleep.

Banished at fourteen.

For masturbating—or so that gross old men could have a few extra wives. I still wasn't sure which was worse. I felt terrible for Jeremiah, for everything he'd been through, but I felt even worse for all those girls who never left. At least he'd escaped, no matter how painful that had been.

But still. Fourteen fucking years old.

What the fuck! What. The. Fuck.

Of course I had bungled it. I wasn't the kind of person people opened up to about things like that—the sad and painful things that had built them brick by brick. I was the good news girl. The one they turned to with a promotion or a birthday. I hyped them up. Made them feel special. People liked me because they liked *themselves* when they were with me. I laughed at their jokes, so they pushed themselves to be funnier. I cheered for their successes, so they tried even harder. They sparkled all the more brightly because I held up the mirror.

Making people feel good about themselves made me feel good about myself. I didn't have much to offer the world, but at least I could do that.

And all that was real—I didn't fake a damn thing—but it was surface-level shit. My relationships were babbling brooks: pretty and frothy. But Jeremiah had pulled me into deep waters, and I didn't know how to swim.

A normal person might have shown a little empathy. Maybe shared a piece of themselves in return. I could have told him that I knew what it was like to have disappointing parents. That my mother hadn't banished me, but she was the reason I banished myself, because she hadn't protected me from the men in her life. I could have told him that their actions don't define us, but we had better lives because of what we did about it.

But I hadn't said any of that.

No.

I said, *Sit there and look pretty, cowboy.*

Fuck a duck. What the actual hell was wrong with me? Thank god he kissed me because at least I couldn't talk when my lips were occupied with his. For approximately two seconds before I'd made it weird again.

Now I was lying in bed *alone.* That was how it should be, no matter how much I wished he were in bed with me. Because Jeremiah was a good man. The kind of man who gave a silly girl his coat when she was standing in the rain. The kind of man who used his body to protect hers from harm. The kind of man who would make a woman his reason for everything.

The kind of man who deserved a woman worthy of that.

And that woman...that woman wasn't me.

I was the last person a man like Jeremiah should get tangled up with.

THE SUN WAS STREAMING through the curtains by the time I pried my eyes open.

Sleep hadn't come easily last night. Even after I'd finished my audiobook, I'd lain awake for hours thinking about what Jeremiah had told me. All the things he'd said, and how I'd given him a big fat nothing in return. Guilt had kept me tossing and turning.

People were looking for me. Good people, bad people, it was all the same to me. They wanted something I wasn't willing to give. If they found me here—if I brought that trouble to Jeremiah, after everything he had been through—I wouldn't forgive myself.

I should tell him. But if I told him what I was running from, wouldn't he be in danger, too? Scratch that, I shouldn't tell him. What I should actually do is leave.

But I was too selfish to do that. I felt safer here than anywhere I'd ever been. It wasn't just the ranch that made me feel that way. It was Jeremiah. He made me feel more than safe. He made me feel...I didn't have words for what this was. My lips felt branded by his. I had never experienced anything like that. Never knowing if he fucked like he kissed felt like cruel and unusual punishment.

And that was the other thing that kept me tossing and turning all night. I was horny as hell over a certain mustached cowboy who seemed to think we had all the time in the world to figure this out. Which we didn't. June was almost over.

Shit! It was almost ten. I'd missed breakfast—both eating it *and* cooking it. Cecily and Amos were probably furious with me. I knew they could handle the workload without me, but they shouldn't have to. Not when I'd promised to be there.

A knock on the door had me tumbling out of bed in a panic. Cecily, maybe? Amos coming to lecture me about responsibility? I pulled my hoodie on as I made for the door and breathlessly flung it open. "Hey—"

Nope. Not Cecily. Not Amos.

Jeremiah.

I slammed the door shut in his face.

"Two minutes!" I hollered, hoping he could hear me from the porch. "Just give me two minutes!"

I raced to the bathroom, did my business, scrubbed my teeth for a brisk thirty seconds, and didn't bother with my hair because as it so happened, I had the kind of wave that looked hot rumpled.

When I opened the door again, Jeremiah was right where I had left him, only now with his hands on his hips and a scowl on his lips. I smiled brightly. "Good morning."

His scowl deepened. "The day is half gone. I didn't see you when I came by this morning, and Amos said you never showed up at the kitchen. Randy said you weren't at breakfast with the other guests, either."

I cocked my hip against the door jam, one ankle crossed over the other, and folded my arms. "Aw, that's sweet. Were you worried about me, caveman?"

My words hung in the air. Jeremiah studied me calmly as the silence stretched a beat past comfortable.

"Are you feeling all right, Lennon? No fever, upset stomach, anything like that?" His tone was as placid as a summer lake under a cloudless blue sky.

It made me nervous.

"No, I'm not sick."

"How about your mental health? You doing okay there? Anxiety, emotional distress, that sort of thing?"

I stared at him. *Yes, not having your dick inside me has caused me immense emotional distress, thank you for asking. I am in agony.* But I would sooner move back home with my mother than tell Jeremiah Bell that pining for his dick had kept me up last night.

"What an odd question," I said sweetly, and then left it unanswered.

"So you're fine?" he pressed. "Physically, emotionally, and mentally healthy?"

"I'm right as rain," I chirped, and then winced internally. Who the hell *said* shit like that? Not the mentally healthy, that was for damn sure.

"Good. That means I can yell at you without feeling bad about it."

My spine snapped straight and my mouth dropped open. "What—"

"Yes, Lennon, I was fucking worried about you." His voice rose with every word. All pretense of calm was gone. Thick tendons in his throat popped out as he loomed over me, jaw ticcing.

"I was fine!"

"No one knew where you were. The last time we didn't know where someone was, he drove off a cliff. I didn't know if you were hurt or sick or just gone." He put a hand to my belly and moved me backwards into the cabin, then kicked the door shut behind him.

Holy shit, he was really worried about me? My breath stuttered. No one had ever worried about me before. People enjoyed my company, and I liked to think they missed me when I wasn't around. But no one had ever claimed responsibility for me like that. I took care of myself. Always.

But Jeremiah...he acted like I was his to keep safe. He had been taking care of me since the day I got here. Protecting me from the cold and rain and cowboys intent on making me bleed.

"I'm sorry." I swallowed past the gravel in my throat. "I didn't mean to make anyone worry about me. I didn't know anyone cared."

"I care. More than I should." He lifted my chin with his fist, his thumb tracing my jaw. "What are you doing here, Lennon? I need to know."

My brows pinched in confusion. But before I could ask him what he meant by that, I heard the swish of paper gliding against the wooden floor. The smell hit the back of my throat and I gagged.

I was dimly aware that Jeremiah was no longer touching me. He stooped to pick it up, then opened the door and peered out. My knees shook.

"No one is there. What is this? Is this for you?"

My hand twitched at my side, but my limbs were lead, too heavy to lift. I tried to breathe, but every breath brought in that same smell.

Vanilla and citrus.

19

JEREMIAH

"Slow, deep breaths through your nose, honey."
With her back to my chest, I eased us both down the
cabin wall until our butts met the floor, keeping her
wedged between my thighs.

"I can still smell my perfume." Her voice was pitched
high with panic.

That's what this was. A panic attack. They were
common enough with our guests—and Liam—that we
were all experienced in handling them. Why would a
scented postcard trigger a panic attack in Lennon? That
question would have to wait until she was calm.

I grabbed her ankles, one in each hand, and gently
positioned her legs so her knees were bent and her feet
flat on the floor. "Press your feet into the floor and

breathe, honey. You're safe. Can you feel me breathing? Breathe with me."

I inhaled, silently counting to four, expanding my belly so she could feel it against her back. Held for two, then exhaled for six. Her breathing slowed slightly, but not enough. It was still too quick and shallow. I breathed again. Inhaled for four, held for two, exhaled for six. This time she matched me.

"Purse your lips like you're whistling when you exhale, all right? Inhale through your nose. Tell me five things you see."

"Um." I felt her shift like she was trying to focus. "The braided rug. Green curtains. Black knots in the pine beams. Blue sky out the window. The bed."

"That's great, Lennon. You're doing so good. Tell me four things you can touch."

"Jeans." She rubbed her palms over my denim-clad knees that were bracketing her. "The breeze from the open door." Her feet wiggled. "My toes," she said, and I chuckled softly. She leaned back against me. "You."

"That's right, honey. I'm right here. You're safe. Nothing can hurt you here." Who the fuck had slipped that postcard under the door? I pushed the question aside and focused on the woman in my arms. She needed me calm now, not murderous.

"Safe," she repeated. Her head tipped back on my shoulder. "Safe."

The next question would have been three things she

smelled, but considering it was a smell that triggered her panic attack in the first place, I thought better of it.

With her face right there, I couldn't stop myself from pressing my lips to her damp temple. Not a kiss. A quick touch like I was taking her temperature with my mouth. Nothing more.

But then I did it again, and that was definitely a kiss.

She was over the worst of it now. A sheen of sweat glistened on her skin. Her legs trembled violently—the surge of adrenaline leaving her system—and I could feel her body tense as she tried to get her muscles under control. I cuddled her closer, giving her a safety net where she could fall apart.

"I've got you, Lennon. I've got you. It's all right."

With a whole-body shudder, she gave in. Big and violent, even her teeth rattled. I held on until it passed and she went limp against me. Still between my legs, she wiggled herself lower down my body and curled onto her side. I stretched out my legs and gave her my thigh for a pillow.

"How do you feel?" I asked.

"Tired." She yawned, and it triggered one of my own.

I sifted my fingers through her hair, pulling it back from her face. My fingertips followed the soft curve of her ear as I tucked her hair behind it, then continued to her jaw. I pressed two fingers there, testing. Her heart-beat had slowed, but it wasn't completely back to normal yet.

"Are you taking my pulse?" She tilted her head just enough that she could side-eye me from my lap.

"Maybe."

"Am I having a heart attack? I felt like I was dying."

"Not a heart attack. A panic attack can feel like a heart attack, though. Have you ever had one before?"

"No, never. I don't know why it happened now. The postcard surprised me, but it's not like this was the first one. I don't know why I reacted like that. It's so stupid. I feel ridiculous." She pressed her face into my thigh like she was trying to hide.

My gaze flicked to the postcard, and my brows pinched. "Sometimes a panic attack is triggered by a memory. Something—a smell, a sound—reminds your subconscious of a time when you weren't safe. But sometimes panic attacks happen when we ignore the danger signs until our subconscious can't take it anymore and we explode. It's your brain's way of telling you to stop gaslighting yourself."

She snorted. "Faking a heart attack is my body's way of warning me I'm in danger? Seems dumb. How am I supposed to run from danger if I feel like I'm having a heart attack?"

I laughed. "No one said a panic attack was a rational response." I paused, then said carefully, "Tell me about the postcard."

For a moment, she didn't say anything as she fiddled with the fabric of my jeans. Then she sighed, pushed to sit up, and snagged the postcard from where it had landed two feet away. "Here." She flicked it to me.

I studied the photograph of a field of wildflowers before flipping it over.

I DID IT FOR YOU

The words jumped out in purple block letters. What did it mean? I brought it to my nose and sniffed. Sweet and citrusy.

"Vanilla and orange?" I asked, looking at her.

She sat next to me and nodded. "Belle Gourmand. It was my perfume for years, but I stopped wearing it a while ago. It creeped me out too much."

"Ex-boyfriend?"

"Maybe? I really don't know. I'm pretty active online." I nodded like this was new information. "My perfume isn't a secret. I'm sure I've mentioned it. It could be a subscriber." She glanced at the postcard in my hand but didn't move to touch it. "It doesn't seem like something anyone I've dated would do. I mean, they seemed normal at the time. But how well can you really know a person, anyway?"

She wasn't wrong. People had a way of shocking the hell out of me. Hell, sometimes I even surprise myself.

"I don't know why I panicked like that. Spraying it with my perfume is creepy, but the messages themselves are pretty tame. I get way worse messages from men online."

"Such as?" I gritted out.

"The usual stuff. Dick pics, graphic fantasies, rape threats."

My molars smashed together. "I need names."

"I don't know them." She worried the inside of her cheek for a moment, then seemed to come to a decision. Her shoulders squared and she met my eyes. "I'm a cam girl, Jeremiah. Subscribers pay me a monthly fee to watch me do 1950s housewife shit naked. Make dinner, dust and vacuum, put together pretty floral arrangements. That kind of thing. I have no idea who my subscribers are unless they tell me. The host company handles subscriber accounts and financial payments, not me."

"You report these threats to the police?" I kept my voice calm, but there was nothing calm about the rage surging inside me.

"The police? You want a cam girl to report rape threats to the police?" She rolled her eyes. "Mostly I just block them and move on with my day. It's not like they can actually hurt me through a computer screen, even if it feels like they can." She flicked the postcard with the tip of her nail as if she didn't want it to contaminate her. "Maybe that's why this bothers me so much. It proves they can find me offline."

No return address. No stamp. No postmark. It hadn't gone through the post office. Someone had hand-delivered it. How had they known she was here? Had they paid someone to deliver the postcard, or was the asshole actually here in person?

"We're circling back to that cam girl shit, just so you know. I'm not going to let it go."

She flinched. "Does it matter?"

"Does it matter?" I repeated incredulously. "Of course it fucking matters, Lennon. Rape threats? Death threats? You can't ignore that."

"No, I mean—" She huffed a small laugh and shook her head. "I mean, does it matter to you *personally*, Jeremiah Bell, that I paid my bills by camming?"

No was the right answer, but it wasn't the truthful one. I didn't care that men had seen her naked. I didn't even care that they had paid her for that privilege. That was before she had ever come to Wyoming. I'd had no claim on her then. I had no claim on her now, but that didn't stop me from wanting her all to myself.

"It matters," I said. "I'm jealous as hell, Lennon. But as long as I'm the only one touching you, it's something I can live with. If camming is something you plan to keep doing, we need to find a way to keep you safe."

"Jeremiah," she said softly. The way she looked at me made my chest hurt. "There's nothing you can do about it. If I report them, they find a way to create a new account and harass me from there. Don't worry about it, okay? It's not your problem."

She actually believed that? I twisted to look at her. "It's not a problem, Lennon. It's a wrong. Problems have a solution. There's no solution for wrongs. You have to cut them out or they will spread like cancer. It doesn't matter if the wrong is happening to you or to someone you know, or to a complete stranger. Wrongs belong to everyone. You see it, you fix it. That's what you do."

"What *you* do, maybe," she muttered. "Some of us are too busy trying to survive, and some of us are nothing but cowards." She lifted her gaze to my face, her dark eyes searching mine. "You're a good man, Jeremiah."

"Am I?" My father's words still echoed in my head. *Sinner. Banished. Son of perdition.* "I suppose goodness is in the eye of the beholder."

She huffed, then grabbed my face with both hands. "Well, it's my eyes doing the beholding, and I'm looking right at you. You're a good man, Jeremiah."

I swallowed past the sudden thickness in my throat. She couldn't absolve me for sins she didn't know I had committed. If I sank to my knees and confessed it all, would she still look at me like that? I wasn't going to find out. Not today, and probably not ever. She would be gone from here in another month. Better for everyone that she didn't carry my sins with her.

So instead I looked her dead in the eyes so she'd know I wasn't fucking around, and said, "I'm going to ruin their lives, Lennon. Anyone who threatened you, I'll ruin them. Is that what a good man would do?"

She considered that, and then her lips tilted up in a little smirk. "I'll allow it."

"Good. Now tell me about the postcards. When did you start receiving them?"

"About two years ago, I think. I got one every week for a couple of months. I thought they were funny at first. They were almost...friendly? I don't know how to describe it. They would say nice things about my outfit or my new haircut. But then they started getting more judgmental. Telling me I shouldn't be with the guy I was dating, or that I always made bad choices when it came to men. The postcards stopped when I moved apartments, and I was relieved. I didn't get one for a couple of weeks. And then they started up again. That's when I got scared. I moved again, and they found me again. My last apartment, it wasn't even really mine. It took them longer to find me, but they did. A postcard arrived a few days before I came here, to Mercy River."

That wasn't good. "Did they always come like this? Hand-delivered, no postmark?"

She nibbled her lip. "No. They didn't have a return address, but they had a stamp and postmark."

Fuck. That was even worse. "Do you remember the cities from the postmark? Were they all mailed from the same place?"

"The cities?" she repeated. She blinked rapidly, then let her head fall back against the wall with a thunk.

"The postmark says where it was mailed from. Holy shit, I'm such an idiot. I never even checked. I just threw them in the trash." She squeezed her eyes shut.

"You're not an idiot, Lennon. But we're going to take this seriously now. I need you to tell me everything."

She opened her eyes and looked at me. "I just told you everything. There's nothing else."

My gut was telling me there was something else here. "What brought you to Mercy River Ranch? How did you find us?"

"The brochure. One of those mailers you send out."

Brochure? I stared blankly at her. "What the hell are you talking about?"

She pushed to her feet. "I'll show you." She went to her bag, rummaged through it, then pulled out a folded brochure and handed it to me. "This showed up. The same day as a stalker postcard, actually."

"I've never seen this before."

I flipped through, feeling like I was looking at an alternate reality. It was a glamourized, dude ranch version of Mercy River. No mention of veterans or first responders, just tranquility, trail rides, and spa sessions. Fucking hell.

I scanned the QR code with my phone. It took me to a website proclaiming to be Mercy River Ranch, but I knew for a fact that it wasn't ours.

"Fuck, Lennon." I scrubbed a hand over my face.

"What? What's wrong?" Her gaze bounced anxiously from my face to my phone and back again.

"You didn't come to Mercy River Ranch by accident. You were lured."

20

LENNON

SHERIFF SHERWOOD HAD SUSPICIOUS EYES. HE KEPT THEM pinned on me while Jeremiah explained the situation, visibly growing more suspicious with every word. Like it was somehow my fault a creepy stalker was sending me perfumed postcards. He had a tough, wiry look to him. Shaggy, salt-and-pepper hair, bushy black eyebrows, and a thick white mustache that covered his upper lip. This was Grace and Emma's father? It was hard to believe. They were made of sunshine. Sheriff Sherwood was all granite.

"My prints are on it. So are Lennon's." Jeremiah handed over the bagged postcard. "It might be a long shot to pull anything from it, but it's worth a try."

The sheriff accepted it without taking his eyes off

me. Apparently, we were all in grave danger that if he so much as blinked, I would immediately commit crimes. "I'll send it to the lab."

We kept the staring contest going as Jeremiah got into the part about the website and how I came to Mercy River Ranch.

"The booking link on the fake website takes you to the booking link on our real website. It's pretty seamless, and unless you're paying close attention to the website address, you wouldn't notice that the fake one is different."

"Smart." His gaze finally released mine. I was offended by the implication that if brains were required, I was off the hook. "You talk to Mateo Alvarez about any of this?"

"Mateo is out on a trail ride with the other guests. He'll be back this evening. The website is gone now. I tried to pull it up to show you when we got here. That means whoever set it up knows we checked it. They're covering their tracks."

Sherwood drummed his broad, blunt fingertips on his oak desk. "This is well within his capabilities."

Jeremiah cocked a brow. "It's a website that links to another website. A high school student could do it."

"You have any high school students working at the ranch? Because whoever built that website wanted Lennon here for a reason. They didn't try to send her to Hawaii or Vermont. They brought her here, to

Mercy River Ranch. Mateo is a computer genius who happens to be a part-owner of the ranch. Maybe it's a coincidence, but I'm not going to stake Lennon's safety on it."

"Wait, what? You can't possibly think Mateo had anything to do with those postcards," I said.

The hitch in Sherwood's bushy eyebrows told me he *could* possibly think that.

"But he's so nice!" I protested.

"Miss Graves, I've been in this world a long time. You'd be surprised how often people say that exact thing when they find out what heinous crime their neighbor committed. *But he's so nice. He mowed my lawn. I never suspected.*" Sherwood set his elbows on the armrests and steepled his fingers. "It's my job to suspect, so that's what I do. I suspect everyone."

Now I felt slightly less miffed about his suspicious eyes, but I still didn't think Mateo was behind any of this. "Psycho stalkers don't have dimples like that. They just don't."

Jeremiah turned his head slowly to look at me. "No," he reprimanded curtly, like I was a misbehaving puppy.

Sherwood's mustache trembled as if he were holding back a laugh. "Dimples notwithstanding, I'll be talking to Mateo and everyone else at the ranch. But let's start with you, Miss Graves."

Oh, hell.

"Me?" The word was barely a squeak. The sheriff's

steely blue eyes narrowed on me again, and I cleared my throat. "What about me?"

"Tell me about your life in New York. What did you do for work? Who did you associate with? Is there anyone you can think of who would want to harm you? An ex-boyfriend, maybe?"

I chewed my lip, thinking. Enemies? No. I had dangerous information, thanks to Benny—information I had no business having. That was why he wanted me out of New York. But the postcards had started a year before I'd even met Benny. This had nothing to do with him. He'd protected me, sent me far away from his mess. I wasn't going to betray him and drag him into mine now.

"I can't think of anyone who would want to harm me. I don't have enemies, really. I'm too busy working to get into shit I shouldn't be in. I'm kind of a jack of all trades, you know? I have a lot of different jobs. I model a little, mostly catalogues and some fit modeling—"

"Fit modeling?" Sherwood interrupted.

"I stand there for eight hours a day while designers fit the clothing to different body shapes. It's exhausting and not very prestigious, but it pays pretty well."

He nodded. "What else?"

I licked my lips. "I'm a cam girl. That's where most of my money comes from." I crossed my hands over my lap, meeting the sheriff's gaze squarely. I wasn't ashamed of who I was or how I paid my bills, but that didn't mean

I enjoyed talking about it with people who thought it gave them permission to treat me like garbage. Hopefully the sheriff wasn't one of those people.

"A cam girl." He leaned forward, looking up at me from beneath his furrowed bushy brows. "Miss Graves, do you mean to tell me you're the first person in the history of the world's oldest profession to not have a single enemy? That doesn't seem likely."

My head tipped sideways. "Prostitution is illegal, Sheriff. I'm a cam girl. Think of it like a stripper, but online. Subscribers can look but they can't touch. And yes, I *am* telling you that my regular subscribers have never threatened me or made me fear for my safety. But of course there are people who harass me. I'm a woman on the internet. They're just trolls using anonymous accounts. I have no idea who they are."

Jeremiah tapped his fingertips on his knee like he was thinking through something. "Wearing a mask isn't enough to protect your identity from someone deter-mined enough to find you. Did you ever meet one of your subs in person?"

My head whipped toward him. "I didn't tell you I wore a mask," I said slowly.

Jeremiah stared back at me. "If one of your subs—"

"Shut *up*," I hissed. My eyes burned. He knew. He fucking *knew*.

Jeremiah's gaze faltered beneath the accusation in mine. He dragged a hand through his hair and nodded.

I gripped the armrests with shaking hands and turned back to Sheriff Sherwood. "My top subscriber didn't find out who I was. I found out who *he* was." Honestly, I couldn't be surprised people were after Benny. He never knew how to shut up. "So, yes, we met in person and started dating. But it's not him. There's just no way." Benny was as gentle as a butterfly. He wouldn't send those postcards, much less trick me into coming to Mercy River. That didn't make sense at all. His problems were the reason I was here.

The sheriff exchanged a glance with Jeremiah. It was clear that neither one believed me. "All right," Sherwood said finally. "Can you think of anything else I should know?"

But I was done. Still shaking with fury, I shoved back my chair with a loud scrape and pushed to my feet. "Why don't you ask Jeremiah? It seems like he knows everything anyway."

I stormed out. If I stayed a second longer, I'd be forced to punch Jeremiah in his beautiful, lying mouth.

THE GOOD THING about running out of clean clothes and being forced to wear my going-out dress was that it was an excellent dress for flouncing. I stomped along the crumbling brick sidewalk, the short skirt bouncing against my thighs with every furious step.

"Get in the truck, Lennon."

God, that voice. Deep and steady. The same voice that had pulled me out of a panic attack only hours ago. I had trusted that voice.

I glanced up. Jeremiah was driving on the wrong side of Main Street at two miles an hour, keeping pace with my angry stride. I stopped, and he hit the brakes.

"I'm not going anywhere with you, you lying sack of shit."

"That's not fair. I might be a sack of shit, but I didn't lie, Lennon. Not once."

Your kiss was a lie. My lower lip trembled, and his gaze dipped there. "Fuck," he said quietly. He scrubbed a hand over his jaw. "Please get in the truck, honey. I'll explain everything."

"I don't want your explanation, Jeremiah. Leave me alone. I want to go home."

Except I didn't have a home. Had I ever? A place that was safe and *mine.* Not my mom's trailer. Not any of the apartments I bounced around every twelve months to avoid a rent increase. Not Benny's place. My shoulders sagged. I was so fucking tired of it all.

"It's a long walk. We won't get there until after dark."

The implication that the ranch and my snug little pine cabin were home only made me more upset. A month from now I'd be gone. Benny's problems didn't look like they were going to wrap up anytime soon, which meant returning to New York was out of the question. I'd been toying with the idea of extending my stay at Mercy River, but now? My stalker had found me and Jeremiah…Well, I had to admit that he was part of my reason for staying.

Not anymore.

I took another step and then stopped again. I didn't really want to spend what was left of the day walking along the side of the road. My thighs would chafe. Biting off my nose to spite my face wasn't really my style, and neither was suffering.

"Fine," I said. "I will get in the truck. But I—" I broke off as Jeremiah shifted into park and climbed out. God, he was tall. I hated that my pulse fluttered. "Um. I don't want to hear one word from you. I realize that doing a little keyboard investigating isn't really a big deal. Everyone does that before a date so they don't wind up getting murdered." It was really hard to stay on my high horse when he tucked me against his side and walked me around his truck to the passenger side, but I did my best. "I understand that I am probably overreacting but, just so you know, I intend to keep doing that for a while longer."

His mouth quirked. He opened the door and guided me in. "All right."

"Good." I flounced into the seat and reached for the

seatbelt, but he was already there, buckling me in like he was afraid I would change my mind.

He rounded the hood of the truck and settled back into the driver's seat. A quick check in his mirrors, and then he steered us to the correct side of the road. Silently. He kept his word, not speaking until we parked at the lodge.

Before he even turned off the engine, I hopped out, making a beeline for the stables.

"Lennon! Where are you going?"

"To pet a fucking horse!" I hollered back. "For my fucking mental health!"

I heard him mutter a stream of curses, followed by the truck door slamming shut. I broke into a jog. The stable was quiet as I entered. My heart sank as I passed empty stall after empty stall. Dammit. I really wanted to pet a horse. There was something about the velvety nose of an animal that made bad things more bearable.

Footsteps sounded behind me, but I didn't turn.

"The horses aren't here. The ranch hands use them for working cattle and other chores, and the rest are on the trail ride Mateo is leading. I'm sorry, honey."

I whirled, hands on hips. "Then bring me a goat!" I bellowed.

He eyed me warily, then dragged his hand through his hair and tugged. "Wait here."

I waited. A moment later he returned with a hen

under his arm. She was white and plump, with a speckled black head and tail, and bright red comb.

"A goat isn't any fun to cuddle, honey, trust me. They'll eat your dress. Or your hair. How about a chicken?"

I held out my arms. "Give her to me."

He transferred her over. She was soft and surprisingly light. I wanted to squeeze her, but I had the feeling her fragile bird bones could not withstand my affection, so instead I gently cuddled her against my chest. She clucked softly. I stroked a finger down her back, marveling at how fluffy she was.

"What's her name?" I asked.

"Henrietta."

"I have had a terrible day, Henrietta," I told her. "My stalker is back and the man who gives me belly butter-flies is a goddamn liar."

"I give you belly butterflies?"

The vulnerable ache in his tone made me want to cuddle him like Henrietta.

"Shut up," I said.

Henrietta made a cute little bock-bock sound. Chickens were delightful. No wonder Holly carried Mother Clucker everywhere.

"I get it now." I rubbed my cheek against her silky feathers. "Don't tell Holly."

Jeremiah chuckled softly. "Your secret is safe with me."

I peered up at him from the safety of chicken feathers. "Is it? Because I don't feel very safe with you right now."

Shocked pain crossed his expression. "You *are* safe with me, Lennon. I promise."

I sighed. "You know, ever since I came here, something felt off to me. The whole ranch was...weird. It was nothing like the website, which makes sense now. I expected there to be other women around, but the only other guests are men. They've been nice, but they have this bond with each other, even though they all came here as strangers, that I just don't have. Now I get it. I'm not supposed to be here. The thing is, though..." I rolled my lips, trying to make sense of the emotions roiling inside me. "You knew that all along. I didn't tell you I wore a mask. You *knew*. You knew I was a cam girl, not a first responder. You knew I shouldn't be here. And you said *nothing*. You kissed me, and you still said nothing. Why?"

"Because you kissed me, and I wanted it to be real." He cupped my cheek, his thumb tracing my bottom lip. His blue-gray eyes bored into mine. "Fuck, Lennon. I didn't tell you because I wanted *you* to tell *me*. It never occurred to me you were tricked into coming here, and I didn't look into you until after that night at Sundown."

Some of the ache in my chest eased at his words.

He went on, "I didn't trust you from the moment you arrived, that's true, and I thought Miguel's accident—"

I jerked back. "What does Miguel's accident have to do with anything? I've never even met him before."

"Lennon." His brows pinched as he stared down at me. "I don't know how or why yet, but there is not a doubt in my mind that Miguel's accident has everything to do with you. Sherwood thinks he was run off the road. It's too much of a coincidence for me to believe your stalker lured you here the same week someone tried to kill him."

"Oh my god." I clutched Henrietta closer as the enormity of my situation finally sank in. "Oh my *god*."

My stalker had created an elaborate setup to lure me here. No one would go to all that trouble without a reason. I didn't know who he was or what he had planned for me, but I sure as fuck wasn't sticking around to find out.

"I have to leave. Right now. I have to..." Fuck, fuck, fuck. I didn't have anywhere to go. Nowhere safe, anyway. "I have to go join a nunnery or something."

He snorted a laugh. "You are not joining a fucking nunnery, Lennon. Give me the chicken."

"No." I dodged his hands. "She's coming with me. For emotional support. And eggs."

"*Lennon.*"

"Fine," I huffed, handing her over. "She'd probably shit all over my car, anyway."

Car. My eyes squeezed shut. The car wasn't mine. It belonged to Benny's friend's ninety-year-old mother.

"I think you're on the verge of another panic attack. Breathe, baby."

I opened my eyes to glare at him. "You're goddamn right I'm having a panic attack. I'm trapped at this ranch with my stalker, and I don't even know what he looks like, by the way, so he could sneak up on me at any moment. I'm scared. I'm—"

Whatever I was going to say next was silenced by the firm, gentle press of his mouth on mine. When my lips relaxed, he pulled back. "Safe, honey. You're safe. I fucked up. It won't happen again."

I searched his face. He meant it.

He touched his forehead to mine. "From now until we find this asshole, you don't leave my sight."

21

———

LENNON

HANNAH'S ROOM WAS SMALL AND BLUE. FROTHY WHITE curtains hung in the window. The dresser, bed, and desk were made of pine—I couldn't escape it, but it was growing on me. A small porcelain statue of an armor-clad knight on a white horse sat on the dresser, and a painting of a young girl in a pink dress reading a book by a stream hung on one wall. It was a tiny oasis of femininity in a ranch that solidly tilted toward rugged. Hannah and I were clearly very different people, but I had a feeling I would like her.

When Jeremiah informed me that I would be staying in his apartment at the lodge, I hadn't argued. Honestly, I was relieved. But now that I was standing in the doorway of his sister's bedroom, I felt like an intruder.

"Are you sure your sister won't mind me staying here?" I gripped the handle of my suitcase, unsure if it was okay for me to unpack. Maybe I should shove it into the closet and leave it at that. It wouldn't be the first time I had lived out of a suitcase.

"I already texted her. It's fine. She said she's only using the top two drawers. The bottom four are empty." He opened and closed each drawer in rapid succession to verify, then nodded. "Go ahead."

"All my clothes are dirty. I need to do a load of laundry before I settle in."

I moved my bags to a corner so they were out of the way and picked up the silver-framed photograph on Hannah's desk. It was Jeremiah and a blonde, twenty-ish-years-old woman who I assumed was Hannah sitting in the rocking chairs outside the lodge, both of them holding mugs and smiling at whoever was taking the photo. Hannah was wearing a long skirt and an over-sized sweater, although it looked like summer, judging by Jeremiah's T-shirt.

"Was she raised at the compound, too? You don't have to answer that. It's none of my business. I'm being nosy," I added quickly.

"It's not a secret. Yes, she was raised at the compound, too. She was my only full-blooded sibling. I shared a father with seventeen other kids, but our mother had difficulty conceiving and staying pregnant.

We were her only two. I'm almost six years older than Hannah."

I sucked in air. "Seventeen kids? Your father has *seventeen* kids?"

"Eighteen, counting me."

"Holy shit. He must have had, what, five wives?"

"Three."

It took me less than a split second to do the math. As long as numbers were in my head, I was good. It was on paper when they screwed with me. "Two of you were your mom's, so the other two wives had eight kids apiece?"

"One had ten, the other had six. Probably more. Eighteen was how things stood when I was banished at fourteen. His wives were still fertile then. They probably had more. He might have taken on a fourth wife, too."

My mind was well and truly boggled. "So you have sixteen brothers and sisters still out there. At least."

His lips flattened. "There were a couple of years where a sibling would show up at my door. Banished brothers, mostly, but the occasional runaway sister. I gave them a place to stay, got them the help they needed. Seven years ago, the compound was raided by the FBI. It's been quiet since, but I keep looking for them."

"Is that how Hannah escaped the compound?"

"The raid? No. And she didn't run away. I went and got her when she was fourteen."

I studied the photograph. Long, white-blonde hair. Crystal-blue eyes behind her glasses. "She's pretty," I remarked. "They couldn't have been happy with you taking her."

"I didn't give them a choice."

The darkness in his tone pulled my gaze to him. His eyes were fixed on the photograph in my hand, eyes steely, mouth a grim slash. "Good," I said, and meant it.

That brought a bit of light back into his face. His mouth softened, and when he turned to look at me, there was a hint of amusement in his blue-gray eyes. "You keep saying shit like that, I might start to believe it."

I gave an exasperated huff. "All evidence to the contrary, you mean? You *are* good, Jeremiah. Annoyingly good. Why can't you see that?"

"As I said, goodness is in the eye of the beholder. Who decides what it means to be good, Lennon? God? Or man's interpretation of God? They banished me as a child for sinning. I am a son of perdition."

"You know that's shit, Jeremiah. You *know* that."

"Wars are fought and populations exterminated by people who claim to know, and yet none of them seem to agree. So, no, I *don't* know. I'm not that arrogant to claim I know the meaning of life." His fingers threaded through my hair, pulling it back from my face. "It's all right, though. I kind of like being damned." He twisted my hair around his fist as he examined it.

"What?" The word burst out of me on a surprised laugh. "You like being damned?"

He tugged me closer, and my breath hitched. "There's a freedom in it. Once you know you're going to spend eternity in hell based on someone else's definition of goodness, you get to decide how to spend your time on earth before you get there. Do you want to know my favorite Bible verse?"

"Yes," I gasped, because now his other hand was gently curving around the base of my throat, his thumb tracing my clavicle.

"Isaiah forty-five, seven. *I form the light and create the darkness. I make peace and create evil. I the Lord do all these things.*" His mouth pressed each word into the delicate skin of my neck. I twisted my head to the side to give him more access. "Righteousness is not goodness. Flooding the world is righteous. Turning a woman into salt is righteous. I don't think anyone would claim those things were necessarily *good*."

It was hard to focus on his words when his mouth was doing wicked things that made me clench my thighs together.

"I may be righteous, but I don't know that I'm good. Because when I close my eyes, the things we do to each other..." His teeth scraped over the pulse point below my jaw. "Are very, very..." He sucked gently at my skin. "*Bad.*"

"Tell me," I pleaded. "Oh, god, please tell me."

"You want to hear all the ways I'd disrespect you? You want me to tell you how I fantasize about putting you on your knees and fucking that sassy mouth of yours? That you ruined my life telling me about facials because now all I can think about is you dripping with my cum? That my thirst for you keeps me up at night? Is that what you want me to tell you?"

Anticipation shivered down my spine. "Yes," I whispered, reaching for his belt buckle. "That's what I want."

"Hell." He trapped my hands in his, stopping me from getting what I wanted, and groaned. "I need a second." His forehead dropped to mine. His chest brushed mine as his breath sawed in and out. "Now I know how Galadriel felt when she didn't accept the ring from Frodo."

It took a moment for my lust-dazed brain to understand what was happening. Jeremiah was turning me down. Heat scorched my cheeks as I reeled back, wrenching my hands from his. *Not so shameless after all, Miss High and Mighty*, my mother's voice cackled in my head.

"Sorry. Oh, god, I'm so sorry. I thought—I mean, you said you wanted—" I stumbled backward, tripping over my own feet.

He reached for me, thought better of it, and gripped the edge of the dresser behind him so hard that his knuckles turned white. "I *do* want. Fuck, honey, I want so badly that my balls are a permanent shade of blue. But we're at the end of a very long day. You've had one and a half panic attacks, found out your stalker lured you here, yelled at me not even two hours ago, and threatened to run away to a nunnery. You need food. You need a hot shower. You need rest."

"But I *want* your dick," I shot back.

He gave me one heated, hungry look that turned my insides molten before squeezing his eyes shut with a shake of his head. "If you still want my dick tomorrow, it's yours."

I studied him, baffled. He was really saying no to a blowjob out of concern for my physical and emotional well-being? Was that something men were even capable of? Heaving a sigh, I pressed a kiss to his cheek. Every muscle in his body strung taut in response, like it took everything he had to hold himself back.

"What did I tell you?" I whispered in his ear. "Annoyingly good."

22

JEREMIAH

By the time we had showered, eaten dinner, and gone back upstairs to our respective rooms, I was exhausted down to my bones. But that didn't stop me from lying awake, imagining exactly what Lennon's mouth would have felt like if I had said yes.

With a groan, I threw back the covers and rolled out of bed. I pulled on a pair of flannel pajama bottoms and tugged a T-shirt over my head, shoved my feet into the L.L. Bean slippers Hannah had given me for Christmas four years ago, and padded down to the library. Maybe I could lull myself to sleep with a book.

The library had been Hannah's idea. No surprise there, since my little sister was a librarian. It had started small, just for her personal use, but as we noticed more guests searching for something to quiet their minds, I built it out. Now we had a bit of everything. Hannah's beloved romance novels took up several shelves, but we also had every genre of fiction imaginable, plus biographies, histories, and poetry.

Poetry was my preference before sleep, since I could start or stop whenever I felt like it. I didn't have to wait until the end of a chapter or even the end of a sentence. The rhythm of it relaxed my brain. I grabbed Mary Oliver and settled into the red wingback chair, kicking my feet up on the ottoman.

Not ten minutes later, the door creaked open. One of the guests, probably. The dining hall was closed, but the library and game room were open. Insomnia was pretty common here. I craned my neck around the wing of the chair.

Lennon.

Wearing nothing but those fucking tiny shorts and tank top. Fucking *great*. I had just talked my dick down, and now I was rock hard again. Her sleep attire was going to be the death of me.

She froze when she saw me sitting there. Her tongue darted out to nervously lick her lips, and that made everything worse.

"You're supposed to be asleep," I ground out.

"*You're* supposed to be asleep," she retorted.

She sashayed right by me, and I turned my head to

track her to the built-in bookcases that lined the wall. A mistake, because it meant I got a glimpse of the curve of her ass with every step she took.

"What are you looking for? I'll help you find it, and you can take it back to your room."

She cocked an eyebrow at me over her shoulder. "Eager to get rid of me, caveman?"

"Yes, Lennon. That's exactly what I'm doing." I dragged a hand through my hair and tugged. "I'm trying *not* to be a caveman. I deserve a sainthood for not throwing you over my shoulder and dragging you to my bed the second I saw you in those fucking shorts."

"Sorry." She squatted to get a look at the bottom shelf, and her shorts disappeared into her ass crack.

Fuck. *Me.*

I bit my knuckles to smother my groan.

Straightening, she pivoted on her slippered toes to face me. Her head tilted sideways as she studied me. "Do you like breasts, Jeremiah?"

"Do I..." My gaze dipped without my permission. No bra. Peaked nipples. Fucking hell. My mouth went dry with thirst. I couldn't push any words past it.

"Like breasts," she finished for me encouragingly. "I happen to be a big fan of them myself." She tucked her chin to look down at herself and pushed her chest out. "And I think mine happen to be pretty nice." She smirked at me. "But you seem preoccupied with my lower half, so I was just wondering. Maybe breasts don't do it for you. Or mine don't, anyway."

Heat washed over my cheeks. I swallowed hard and looked away. "They do. Everything about you does it for me."

"Good to know." Her hair swished as she spun back to the shelves.

I struggled to regulate my breathing. Breathe in. *Don't stare at the hair I want wrapped around my fist.* Breathe out. *The flare of her hips that would give me some-thing to hold onto.* In. *The ass I want to smack for being such a goddamn brat.* Out. *Fuck, she's beautiful.*

She chattered on like she was completely unaware of her effect on me. But I wasn't fooled. She knew exactly what she was doing.

"Usually I listen to an audiobook before I go to bed, but I can't find my earbuds. The sound quality just isn't the same coming straight from my phone, you know? So I thought maybe I'd try an actual printed book for a change."

She pulled a book from the shelf, flipped it over to read the back, then opened it to the first page. She chewed her lip. It took her a while before she finally sighed and slipped it back in its place. "I'm a terrible reader, though. It's frustrating. I love stories. Hearing them or seeing them acted out on stage. It's only when they're words in front of my eyeballs that I lose the plot."

She pulled out another book, read the first page, then slid it home again. "I should probably just go to bed."

But she didn't leave. She stayed right where she was and kept talking. "Grace thinks I'm dyslexic. I don't know if she's right, but I think I'll get tested when I get back to New York. She says there's no cure, but there are methods that can help me if I am." She traced the spine of a thick green volume with almost wistful reverence. "I hope I am. I'd rather be dyslexic than stupid."

"Stupid?" I slammed my book shut and frowned at her. "What the hell are you talking about?"

She gave me a sardonic look that I didn't buy for a second. "When you're sixteen years old and stumbling over words that wouldn't faze a fourth grader, people tend to doubt your intelligence. My mom and teachers certainly did."

"You're not stupid, Lennon. That's ridiculous."

"Oh, yeah?" She crossed her arms over her chest. "I never finished high school. I dropped out at sixteen so I could move to New York and model—real smart, right? I don't even have a GED. I couldn't pass the test."

"That doesn't mean shit, honey. There are lots of different kinds of intelligence."

She rolled her eyes. "People only say that when you're dumb."

"You *are* smart. Hell, you're the first outsider to ever beat us at Blood Ball, and I'll let you in on a little secret:

It wasn't your physical prowess. You beat us with your creativity and your brain."

"And because you wouldn't let them near me."

I chuckled. "Lennon, baby, they were never going to make you bleed, whether I was there or not. You knew that, and you used it against us."

"Then why did you protect me?" she challenged.

I stopped fighting myself and let my gaze land on her perfect tits. I scrubbed a hand over my mouth and then met her eyes straight on. "I didn't want them touching you."

Her lips parted. "Oh," she sighed.

"Yeah. Now find a book that interests you and bring it on over here. I'll read it to you."

She stared at me like she thought I was joking. "Really?"

"Of course, really. Choose your book."

Her gaze drifted over the hundreds of books lining the shelves, and she shook her head. "That would take forever. Whatever you have in your hand is fine."

"This?" I held up the book. "It's poetry."

She shrugged. "Whatever."

I figured she'd take the matching chair next to me, but she bypassed it and slid her knee between my thigh and the armrest.

"Scooch," she said.

I shifted over and she wiggled in sideways so her butt was on the cushion and her legs draped over my lap, her head resting between the wing of the chair and my shoulder. I held the book with one hand and propped it against her bent knees. There was nowhere for my other hand to go but her shin unless I held it in the air. Fuck, her skin was soft.

"You're killing me, kid," I grunted.

She grinned. "I know."

I read. She was asleep in five minutes.

23

LENNON

"Nice of you to make an appearance," Amos groused. "Thought maybe you'd quit without giving us your two weeks' notice."

"I can't quit a job that I was never hired for in the first place." I breezed past him, heading straight for the sink to wash my hands. "You don't even pay me. In fact, *I* pay *you* for the privilege of frying bacon and playing cowgirl. I mean, I pay the ranch. And the ranch pays you."

Amos grunted but didn't argue. I grinned, drying my hands on the towel. He narrowed his eyes and pointed his metal spatula at me. "You're on biscuits, city girl."

"No problem."

"Where were you yesterday?" Cecily asked. "And *what* are you wearing?"

"A pipe burst in my cabin's bathroom." Feeling guilty about lying, I dodged her gaze and reached for the flour. Sheriff Sherwood had told me it would be better to say nothing about the postcards unless I absolutely had to. Stalkers wanted attention, and even negative attention might encourage him to keep going. Jeremiah had pointed out that everyone would notice I had moved into the lodge, so we agreed on a cover story. "I had to move my stuff to the lodge. I should have called. I'm sorry. As for my outfit..." I twirled, showing off the ankle-length skirt. "Do you like it?"

"Um." Cecily rolled her lips together, clearly struggling to find something nice to say. "It's pretty," she ventured. "But it's not very *you*."

I laughed. She wasn't wrong. From what I found in her drawers, Hannah favored long, flowy skirts and cardigans, whereas I preferred clothes that showed off my figure. "That's because it's not mine. It's Hannah's."

"Hannah?" Her brow furrowed.

"Jeremiah's sister. I'm staying in her room. I meant to do laundry yesterday, but with...um...everything, I never got around to it. Jeremiah lent me some of Hannah's clothes." I measured out the sugar and added it to the flour, along with the baking powder and salt.

"That's awful. About your cabin, I mean. You're not thinking of leaving the ranch early, are you?" Her eyes went wide. "You can't go yet. I was hoping you might decide to stay longer. Lots of guests stay the whole summer." She wrinkled her nose. "I promise I'm not just saying that because we're down a man and need the help."

I laughed—but could I? Could I stay longer? Benny was out on bail, and his trial was scheduled for August. His murky business associates were still keeping close tabs on him to make sure he didn't cut a deal with the feds. Why not stay in Wyoming for the rest of the summer?

"I'm not leaving early. I'm paid up through July, so I might as well get my money's worth." Not to mention, I had nowhere else to go. "And the lodge is nice. I don't mind staying in Hannah's room until they fix the pipe." *And find my stalker.*

"But Jeremiah's there. That's gotta be awkward, right? I mean—" She cracked an egg with too much force. Pieces of shell crumbled into the bowl. Frowning, she tried to fish out the slimy white flecks but quickly gave up and emptied the bowl into the trash. "Shoot."

"Stop yapping and focus on what you're doing," Amos said. "We've got cowboys to feed."

JEREMIAH HAD TOLD me to stay put at the lodge and he'd come get me after his morning chores, but I was feeling better about everything after making breakfast with Amos and Cecily. I couldn't imagine either of them writing those creepy postcards. Hell, with the exception of Brian, there wasn't a single person on this ranch I thought was capable of it—and I doubted Brian had the tolerance for a long game. The more I thought about it, the safer I felt.

Safe enough to walk to my cabin by myself in broad daylight to grab my earbuds, anyway. I wasn't stupid enough to go out after dark without Jeremiah or someone I trusted.

I ran up to Hannah's room to change out of her bohemian prairie chic skirt. I'd given it a fair try, but she was narrower through the hips than I was, and I had a few inches of height on her, so the skirt hit at an unflattering point two inches above my ankles. Laundry remained undone, and I wasn't going to rectify that now —if death by stalker was inevitable, then I wasn't spending my last few hours on this earth doing my least favorite chore—so I changed into my last clean outfit, a short white dress with blue flowers.

I hummed to myself as I headed down the quarter-mile dirt path that led to the cluster of guest cabins. Considering yesterday's upheaval, I was in a remarkably good mood today. And why shouldn't I be? The sun was shining, the air was fragrant with wildflowers and ponderosa pine, birds were chirping, and I still wanted Jeremiah's dick.

Yes, I was in danger. Probably. Maybe my postcard stalker just wanted to talk. Regardless, that same danger had existed two days ago, too. The only difference was that I was *aware* of it now. I couldn't actually do anything about it, and what did I do when I had problems I couldn't do anything about? I pretended they didn't exist. It wasn't lying to myself. It was procrastinating the truth.

So that's what I did.

I pretended I wasn't scared of every shadow darkening the sunlit path.

I pretended I didn't feel someone's stare on the back of my head.

I pretended that I was looking behind me for a friend, not a murderer.

I did pretty well pretending until my cabin came into view and the partly open door stopped me in my tracks. Someone was in my cabin. Someone was—

A cart loaded with rags, disinfectant sprays, and a bucket pushed across the braided rug, guided by an unseen hand.

Someone was cleaning my room.

Jesus, I was paranoid.

"Hello?" I called, stepping inside.

A woman with a brown ponytail poked her head out of the bathroom. "Oh, hi. Housekeeping." She came fully into view, mop in hand. "Sorry, I thought you had left."

"Just the cabin, not the ranch." I glanced around. She'd already stripped the bed. I opened the drawer of the nightstand and found it empty. "You didn't happen to find my earbuds, did you?"

"Purple case?" she asked. I nodded, and she reached into her pocket. "Here you go. I was going to turn them in to the lost and found at the lodge."

I slipped them into my bag. "Thanks. It's great to see another woman around. I was beginning to think women were going extinct."

She laughed. "I've been around the whole time. Housekeepers tend to be more invisible than cowboys. Maybe it's their hats."

"Right." I smiled. "Do you mind if I take a quick look in the bathroom to make sure I grabbed everything?"

She shrugged as she plugged in the vacuum. "It's empty but go ahead." She hit the button, and the vacuum roared to life.

I stepped over the cord on the way to the bathroom. Empty, like she said. I hadn't noticed anything missing when I'd showered last night, but every time I packed my things, I felt like I was leaving something behind.

"Thanks again!" I shouted over the vacuum. She nodded and waved in return.

The smell knocked into me as I crossed the threshold. Vanilla and citrus. My hand clenched my purse strap so hard my nails bit into my palm. Slowly, I looked down, already knowing what I would find.

A postcard. The photo was of a waterfall this time. I picked it up, my hand shaking.

YOU'RE MAKING A MISTAKE

I scanned the yard and treeline, but saw no sign of anyone. My heart in my throat, I turned slowly to look at the housekeeper. *Her?* No, it couldn't be. That was ridiculous. But I couldn't force the words out to ask.

It took her a moment to feel my eyes on her, but then she did a double take and turned off the vacuum. Her brow furrowed. "Are you all right?"

She wasn't my stalker. She was the housekeeper. I was being silly.

"I…" I cleared my throat. "Did you see anyone just now?"

"Other than you? No. Is everything okay?"

I forced a tight-lipped smile. "Everything is fine."

I shoved the postcard into my bag and jogged down the porch steps.

Everything is fine. Everything is fine.

I pretended I couldn't smell it. I pretended it wasn't there in my bag, a companion to every step I took.

Maybe I felt someone's furious gaze following me down the path.

But I pretended I didn't.

"FINALLY. A HORSE." I nabbed an apple from the basket and held it out on my flat palm to the only horse cooped up in the stables on this gorgeous summer day. Alibi, according to her nameplate on the stall door. She bobbed her head as she lipped it up. "What do you say, girl? You want to be my getaway ride? We can live in the mountains and everything will be fine."

"You're not going to get very far on a lame horse," Jeremiah's amused voice said from behind me. "Alibi has a bruised frog."

"A bruised what?" I leaned back to look her over. Admittedly, I was no horse expert, but she seemed okay.

"The frog is part of her hoof. Probably stepped wrong on a stone last night. She'll be all right in a day or two." He set aside his pitchfork and rubbed her nose. "You want to tell me what you're doing here when I told you to wait for me at the lodge?" His voice was as unruffled as ever, but a muscle popped in his jaw.

Probably not the time to tell him I'd gotten another postcard. That suited me just fine since I was deep in denial, anyway. I knew I couldn't stay here. Sooner or later, I was going to have to figure my shit out. Where was I going to live? What was I going to do for money? How was I going to feel safe ever again?

All questions for another day. Right now, I only had one question I wanted an answer to.

"Do you keep your promises, Jeremiah?" I leaned back against the wall, letting him get a good look at me.

His gaze shot to mine, and I couldn't resist issuing a challenge with a flick of my eyebrow, running my tongue over my lower lip. He swallowed thickly. "Haven't broken one yet."

"Good. Then I'm here to collect." I pushed off the wall, grabbed his hand, and tugged him into the empty stall across from Alibi's that he had just finished mucking out, swiping a freshly washed saddle pad from the stack as I went.

"Lennon." His voice was low and rough. "Someone might see."

"Look around. One horse, zero people." I slid the stall door closed. It came up to my chest. "Anyway, someone might see *you*. They won't see me."

His brow furrowed. "What—"

I spread the blanket right next to the door and pressed his shoulders to turn him perpendicular. "Turn this way. Back against the wall, Jeremiah. You're going to need it." I rolled up on my toes to press a kiss to the hinge of his jaw. "I fully intend to make your legs shake."

And then I dropped to my knees in front of him.

His lips parted as he took an audible breath. He didn't say a word as he stared down at me with focused intensity. I couldn't read his expression. He wasn't...oh, god. He wasn't going to turn me down, was he? I would be forced to join a convent for real.

And then his throat worked on a swallow and he reached for his belt. There was a faint tremor in his hands as he slowly undid the buckle and flipped open the fly of his jeans. His cock tented his boxers, and I licked my lips in anticipation.

I tucked my fingers around the waistband of his jeans and boxers and dragged both together down his hips and thighs. His dick sprang free, hard and ready for me. I rocked back on my heels to admire him. Fuck, he was beautiful. Short, dense blond curls around the base. His cock was thick and long, the smooth head rising above his foreskin. Uncut—a first for me.

My gaze flicked up to his and I found him watching me intently, like he wasn't sure what I would do next. I couldn't stop my smile. Oh, I was going to *enjoy* this. I kept my eyes locked on his as I flattened my tongue at the base of his dick and licked up the length of him.

His hips bucked in surprise. "Oh, *fuck*," he bit out, so I did it again, with more saliva this time. He made a sound of pure gibberish that wiped my brain clean of everything but him. No stalkers. No danger. Only this man and his gorgeous dick.

I swiped my tongue over his slit, tasted musk and salt, and planted a wet kiss there before parting my lips around him. When I sucked gently on the tip, his shoulders fell back against the wall, and he groaned. I purred, taking in more of him. He was big enough that I needed to take my time and go slowly. I sucked hard as I withdrew, took a breath, then slid my mouth back down, taking a little more each time.

God, he was lovely. And that wasn't a feeling I normally had about blowjobs. This was different. The sounds he made as I worked him over made me press my thighs together against the ache there. When I cupped his balls in one hand and sucked him deep, his hands shook as they clasped my head.

"Lennon," he gasped out. He fucked my mouth as I sucked him, his hips undulating. "Lennon, honey." His hands spasmed on my head, and then he reached a hand down to cup my chin, trying to jerk me away. "Fuck, honey, I'm going to spill."

Like hell would he rob me of that. I had *earned* this. I shook my head and sucked deeper, humming my contentment around a mouthful of his cock. "Mmm."

He made a sound that was half-sob, half-moan. I lifted my gaze to see him shove the heel of his palm into his mouth and bite down to muffle his shout of pleasure. With his other hand fisting my hair to hold me in place, he came so hard that I struggled to keep up with him. He erupted again and again. What I couldn't swallow dribbled from my lips.

When he finally sagged against the wall, I lifted the hem of my dress and delicately wiped my mouth, then took his softening cock in my palm and gently licked him clean. He watched me through half-lidded eyes, his chest rising and falling on labored breaths.

By the time I zipped him back into his jeans and stood up, brushing off my knees, he still hadn't said a word. His silence was starting to make me nervous.

"Are you okay?" I asked.

His mouth opened and shut a few times like he was struggling to find words before he said, "Men talk about blowjobs a lot. So much that if you haven't done it before, you might be a little suspicious that they're making shit up, because nothing can really be *that* good." He shook his head slowly. "I stand corrected. Hell, after that, I don't think blowjobs are hyped *enough*. I wasn't fuckin' prepared for that, Lennon."

I laughed, feeling proud of myself. "You talk like you never had one before."

"I haven't."

He said the words easily, like they were the god-given truth. I squinted at him, trying to find the joke. "Ha, ha, very funny. What kind of man hasn't had a blowjob before?"

He rubbed his jaw. "Well, Lennon, I reckon that would be a thirty-eight-year-old virgin."

24

JEREMIAH

LENNON ALWAYS HAD A RETORT FOR EVERYTHING, SO seeing her shocked speechless was pretty damn funny. Gaping at me, she grasped the top of the stall door for support, like my virginity had knocked her physically off balance as well as emotionally.

"No," she said finally. "You're not."

I smirked. "I think that's the kind of thing a man knows about himself, honey."

"It's not possible."

"With God, all things are possible," I intoned in my best preacher voice and then bust out a chuckle at my own joke. I was feeling good and relaxed. Looser than I had in years. Warm and gooey like the inside of a chocolate chip cookie fresh from the oven. I felt so good I didn't even care that I was using words like gooey.

But she looked properly horrified. If she had pearls, she'd be clutching them. "Oh, hell. Are you waiting for marriage? Because sex is a sin?"

"It's not that. Until today, I wouldn't have said I was waiting for anything. Sex just hadn't happened, that was all. The timing never felt right. The woman never felt right. Now I think that's what I was waiting for the whole time. I was waiting for it to feel right." I tucked her hair behind her ear, letting the silky strands slip from my fingers. "I think I was waiting for you."

Her nose wrinkled. "Oh, *no*."

I laughed.

"It's not funny!" She smacked my arm. "What do you mean, it never felt right? You're a man. Sex always feels right when you're a man. How could it have never happened? Look at you! You're beautiful. You're kind. You're the kind of man women wish for when they toss pennies into wells."

"Lennon, I was beaten so badly for touching myself I still have scars. I was banished from my family for sinning. That kind of thing will make even the horniest teen boy think twice before he tries to get into a girl's pants. My foster parents sent me to therapy, and that helped. But I can't be casual about being inside another person. I don't take it lightly."

"Jeremiah." She rolled her lips together, brows

drawn together, her dark eyes troubled. "I like you so much. But if you're waiting for sex to be special, you need to keep waiting. You've got the wrong girl."

"Do I?" Wanting my hands on her, I slipped my arms around her waist and pulled her closer. "Sure doesn't feel that way to me." I nuzzled her throat and felt her pulse jump like a jackrabbit. My lips curved. "You're lying to yourself, honey."

She arched away from me with a scowl. "I don't do that. You're the one who seems to have forgotten that I'm leaving in a month."

"So stay. Stay for the whole summer." *Stay forever.* But I knew better than to say that out loud. She was as skittish as a newborn colt. "I want you to stay, but if all I get with you is another month, then I intend to make the most of it."

"The orgasm has clouded your brain. Most men think they're in love with me after a blowjob. It will pass."

I chuckled against her throat and then nipped her skin, making her suck in a sharp breath of air. "Who said anything about love? I want to fuck you, Lennon. This doesn't have to be forever to be right, and it doesn't have to be love to feel special. *You* make it special. It's right because it's you and me together. I wish I could make sense of it, but I can't. All I know is that seeing you every morning is the best part of my day. You make me laugh. You play in rainstorms. You drive me crazy and make me ache." I cupped her ass and pulled her fully against me, letting her feel how hard she was making me again. "It's chemistry, honey. There's no use denying it."

She whimpered and dug her nails into my biceps. I spun us slowly in a half-circle, as if we were dancing. It was a pleasure to give her words back to her. "Back against the wall, Lennon. You're going to need it."

Her eyes went round with horror. "I am not going to take your virginity in a horse stall. Absolutely not."

"No," I agreed. "I don't have a condom, anyway. But you seem to have doubts about what we have together. I'm thinking an orgasm will get us on the same page. Spread your legs, honey." I wedged my thigh between hers and nudged her boot with mine. "I think this is what kids these days call *heavy petting.*"

"The kids absolutely do not call it that." She narrowed her eyes even as she widened her stance. "Have you ever done this before?"

I swallowed my chuckle. "No, but I've always been a quick learner."

She heaved a beleaguered sigh. "Wonderful. I'll take one for the sisterhood and teach you how to find a woman's clit. I guess I have nothing better to do today, anyway."

I cupped her jaw, tilting her chin up so she had to look at me. "I don't need to find every woman's clit. Just yours."

"I—"

I kissed her because I would die if I didn't. I kissed her until her mouth was pliant under mine and her body melted against me. With that smart mouth busy, I slid my hand under her skirt and up the silky skin of her thigh until it met the lace hem of her underwear. My thumb ghosted over the gusset and found the cotton warm and damp.

We both stopped breathing.

I lifted my head and looked at her. "Now, why were you kicking up a fuss when your body is begging for me?"

"Don't take it personally. It's been a while. Some of us aren't cut out for thirty-eight years of celibacy."

"You're awfully sassy for a woman standing in a horse stall with soaked panties." I rubbed my thumb back and forth over her mound and then slipped it under the hem. *Wet.* Thirst coursed through my veins. "*Fuck*, honey," I groaned. Her hands spasmed on my shoulders.

Eagerness made my hand tremble. I twisted my wrist for better access and slid my middle finger between her folds. The tip of my finger brushed her entrance. "Tell me I can touch you," I begged.

"Yes," she breathed.

I pushed one finger inside. Fuck, I had never felt anything like this. Soft, wet heat. The clench of her pussy around my finger. My dick twitched with jealousy.

She started to moan and then bit it back, her teeth strumming her bottom lip. Goddammit, I would make her pay for that. Someday she would scream my name and beg for me. I just needed to learn how to make that happen. I pumped my finger in and out and then dragged it upward, spreading moisture everywhere. Her breath hitched. *There.*

"Right here?" I tapped gently. She pressed her lips together, and I grinned. Tight little circles with the pad of my finger made her hips tilt. "You like that?"

"My last boyfriend left cash on my nightstand." She said it like a challenge. Like she thought that would deter me. It didn't. Not even a little bit.

"My wallet is in my back pocket. Take what you want." I curled my finger inside her and this time she couldn't hold back her moan. I laughed darkly. "You don't want my money, Lennon. You want me. And that terrifies you."

She growled. "It should terrify *you.*"

"It doesn't." I pressed the heel of my palm against her clit as my finger pumped in and out of her. She arched into me. "Stop fighting me and show me how to make you come."

She huffed, and for a moment I thought she would say something else snarky. But then she relented. "Like that, but...more."

I wasn't sure a second finger could fit, but it did. My thrusts turned short and deep as I focused more attention on my thumb circling her clit. I was rewarded with her pussy walls squeezing around me. Her breathing turned erratic.

"Like this?" I rasped.

She didn't answer—not in words. She cried out as she shattered around me, slamming her back against the wall and pushing her pussy into my hand, her hands digging into my shoulders for balance.

I held her tightly as the last quakes subsided, then gently eased my fingers from her body. She had soaked my hand with her orgasm. I lifted my fingers to my lips, inhaled the scent of her arousal, and sucked them clean. The taste of her only made me thirstier.

I kissed her, knowing she could taste herself on my tongue. "Are we on the same page now?"

She made an incoherent sound that I took for agreement.

"Good." I tugged her against me and kissed her again. "Let's go get cleaned up before dinner."

I stooped to get the saddle pad. Her bag was next to it, the corner of a postcard sticking out. My heart jumped into my throat as I slid it out and straightened. I flipped it over and found the telltale purple message on the back. Fuck.

"Lennon." I struggled to keep the anger out of my voice. "What the hell is this?"

25

LENNON

Amos blocked the doorway, his beefy arms crossed over his broad chest, his face impassive.

"Come on, Amos, don't you think you're taking this too far?" I wheedled. "We're supposed to be doing a gymkhana out by the stables. Jeremiah is probably over there now."

"Jeremiah told me to keep you here until he came and got you himself." He eyed me suspiciously. "What kind of trouble have you gotten yourself into, city girl? You steal somethin'?"

"Do I really look like a thief to you?" I demanded.

"What's that?" Amos placed one hand behind his ear and cocked his head like he was listening to someone. "The ancestors say yes."

I pointed at him. "Rude, but fair."

I sighed. I didn't want to stay in the kitchen all day. *Where was he?*

After Jeremiah had found the most recent postcard in my bag and I had confessed to going to my cabin alone, he'd practically put me on house arrest. It had been less than twenty-four hours of this nonsense, and I was ready to find my stalker and turn myself in.

Maybe I'd be less cranky about it if his overprotectiveness extended to our sleeping arrangements, but noooo. The three locks on the door that separated his living quarters from the rest of the lodge were good enough. I had slept alone in Hannah's room last night.

Apparently *I want to fuck you, Lennon* did not mean *I want to fuck you right now.*

Just as well, I supposed. How did one go about deflowering a man like Jeremiah, anyway? I'd lost my virginity at sixteen to a senior I liked well enough, although we'd never seriously dated. I was freshly emancipated and wanted to get it over with before my big move to New York. Virginity didn't seem like the kind of thing I wanted to drag around with me to photo shoots. I wanted to be an adult, not a kid.

Bishop had been nice enough. Mostly I remembered his Star Wars sheets and the Chewbacca poster on the ceiling above his bed that I'd stared at the entire time. It was like losing my virginity to a Wookiee.

Jeremiah deserved better than that.

Jeremiah deserved better than *me*.

I was a good person. I believed that. I didn't lie, cheat, or steal. I never took my bad day out on strangers on the street, and berating waitstaff was as unthinkable to me as murder. I tied the weight of my soul to how I treated people, not the purity of my vagina.

But it didn't matter if I was a good person, because my life was absolute shit. For as long as I could remember, I had been on the run from something. Mom's handsy boyfriends, landlords with hidden cameras, photographers who promised the world if I took off my top. And now I had run from Benny's mess straight into my stalker's trap. What had I done to deserve that? Nothing. But Jeremiah didn't deserve it, either.

He had waited thirty-eight years for this. He deserved to be with someone who wasn't a walking disaster. Someone who would still be here after the first frost. Hell, why not shoot for the stars and make it someone unlikely to get him killed.

That someone wasn't me.

I should walk away, but I wasn't going to. And miss seeing my carefully restrained cowboy come undone? Hell, no. Every cell in my body longed for him. Even my teeth ached from it. He was the first person to ever truly feel like mine, and I was going to hold on to him with both hands for as long as I could.

So maybe I wasn't such a great person after all.

"I REALLY THINK I could have survived the ten-minute walk from the lodge to the stables without being kidnapped or murdered," I said. "Only someone completely unhinged would think they could get away with attacking me in broad daylight with a whole team of Tier 1 operators running around. You didn't have to come get me."

He shot me a look. "Stalkers don't tend to be the most reasonable, rational people. Both of those postcards came in the middle of the day, when we were right there and could have seen him. He's cocky. I don't like that. He thinks he can get away with everything, and so far he's been right. That makes him reckless and dangerous."

Jeremiah didn't hold my hand as we walked down the dirt path to the stables. Instead, he kept one hand resting lightly on the back of my arm, like he was afraid someone might snatch me up if he let his guard down for even a second.

"Anyway, if I hadn't come to get you, I couldn't do this."

He pulled me against his side and lowered his mouth to mine. It was the kind of kiss that was just a kiss. A kiss that didn't go anywhere. A kiss that didn't ask for more. The kind of kiss a husband greeted his wife with after a long day of work on all those happy family sitcoms from the 1950s. The kind I had never experienced before in real life.

Strange to have it now, with a man I wasn't even technically dating.

"If he's so cocky and unhinged, what's to stop him from doing something truly insane, like snatching me from my bed in the middle of the night?" I asked as we continued on.

"Nothing. That's why you're staying with me at the lodge."

"Maybe I should stay in your room," I suggested innocently. "Just in case."

He raised a sardonic eyebrow at me. "No ulterior motive, Miss Graves? You're not after my virtue, are you?"

I smacked his stomach. My hand practically bounced off his abdominal muscles. *Jesus.* He laughed at the look on my face.

"I am absolutely after your virtue, cowboy, and I'll tell you why." I stopped walking and tugged his arm until he did, too, and turned to face me. "Do you watch horror films?"

He shook his head.

"Well, I do. I love them. And one thing I've learned after literally dozens of slasher films is that virgins tend to survive the massacre. The slut standing next to them is the one who dies first. That's me." I pointed at my chest with both index fingers. "I'm the slut standing next to the virgin. And since I have no intention of ending my slutty ways, the only solution is for you to stop being a virgin. Fortunately, I'm here to help."

For a moment he stared at me like I had lost my mind. Then he threw his head back with a howl of laughter. "Lennon," he gasped. "Fuck."

"Do you want me to die, Jeremiah? Because that's what happens to sluts in slasher films."

"You're not going to die. I promise you, there's no safer place for you to be than right by my side. And if you want to share my bed, all right. But I'm not rushing this."

Shit. I was no better than a teenage boy pressuring his girlfriend, whining the whole time about not wanting to use a condom. "Right." I bobbed my head excessively to make up for being a trash human. "Of course. Losing your virginity is a big deal. It should be special."

"I told you. It's special because it's you. That's all I need. If it were just about me, I'd take you up against this tree right now."

I eyeballed the tree in question. It looked sturdy enough. "Then why are we waiting?"

He gave me a quizzical look, then dropped a kiss on my forehead. "I thought it was obvious, Lennon. I'm wooing you."

THE GYMKHANA WAS SET up in the large arena off the main horse barn. It was kind of like the field day we had in elementary school, except the games and races were played on horseback. As I had now had a grand total of three riding lessons with Jeremiah, I did not expect to win. But it looked like fun and I was down to try.

Jeremiah didn't stick around for the event. He turned me over to Liam and Holly like I was being sent to the principal's office and disappeared with Mateo. Whatever they were up to, it was about me. That made me nervous. Benny's problems had nothing to do with the stalker postcards, but I didn't need federal agents and mafia kings added to the mix. One problem at a time.

I would rather have Jeremiah with me, but Liam was a close second. The man was built like a fortress. Nothing was getting past him. Despite his ocean-blue nail polish—courtesy of Blair—there was a mean grumpiness to him. I got the feeling he would enjoy a fight.

"We've got the egg race, the bucket race, and musical saddles." Liam took up a ridiculous amount of space with his legs akimbo and his arms loosely at his sides. "Holly is going to be no more than two feet from you at any given time. She'll be your shadow. Even if someone managed to get past me—to be clear, they fucking *won't* —she'll be right there. Nothing bad will happen to you on Holly's watch."

Holly gave a toss of her black hair. Her smile reminded me of a serial killer. Not that I had ever met one in real life, but if I had, that was probably how they would smile at me right before they put the knife in my chest.

I turned back to Liam with a dubious look. "Has it occurred to you that Holly might *be* the bad that happens to me?"

He didn't respond. His gaze was already tracking the field, searching for threats. Ignoring the one standing right next to me.

Holly grinned. "Come on, city girl. Are you ready to play?"

I spun back to Liam. "You heard that, right? That was clearly a threat."

He gave the tiniest shake of his head.

I sighed and trudged forward.

Holly was going to kill me.

26

JEREMIAH

"Jeremiah Ezekial Bell!" Lennon's voice boomed from the office doorway, startling Mateo and making my spine snap straight like a guilty child.

"That's not my middle name," I said automatically, but I was more concerned with Lennon looking like something my dog had dragged through the mud. She was soaked through and filthy. Next to me, Mateo slapped a palm over his mouth and nose, whether to hide his laughter or ward off the stench, I didn't know.

"Then what's your middle name?" she demanded.

"I don't have one."

"Well, you do now. Congratulations." She stared at me, fuming. "Aren't you going to ask?"

"Honestly, I'm a little afraid to." I eyed her warily.

"I'll ask," Mateo cut in. "Lennon, what the fuck is that smell?"

Lennon stormed forward like a furious hurricane. Mateo and I pushed our chairs back in a hurry. She slammed her hands on my desk and leaned in. "That is the smell of an innocent woman who was hit with raw eggs, pushed into a horse trough, and then somehow found herself in a wheelbarrow full of horse dung. *That* is what you smell, Mateo. You smell me."

Mateo vibrated next to me, covering his cough with a laugh. I glared at him, sending a silent message with my eyes. *Are you trying to get us killed?*

"What happened, honey?" I sensed more than saw Mateo's head whip toward me at the endearment. Shit. I had told them about Lennon's stalker because that was necessary for everyone's safety. But I had left my feelings out of it.

"Holly happened to me," Lennon gritted out.

Goddammit.

Mateo shook his head. "You left her with Holly? Jesus, Jay."

"I left her with Liam," I said defensively. "I would never leave her with Holly."

"And Liam assigned Holly to shadow me," Lennon said.

"Seriously?" Mateo pushed his glasses up on his nose and cocked his head. "Did you do something to piss him off?"

Lennon threw up her hands. "How the hell should I know? I've barely talked to him since I got here. He's not exactly a stimulating conversationalist, you know. All he does is grunt."

"It's all right." I tried to soothe her with my voice because I sure as fuck wasn't going to actually touch her. "Tell me what happened."

"I don't know what happened." Frustration laced her voice. "I don't know how I managed to smash an entire carton of eggs on myself. I don't know how I fell into the water trough. I don't know how I tripped on nothing and ended up in the wheelbarrow of horse manure. But every time, Holly was right there. And I *know* I didn't do it to myself."

I exchanged a look with Mateo. Yeah, that was Holly, all right. No one ever saw her coming. She was like a fucking ghost assassin.

I pushed to my feet. "How about I take you upstairs so you can shower?" I ignored Mateo's knowing smirk as I rounded the desk. "And, um..." I looked around frantically. What would make Lennon happy again?

"Ice cream." Mateo snapped his fingers. "You want some ice cream, Lennon?"

Her eyes narrowed. "Don't try to handle me, Mateo. I *will* have my revenge." But then she cocked her head. "Skittles and Diet Coke. That's what I want."

"Fine," I agreed immediately. "But we'll have to go to

town. We don't keep Skittles on hand. No one's ever requested them before."

"So we'll go to town," she snapped, like I had put up a fight.

"I'll drive." I gave her a wide berth as I made for the door.

"And a hug."

The words stopped me in my tracks. I pivoted slowly. "Give the woman a hug, Mateo."

Mateo shook his head rapidly, his gaze pingponging between us.

"From you, Jeremiah," Lennon clarified. Her eyes glittered with evil joy. "I want a hug from you. It's the only thing that will make me feel better about being assaulted by one of your staff."

"Holly didn't touch you," I protested.

"I know what she did, and so do you." The only thing wider than her open arms was her shit-eating grin. "Come here, cowboy."

With a grimace, I stepped into her embrace. Her arms banded around me and her low laugh tickled my ear. Suddenly I didn't care that she was filthy and smelly. Lennon was in my arms. I had everything I wanted. I held her tighter and nuzzled her neck, searching for a clean spot to lay my lips.

"You're enjoying this." She smacked my arm with an annoyed huff. "You're not supposed to *enjoy* it."

"Interesting," Mateo said thoughtfully behind us.

I knew I would have to explain myself sooner or later, but not yet. For now, I ignored him and dragged my girl upstairs to get clean.

"Skittles and Diet Coke, huh?" I watched her shake out a palmful, then carefully select one of each color and pop them into her mouth in one go.

"It's my comfort meal."

After we'd showered—separately, despite her altruistic plea to save water, because I didn't trust myself having Lennon naked and wet within arm's reach of me—I'd driven her to Sunday's Sundries on Main Street. We'd taken her candy and my vanilla cone to the picnic tables out back, where Mercy River snaked through the town.

I shook my head. "Skittles and Diet Coke isn't a meal, honey. It's a snack."

She was quiet for a moment as she uncapped her soda and took a sip. After wiping her mouth with the back of her hand, she said, "My mom promised me my twelfth birthday would be special. We'd go out for pizza and she'd bake me a cake herself. Normally, I'd know better than to believe her. She made a lot of promises she never kept. But this time, I figured she'd actually follow through. Her boyfriend had dumped her two weeks before, so she was in that short window where she was done crying about it and in her *I don't need a man* phase before she inevitably decided she did, in fact, need a man." She squinted at the river. "When I came home from school, she was getting dressed to go out. Not for me." Her tone turned sardonic. "She'd met someone. He was *so* sweet"—Lennon rolled her eyes—"and he wanted to take her to dinner."

"She left you alone on your birthday?" We didn't celebrate birthdays at the compound. There were too many kids to give anyone special attention for a day. Being an only child, that probably hit different, having your mom choose to spend time with someone else.

Lennon nodded. "She had completely forgotten about the cake, but she told me to order myself pizza for dinner. Only..." Lennon rolled her lips, then shrugged like it didn't matter. "She hadn't left any money. Your ice cream is melting."

I blinked through my fury and realized a stream of melted ice cream was making its way to my hand. Feeling ridiculous, I licked it up.

"I scrounged around for loose change. I searched her drawers, the couch cushions, all that. Got sixty cents for my trouble. So I searched the neighborhood. I checked near cars and front steps and along the road to the gas station. I ended up with a few dollars. It wasn't enough for a whole pizza, but I could buy something to eat. A hotdog probably would have been more filling, but gas station hotdogs are disgusting." She wrinkled her nose at me, her lips tipped up in a genuine smile. "Anyway, it was my birthday. I wanted something yummy. So I bought my favorite candy and a Diet Coke because the regular Coke wasn't on sale."

"Lennon," I rasped. My chest hurt. "I'm so sorry, honey."

She frowned at me. "No. Don't do that. This isn't a sob story, okay? When I'm feeling down about something, I have Skittles and Diet Coke because it reminds me of my twelfth birthday and it makes me feel better. It's a *good* memory, Jeremiah."

"How? Your mother—" Anger choked the words in my throat. I hated that Lennon had been treated as disposable by the person who should have loved her the most.

"Because I proved I didn't need anyone else. I could take care of myself. And I do. Maybe not in a way you approve of, but I'm happy and healthy." She made a silly face and popped another handful of Skittles in her mouth. "That stalker thing isn't my fault, you know. You can't hold me responsible for him. But I'm going to figure it out and I'm going to fix it. I promise."

"Lennon. I approve of you. I more than approve of you." How could she doubt that? "You're smart and so fucking strong. So fucking beautiful."

She stared at me in surprise. Then her gaze faltered and dipped to my cone. "Eat your ice cream, Jeremiah."

I kept looking at her, waiting for her to give me her eyes again. She didn't. My girl was a coward about the strangest things. I shook my head. "I've never known anyone as scared of compliments as you are."

"I'm not *scared*. I just don't believe them."

I cocked my head, genuinely perplexed. "How's that? You're the most confident woman I've ever met."

"Well, sure. My taste is impeccable." She smirked as she tilted her soda to her lips. "*I* think I'm great. But I find it impossible to believe that anyone else does."

I hated everyone who had given her a reason to doubt me. Her mother was at the top of that list.

But I was going to rectify that. Before Lennon Graves left Mercy River Ranch, she would know down to her bones exactly how wonderful I found her.

"You know I'm going to have to do something about Holly, right?" Lennon sounded almost apologetic. "It's part of that whole taking care of myself thing. If I let it slide, how will I ever trust myself again?"

Oh, fuck. "I need you to listen to me very carefully, honey. Leave Holly alone."

"I know, I know. You were a team of some kind of special forces." She flicked her wrist. "Holly's not going to actually *kill* me—"

"Holly wasn't special forces," I interrupted. "She was a contractor assigned to a special forces team. She did jobs that—never mind. Just trust me on this, okay? She has different rules."

She gave my thigh a reassuring pat. "I know you're worried. You think I'm punching above my weight class—"

"I don't think that," I interrupted. "Holly has trained skills, but you're creative. It's like watching two super powers with nuclear weapons duke it out. I'm scared one of you will hit that red button and vaporize us all."

27

LENNON

"Cheers to the end of a shitastic day." Emma raised her plastic cup of sauvignon blanc.

I tapped my cup to hers and drank even though my day had been pretty lovely, actually. On the other hand, with my postcard stalker on the loose, maybe every day was a teeny tiny bit shitty. Although it was hard to complain when having a stalker meant I got to curl up with a warm cowboy every night.

A cowboy who still refused to put his virgin dick in me.

Maybe I had something to complain about, after all.

Emma had gathered the three of us—Tamilee, Cecily, and me—to decompress over a glass of wine so she could go home to Blair in a good mood. We'd set up lawn chairs in the horse pasture to enjoy the view. Sunset wasn't for another few hours—June days were long and bright in Wyoming—but the mellow evening light cast everything in a warm golden glow. Mountains and horses nibbling on pasture stretched out before us. Behind us, my favorite cowboy was practicing roping in the ring.

It was tempting to turn my chair around and watch.

"Are you going to tell us what Liam did to piss you off?" Tamilee asked.

"How do you know it was something Liam did?"

Tamilee raised her eyebrows. "Mmhmm."

Emma huffed. "I met someone last week. We were going to have a lunch date today, but he called and cancelled at the last minute. Said he had an emergency. So of course I said that was fine, and we could reschedule anytime. He said no, he was moving to Canada. Where in Canada? I asked. He went completely silent. Like, are you fucking kidding me? You can't name a single province or city in Canada?" She snorted and took another gulp of wine. "Fucking Liam. I know he had something to do with it. He never thinks anyone is good enough to be Blair's stepfather. I'm not looking for a new husband!" Frustration seeped into her voice. "I just want to get laid!"

Cecily rubbed her back in soothing circles. "Honestly, Liam probably did you a favor. If the man couldn't name a single province or city in Canada, do you really think he can find your clit?"

Laughter made wine shoot out my nose. "She has a point, Emma."

"Yeah, probably." Still looking disgruntled, she swirled the wine in her cup. "What about you, Lennon? I heard you had a terrible time at the gymkhana the other day."

I growled into my wine. "I know it was you, Holly!" I shook my fist at the sky, like she was watching me from the clouds.

Tamilee shook her head. "What did I tell you about that? Don't let her get under your skin."

"She didn't get under my skin. She got egg all *over* my skin. Egg and manure."

All three of my new friends reeled back like I like I was still covered in it with a collective "Ew!"

"I mean, I can't prove it. But I know it was her."

Cecily leaned toward me. "Want me to kill her?"

She looked so deadly serious that I cracked up. "Thank you, but I was thinking more along the lines of humiliations galore."

"Got it." Cecily bobbed her head. "We can Carrie her."

"Carry her where?" I asked.

"No, Carrie her like Stephen King's *Carrie*. We don't have a prom, but we have karaoke night, which she always makes a big deal of because she's so damn good it's honestly sickening. We could pour a bucket of pig blood on her while she's singing. Or"—Cecily snapped her fingers—"chicken blood. That's poetic justice, don't you think?"

My eyes went wide. "Jesus, Cecily. That's dark."

"I'm kidding." She gave my shoulder a playful shove. "Of course we're not going to pour blood on anybody. That's gross. Anyway, that movie didn't end well for Carrie's tormentors, and Holly would go absolutely apeshit on our asses. But you know what we could do? We could team up and do a karaoke song together." The bright fervor in her eyes looked almost manic. Too much wine. "That would be so fun."

"Um, maybe." Truthfully, I couldn't sing to save my life. But karaoke night sounded like fun, anyway. Even if it did mean watching everyone clap for Holly. Ugh.

"This has been fun, but it's time for me to head out." Tamilee stood and stretched, making her back crack. She squinted at the stables behind us. "What is that man still doing here? He's usually turned in by now."

I glanced over my shoulder to where Jeremiah was roping a fence post. "He's waiting for me. I'm staying in his sister's room while my cabin is getting fixed, remember?"

Cecily frowned. "That doesn't explain why he's waiting for you. You can walk the fifty feet back to the lodge alone."

She didn't know that Jeremiah didn't let me go even

one foot alone. My postcard stalker was almost certainly someone here at the ranch. Of course it wasn't Cecily, Emma, or Tamilee, but the more people who knew, the more likely it was that the stalker would go into hiding before we could find him—or worse, do something rash. So I just hummed and shrugged as I took another sip of wine.

"Hmm." Emma studied me with a thoughtful tilt of her head. "I'm beginning to think that kiss outside Sundown wasn't a drunk one-off. Spill, Lennon. What's going on with you two?"

"How could something be going on when I'm leaving next month?" God, I hoped I didn't sound as wistful as I felt. Look at him standing there, his sleeves rolled up to his elbows like he knew his forearms gave me impure thoughts. And that mustache. Christ. "We're friends."

Friends who kissed. I giggled because I had also had a little too much wine. "Jeremiah is a good friend of mine, who happens to be a bullfrog. Like the song." For some reason, that struck me as hilarious and I dissolved into a fit of giggles.

Emma laughed. "Okay, goofy girl. I think it's time for us to pack it in." She pushed to her feet, then helped me up too.

Jeremiah must have been watching us, because he immediately started walking toward us, rolling his rope as he came.

"Here comes your bullfrog," Emma murmured with a low laugh.

Ohhhhh.

That gave me an idea.

"Did you order something?" Jeremiah entered the apartment carrying a big gray poly mailer three days later.

"Sure did." I swung my legs off the sofa and excitedly rolled to my feet. I wasn't sure it would get here in time. "Give me that."

He stepped back from my reaching arms, eyeing me suspiciously. "Why are you making that face?"

"What face?"

"The evil genius face. Like a villain who's cackling and stroking a cat while plotting the destruction of her enemy. That's the face you're making."

"Maybe because I *am* plotting the destruction of my enemy." I leaned forward like I had a secret. "I'm going to win karaoke tonight. Now, give me my package."

He handed it over. "Karaoke is not a competition. It's a fun, casual bonding experience."

"Don't be ridiculous, Jeremiah. Everything is a

competition. I'm going to win, and you're going to help me. You owe me."

He crossed his arms. "What do you mean, I owe you? What do I owe you for?"

"Lots of things. For snooping on me instead of asking me for the truth. Figuring out I shouldn't be here and then not telling me. Leaving me with Holly." I flicked my wrist. "Pick one."

"I left you with Liam."

"So you have two other perfectly good options to choose from."

With a deep sigh, he pinched the bridge of his nose. "Lennon, honey. You're talking about a suicide mission. Holly loves karaoke, and she's not going to take kindly to being knocked out of the spotlight. Trust me, whatever you're planning, you don't want to do it."

"I do. I really, really do." I squeezed the package to my chest giddily.

"Tell me why this is so important to you."

I chewed my cheek, searching for the right words. "I told the sheriff that I don't have enemies, but the more I think about it, the more I realize that's not really true. I have enemies. The trolls who harass me online. The postcard stalker. They know how to hit me right where it hurts. But I can't hit back. I don't know who they are. They're ghosts. But Holly...she's not some anonymous troll typing mean shit at three a.m. She's flesh and blood. She has feelings. I can finally hit back."

"Dammit." Jeremiah planted his hands on his hips, staring at me. "All right. What do you need? You want me to sneak the machine up here for extra practice time?"

I laughed. "So I can make the squirrels out our window regret their life choices? No, thank you."

He tilted his head in obvious confusion. "What do you mean? You can't sing?"

"Not a single note," I admitted cheerfully. "Female cats in heat have better vocals than I do."

He blinked slowly. "Are you telling me you're willing to humiliate yourself just to piss off Holly? You understand there's no real winning here."

My grin widened. "Oh, it's much worse than that, I'm afraid. See, I'm not only willing to humiliate myself. I'm willing to humiliate you, too." I ripped open the seal and pulled out the shrink wrapped bag inside. "I need scissors."

Shaking his head, he moved to the efficiency kitchen and rummaged through a drawer. He pulled out the scissors, stared at them for a moment, then shook his head. "Like falling on my own sword," he muttered, but he handed them over anyway. "I don't know why I'm helping you. This is a terrible idea."

"Men do all kinds of silly things for sex."

He cleared his throat. "I was under the impression I was going to get sex anyway."

I looked up. There was something about his expression that made me want to throw aside my evil karaoke plans and drag him to bed. Maybe it was the heat that made his blue eyes darken to twilight. Or the way his cheeks flushed whenever the subject of sex came up. "We could do that right now, if you want."

He quirked an eyebrow at me.

"Fine," I grumbled. "Keep wooing me, then."

He grabbed the hand that was closed around the scissors blades and lifted it to his mouth, pressing a kiss to the inside of my wrist. "All right."

I rolled my eyes despite the swoop of butterflies in my stomach. "Can I have my hand back, please? I have a nemesis to overthrow."

"I still don't understand how singing badly is going to do anything but make everyone feel sorry for you. Is that it? Are you going for the pity vote? You do understand that there isn't actual voting involved, right?"

"But there's applause, isn't there? And she'll be able to tell that people clapped louder for me than for her."

"She has a really good voice, Lennon. What makes you think they'll clap louder for you?"

"Two reasons. One, it's not quite a pity vote, but people really do love watching hot people be bad at things." I snipped open the shrink wrap and pulled out the fuzzy green thing inside. "And two, I have a secret weapon." I gave the fuzzy green thing a couple big shakes to bring it back to life. It unfolded down to my ankles.

"Lennon." Jeremiah's voice held the smallest tinge of fear. "What the fuck is that?"

28

LENNON

HOLLY TRULY HAD A GORGEOUS VOICE. DEEP FOR A woman. Softer and sweeter than I had expected from a psycho bitch. She'd chosen *With or Without You* by U2 which was an interesting choice because it was so emotional and I didn't think Holly had emotions. She kept her eyes closed until she got to the refrain. Was it my imagination, or did she look right at Mateo as she sang the heart wrenching line where someone gave himself away?

Curiosity pricked at me. What was their deal? And why did I genuinely care? Because I *did* care, that was the crazy thing. These people. The animals. This place. All of it mattered to me. The cowboys, Emma and Grace and Tamilee, Amos and Cecily.

Even Holly, somehow. I hated having enemies, but having a nemesis was fun as hell.

I had been here only a month and felt more connected to the people and place than I did after a full decade in New York. That wasn't New York's fault. It was all me. I had closed myself off. Never made any real friendships. At Mercy River, I cracked myself open. Maybe it was the wide open vistas that made me feel brand new. Or maybe it was because my stay here was temporary and therefore felt safer. Who cared if people got to know me? I would be long gone before they could be done with me.

Or maybe it was the cowboy standing in front of me wearing a fuzzy green frog onesie and a scowl.

He kept showing up.

Even when showing up meant wearing a frog onesie.

I didn't know what was more terrifying: that eventually he'd figure out I wasn't worth it, or that I was starting to believe I actually was.

"Any chance you're going to change your mind?" he asked.

"Nope. But listen, you don't have to go out there with me. Emma said she couldn't remember a single time you had done a song. Do you get stage fright?" The slightest twinge of guilt had taken hold. Holly was his friend. More than that. They'd taken gunfire together. That was not a bond I wanted to break.

He rubbed his fuzzy green head. "Well, I don't know. I've never been on a stage."

"You don't have to," I repeated. "I can't sing a note, but I think my outfit will make up for it."

I twirled to give him the full picture. Cowboy boots and a ridiculous red cowboy hat that no real cowboy would ever wear. I'd had to order it online. Cutoff denim shorts that barely covered the crease of my thigh. A red plaid flannel that I'd borrowed from Jeremiah. I'd tied it in a knot at my waist so an inch of skin showed above my shorts.

His gaze licked down my body like a flame. I felt hot everywhere. "You're wearing my shirt."

"It's mine now," I taunted.

He grabbed the knot and pulled me against him. His lips stopped an inch from my mouth. "*Mine.*"

His mouth descended before I could ask whether he meant the shirt or *me*. He kissed me like he didn't care who was watching—although no one was. We were safely hidden behind the haybales stacked tall to provide a backdrop, since the lodge dining room didn't have an actual stage. I didn't want anyone to see Jeremiah before our song. Still, anyone could have walked around and found us.

I didn't care, either. I didn't care about secrets or revenge or stalkers. Jeremiah was kissing the fuck out of me, and nothing else mattered. Not even besting Holly.

"You really don't have to," I whispered as he pulled away.

His lips quirked. He rubbed his nose along mine. "Sure I do."

"I meant you don't have to do the song with me."

"I know what you meant."

I leaned back so I could fully look him in the face. "Why? You and I both know that this is supremely silly. All of it. My feud with Holly—although I want it on record that she started it—and what I'm about to make you do. A grown ass woman shouldn't be behaving like this. I don't know why it matters so much to me."

"It matters to you. That's enough for me."

"Don't you think you should be the voice of reason here?"

He laughed. "I already tried that. It didn't work. So, okay. I'm in."

I chewed the inside of my cheek. "All right. You really don't have to do much for this to work. You're out here wearing a green frog onesie. That's enough to blow their minds. Just stand there and look cute, okay?"

He smirked. "Let's do this."

29

JEREMIAH

THIRTY-EIGHT YEARS.

Thirty-eight years I had wandered in the dark, lost and seeking. *What is my purpose?* I asked the church elders, and the church elders spewed bullshit. *What is my purpose?* I asked God, and God stayed silent. *What is my purpose?* I asked myself, and I answered *fuck if I know.*

Then Lennon Graves belted out the first lyric offkey.

And God said, let there be light, and there was light.

My world was illuminated.

And I knew.

I was put on this Earth to don a fuzzy green bullfrog costume and shake my ass like I was selling it so my girl could have the dubious honor of receiving more applause than her sociopath nemesis.

Not because it was the right thing to do. There was no honor here.

Not because justice required it. Their war would only escalate.

But because she wanted me to. That was enough.

This karaoke contest was without a doubt the stupidest thing I had ever been a part of. I didn't care. It made no fucking sense, but I had never been more sure of anything down to the very marrow of my bones.

My purpose in this life and every other was to make Lennon Graves happy by any means necessary. And right now, that meant letting her call me a bullfrog and dancing my ass off.

The song was *Joy to the World*, and from the moment Lennon declared I was a bullfrog, our audience lost their damn minds. Lennon sang, if you could call that noise singing, and I danced. I gyrated my body. I waved my arms. I made a goddamn fool of myself. It was...not good. None of this was good. Not Lennon's singing, and definitely not my dancing.

She took one shocked, wide-eyed look at me and half-wheezed, half warbled the next line. That was the last time she looked at me for the rest of the song. Apparently my ass shaking ruined her concentration.

My friends had a front row seat to the whole thing. The guests and ranch hands and some of the staff were there, too. People I had worked hard to earn the respect of who might be having second thoughts about my leadership right about now. There was shocked silence as Lennon's truly terrible voice rang out, and then they erupted into hoots and hollers.

Seb stomped his feet in time to the music. Put his thumb and index finger to his lips and let out a piercing whistle. Mateo laughed so hard tears streamed down his face. He had to push his glasses to the crown of his head to wipe his eyes. Even Liam, grumpy son of a bitch that he was, clapped along with the music, his shoulders shaking with suppressed laughter. Holly sat there, mouth agape, like a woman turned to salt.

Later, she and I would talk. There were things that needed to be said. But right now, I had one job and that job was shaking my ass.

"Everybody!" Lennon hollered. She brought her arms up in a wide arc until her palms met in a loud clap over her head.

That got everyone on their feet, clapping and stomping to the final verse. She sang about spreading joy all over the world, to all the children and the animals, and my heart damn near burst out of my chest.

The audience went wild. When Lennon threw herself into my arms, my heart went wild right with the rest of them. Laughing, I spun her in a circle.

Joy. That was Lennon. She was joy to the world. She was joy to me.

My hand stayed on Lennon's lower back as our friends surrounded us. I hooked my index finger into the belt-loop of her cutoff denim shorts, my thumb gently rubbing her soft, bare skin above the waistband.

"Whimsy!" Mateo hollered, jabbing both his index fingers at my chest. "That's what I'm talking about! Fucking awesome, man. And *you*." He threw an arm around Lennon's shoulders and smacked a kiss on her forehead, making her giggle. "Incredible. How did you convince him to do it?"

Her gaze slid to me, dark eyes full of wonder. "I really don't know."

Emma and Grace enveloped her in a hug. I stayed attached at her beltloop while they laughed and jumped up and down.

"Is Blair here?" Lennon asked when they separated.

"Oh, she's here," Emma said with an amused eyeroll. "The ranch kids usually keep to the back row where they mock us all relentlessly. They're *way* too cool for karaoke."

"You're coming outside for the campfire, right?" Grace asked. "I want you to meet my fiancé. Alex is out there building the fire with some of the other ranch hands. But he saw your song and about died laughing."

"I'd love—" I tugged at Lennon's beltloop and let my eyes communicate everything I couldn't say out loud in polite company when she sent me a look over her shoulder. The tip of her tongue swiped along her lower lip and then she cleared her throat. "We'll be out right after we change into something less flammable."

Emma laughed. "We'll save you a seat."

I inched Lennon backward toward the exit. Everyone wanted to stop and talk to us. When we finally cleared the crowd, she paused on the first step of the staircase leading to our apartment and turned to me with her lower lip pushed out in a mock pout.

"No one said anything about my amazing singing." Her voice shook as she struggled to hold back her giggle. "They were all too busy gawking over your dancing."

I caged her in. Dipped my head to that tempting mouth and nipped her lip. "Honey, if you don't get your ass upstairs, I'm going to put on another show for them right here and now."

Her eyes heated like melted chocolate. She was the most decadent dessert, and I meant to indulge in her tonight.

She darted up the stairs with me right on her heels. It took me a beat longer than usual to unlock my door with her pressing distracting kisses to my neck and palming my hardening length.

We fell into the room in a tangle, tugging at clothes

and fumbling with zippers. She got hold of mine and unzipped the frog onesie down to my waist, then sank to her knees to bring it lower, her eyes locked on my tented boxers with a look that made my dick twitch eagerly. But I had something else in mind, so I grabbed her under her armpits and hauled her to her feet.

"Not this time, honey. It's my turn."

My bedroom was twenty feet away but it was still too far. With my mouth on hers, I backed her up until the couch hit her knees, undoing her shorts as we went. She tumbled backwards onto the couch and I followed her down, sinking to my knees between her thighs.

I slid open the top button of my flannel and laid a kiss between her breasts. Her breath hitched. I kept going, unbuttoning and kissing her until I reached the knot. She watched me with half-mast eyes as I untied it and kissed her there, between her navel and her silky pink underwear.

Her chest rose and fell with rapid breaths. She arched her hips so I could tug her underwear over her ass and down her legs.

I couldn't breathe for beauty. I leaned back and pushed her thighs wider to gaze down at her.

"Jeremiah," she said quietly. She reached one hand to me. Threaded her fingers softly through my hair. "You don't have to."

It felt like I did, though not in the way she meant. *Have to*, my body begged.

"My soul thirsts for you, my flesh yearns for you, in a dry and weary land where there is no water." Holy words that my lips whispered to a holy place, where she was abundantly wet.

And I drank.

30

LENNON

THE FIRST TOUCH OF HIS TONGUE WAS BLISS.

The second nearly rendered my soul from my body.

There was nothing tentative about the way Jeremiah ate me. Nothing gentle about the way his hands clenched my hips, wrenching me upward, grinding me against his feasting mouth. Teeth and tongue and lips. He used them all to take his fill of me.

I came before I knew what was happening. It barreled into me like a freight train, giving me no time to prepare. My back arched and I cried out as the pleasure seared through me.

But he didn't stop. My body jerked as his tongue hit my over-sensitized clit. "Jeremiah," I gasped. "Wait, please, oh my god—"

He pulled back, frowning like I had cancelled Christmas. He dragged the back of his hand across his damp mouth. "More," he demanded.

And then dove back in.

Oh god, oh god—

His touch bordered on pain. I shrieked and my thighs clamped around his head. With a dark chuckle, he turned his head and pressed a kiss to my inner thigh. "Too much? Right there"—he tapped my clit gently with his finger—"that's too much?"

I nodded, slowly letting my legs fall open again. "I need a minute."

"I'll wait."

But then he slipped his hands under my ass and lifted me to his mouth like a chalice. I tensed. With a soothing murmur, he slid his tongue inside me. He took a long, lingering lick and then another.

"Does that hurt?" he asked, and then did it again.

It didn't hurt. His tongue turned my insides to hot liquid. I was melting like a lit candle. He arched an eyebrow at me, the only way he could communicate when his mouth was full of my pussy, and I said, "No, it doesn't hurt."

His tongue was gentle as he savored me. He kept going like he wanted nothing else but this. My pussy, his mouth. He made a sound of utter contentment as his tongue swept inside me again and again. This wasn't for my pleasure. It was all for his.

I stared down at his golden head between my thighs. The broadly muscled shoulders. His beautiful, capable hands that held my body to his mouth. It was the most gorgeously erotic thing I had ever witnessed, this man on his knees bringing us both pleasure.

My pussy squeezed and he made a low, hungry sound.

"More," I pleaded.

He gave it to me, pressing eager, open mouthed kisses all over my pussy before once again finding my clit. He swirled his tongue around the slip of flesh, gently at first, like he was testing how much I could take. I pushed against his mouth, giving him my answer.

His hands wrapped my thighs, pulling me open, and his mouth latched onto my clit. He sucked gently and then more firmly as I moaned. And then I was coming again, hips bucking against his mouth, my head thrown back as stars exploded in my vision. His fingers dug into my hips with bruising force and he groaned, shoulders straining forward.

"Oh, my god." I blinked at the ceiling. "Oh, my *god*."

He made a happy sound and pressed his cheek to my belly. I sifted my fingers through his hair, craning my neck to look down at him. He looked back at me with a sated, almost sleepy smile.

"Defiled your bullfrog onesie. Sorry about that. You tasted too good. Couldn't stop myself from spilling."

I snickered. "So your deflowering will have to wait?"

"At least ten minutes."

I laughed softly. His hair slipped through my fingers like spun gold. I gave him a little scratch with my nails and he made that happy sound again. My chest felt tender as I looked down at him. Warm and achey. This must be that love hormone that released with the orgasm. I had thought it was a myth.

I had orgasmed before, but it had never left me like this. As though something precious had been placed in my care. It was beautiful and terrifying all at once. I wanted to cuddle him closer, heal all his hurts, and I didn't know what to do with any of that. The only person I knew how to take care of was myself.

I squirmed under the sudden heaviness of his body. Half laughing, half groaning, Jeremiah levered himself off of me. He dropped a kiss on my forehead before getting to his feet.

"Come on." I let him pull me to my feet. He smirked as his shirt tumbled to the tops of my thighs. He caught hold of the plackets and tugged. "Looks better on you than me. You can keep it."

I want to keep you. But the words lodged in my throat, choking me.

"I think this is going in the trash." He stepped out of the frog onesie and headed for the kitchen.

I snatched it from him before he could make good on his threat. "Don't you dare! I'll put it in the wash."

He laughed but let me have it. "You know I'm not wearing that again."

"Not for karaoke. But unfortunately for you, giving me the best orgasm of my life while rocking a frog onesie unlocked a new kink in me. I'm going to need a repeat performance."

His gaze was heated as he caught my hand and pulled me toward his bedroom. "Anytime."

The way he looked at me made my insides clench with longing. *Anytime.* I yearned for that. For years stretched out before us, filled with love and sex and inside jokes and Jeremiah in a frog onesie. All the things I couldn't have.

But right now, he was mine. And I was going to make the most of the time we had left. I stretched up on my toes and kissed him.

An acrid smell made my nose wrinkle. It must have hit him at the same time because his eyebrows drew together, and then his expression cleared as he remembered. "The campfire. Our friends are waiting for us."

"Or we could—"

Shouts pierced the air.

31

JEREMIAH

By the time the sheriff arrived, the flames that had engulfed Lennon's ancient Volvo had been extinguished. The ranch had fire extinguishers and hoses stationed all over the property, and they'd come in handy tonight. We were fortunate that Lennon's car had been parked far enough back from the lodge that the fire hadn't spread to our pine buildings.

"The fire marshal will be out first thing in the morning." Sherwood stood with me off to the side.

"I want him here tonight," I bit out.

Sherwood scrubbed a hand over his face. "You know that's not going to happen. He's two hours away, and no one was hurt. He can do his investigation tomorrow."

Most everyone had gone home after answering the

sheriff's questions, but there were still a few stragglers either looking to help or looking to gossip. Mateo, Holly, Seb, and Liam had closed ranks around Lennon, forming a half circle with their backs to her. Grace had an arm wrapped around Lennon's waist as they both stared at the burned remnants of Lennon's car. Lennon's expression was completely devoid of emotion. Fucking eerie, seeing all the life drained out of her like that.

I stabbed my fingers through my hair and tugged. I wanted to hit something. "It's arson. You know it's arson. Her car didn't spontaneously combust."

"I don't disagree. But he needs daylight to run a thorough investigation. And even then, we'll know the what but not the who or why. We're not going to be able to pull prints off that, even supposing he left something behind."

He wasn't wrong, but hell. That only pissed me off more. "He's escalating fast, and we're standing around with our thumbs up our asses." I shook my head. A sternly worded postcard was one thing, but a fucking fire? "Since Lennon's been staying with me, he doesn't have access to her like he used to. Keeping her safe is pissing him off."

"It's more than that. She moved in with you a full week ago. The fire wasn't planned. Too many potential witnesses around. My guess is, something happened tonight that made him angry enough that he took immediate action and got lucky no one saw him." He studied me in the darkening dusk. "Heard you and Lennon had quite the duet tonight."

"You think he didn't like my bullfrog onesie?"

"I think he doesn't like to share."

My jaw clenched. *Same.* I especially wasn't going to share Lennon with a stalker who set her car on fire. My gaze went to her again. Even surrounded as she was by people I trusted with my life, I had to verify her safety with my own eyes. Cecily had joined them now.

"Whoever lured her here isn't a stranger, Jay. It's someone familiar with this ranch and with you. He knows damn well you wouldn't get into that frog costume for just anyone, much less shake your ass like a fool."

I didn't need the reminder that Lennon's stalker was likely right here under my nose. It was a constant worry in the back of my mind. That was why I didn't let her go anywhere alone.

We'd done a light background investigation on everyone here—including the guests, which I didn't take lightly—and no leads had turned up. Mateo had started in on Lennon's camming subs, highest donors first, but we still had nearly a hundred to go. Benny Davis was her biggest supporter, but also the least likely to be stalking her. The man was shady as hell, but all his criminal activities were financial in nature. Anyway, he'd had no reason to stalk her when they were dating, and now he was under house arrest while he awaited trial. Whatever he might be guilty of, he wasn't stalking Lennon.

"Get some sleep, Jay. Have Lennon do the same. The fire marshal will be here at nine a.m. We'll talk next steps then."

I was striding toward her before he finished speaking. With a brisk nod of thanks to our friends, I maneuvered Lennon into my arms. Grace stepped aside with a tiny, empathetic smile, but Cecily held on a moment longer, her eyes searching my face as though wondering if I could be trusted.

"I have her. Thanks, Cecily." My gaze flicked between Lennon's friends. "No one goes anywhere alone. Alex is still here to get you home?"

Grace nodded. "We'll make sure Cecily is safe, too."

"Good."

Lennon didn't respond as her friends hugged her goodbye. Her gaze stayed pinned to her car, but I doubted she really saw that, either. I stepped in front of her and slid my hand under her thick hair to the back of her neck.

"Lennon." I squeezed gently. "Look at me, honey."

She blinked a few times like she was coming out of a trance. Her eyes slowly focused on mine. "Jeremiah."

"There's nothing more we can do tonight. Let's go upstairs."

She looked around like she wasn't sure where we were or how we got here. But she didn't protest as I took her by the hand and led her into the lodge. I nudged her up the stairs in front of me, keeping one hand on her lower back so she'd know I was there. I would always be there, if she let me.

She halted at the top of the staircase, and I reached around her to unlock the door. Her sudden sharp intake of breath had my gaze snapping to her face. But she wasn't looking at me. She was looking at the postcard taped to the door.

Before I could stop her, she snatched it off the door and flipped it over to read the message.

IT WAS SUPPOSED TO BE US.

Bold, angry letters.

This postcard was different. It didn't smell like vanilla and oranges. It smelled like lighter fluid.

Lennon's hand clenched into a fist around the postcard. Color rose in her cheeks. "Fuck you," she hissed to the postcard. "Fuck. *You*. There is no us."

"There she is," I muttered, gently prying her fingers open. "Please don't destroy the evidence, honey."

"My *car*. He burned my car." The helpless fury in her voice made me want to hit something.

"I know." I managed to get the door unlocked and both of us inside while only touching the corner of the postcard. It was doubtful we'd find prints, but maybe his anger had made him careless.

"I'm trapped here. *Trapped*."

"You're not trapped. I'll take you anywhere you want

to go. Or you can stay." *Please fucking stay.* I stole a glance at her as I carefully slipped the postcard into a sandwich baggie and sealed it shut.

She didn't seem to have heard me. She faced the window, hands planted on her hips, her brow pinched. "It feels like a big jump. I mean, two years of postcards and then boom, he sets my car on fire? That escalated quickly, don't you think?"

I rubbed my jaw, frowning. "Sheriff thinks that might have something to do with me. He doesn't want to share your attention."

"Well, I don't want to give him *any* of my attention. I just wish I knew who he was so I could tell him to his fucking face." The furrow between her eyebrows deepened and she shook her head slowly, like she was thinking something through. "But it's not like you're my first boyfriend. So why now?"

My brain stuttered. Did she just call me her boyfriend? *Focus, you dumbass virgin. You have a stalker to catch.* I cleared my throat. "You said the postcards started two years ago? Have you dated anyone seriously since then?"

She chewed the inside of her cheek. "It was serious with Benny. If he asked me, I probably would have married him. And, yes, I wouldn't have been with him if he didn't have money. But if I hadn't liked him, no amount of money could have kept me there. Which is more than a lot of marriages have. Maybe it wasn't storybook love, but we cared about each other and we took care of each other. It was honestly the healthiest relationship I ever had."

The jut of her jaw told me she expected condemnation. But she wasn't going to get it. Not from me. All I had to give her was respect.

"All right. So it was serious with Benny, but would your stalker know that?"

She blew out a heavy breath. "There were photos of us. Dinners, galas, that kind of thing." Her head tilted as she mulled it over. "Nine months ago. That's when I started dating Benny, and that's when the postcards started getting...I don't know...judgmental. Telling me I was making a mistake, that kind of thing. And then six months ago, I started getting the brochures for Mercy River Ranch."

I nodded slowly. "So the stalker does escalate when you're in a relationship."

"But it still doesn't make sense. Benny and I were heading to marriage. That's permanent. Being here with you is..." Her face scrunched like the words physically hurt her.

That same pain echoed in my chest. I rounded the counter to get closer to her. Cupping her face in my palms, I forced her to look at me. "Lennon."

I could feel her swallow against my fingertips. "Being with you is wonderful, but it's temporary. If Mr. Stalker doesn't like the attention I'm giving you, all he has to do is wait another four weeks and I'll be gone again. He didn't need to set my fucking car on fire."

"Lennon." I tried to keep my voice gentle, because she wasn't going to like what I had to say next. "I don't think your stalker has any intention of letting you leave this ranch."

"Shit," she whispered. Her eyes widened as the realization hit. Of course he hadn't lured her out here just to let her leave again. "Shit."

"He's getting careless. That fire tonight was brash. Anyone could have seen him. He was so angry he couldn't stop himself. He's going to fuck up, Lennon. It's only a matter of time. He's getting careless."

"I'm not going to sit around and wait for that to happen." She wrenched free and paced the small living room. "Every time I do something he doesn't like, he pops in to let me know. I move into your apartment, he tells me it was a mistake. I sing a duet with you, he sets my car on fire. What a little bitch." The scorn in her voice had me biting back an inappropriate laugh. "I did not rescue myself from my mom's handsy boyfriends and New York's insane rental prices to be taken down now by a delusional *man*. Absolutely the fuck *not*."

She stopped. Turned to look at me.

Ah, hell. That gleam was in her eye, and that gleam meant trouble.

"I have an idea," she said.

32

JEREMIAH

"This is a terrible idea," Liam said. He rubbed Indigo's nose as he held him steady.

"Have to agree with Liam. I don't like it." Seb attached my extra sleeping bag to the back of Indigo's saddle. He might not like it, but that didn't mean he wouldn't help me do it.

"This guy set her car on fire over a frog onesie," Mateo chimed in. "How do you think he'll react when he discovers you and Lennon are gone? He's gonna lose his shit."

"That's the idea." Sleeping bags, sat phone, food. Extra supplies, because I wasn't taking chances. Rifle, for the same reason. "People will notice we're gone. He'll be one of them. Tell anyone who asks that we're planning a three-week trip up near Yellowstone, and we'll leave Friday. Tonight is the trial run to get Lennon acclimated. Got it?"

They stared at me like I'd lost my mind.

"Three weeks in a tent?" Seb scratched his jaw. "You think Lennon will go for that?"

"It's what you're telling people. We're not actually doing it." But I remembered the way she woke up every morning to see the stars. I remembered the way she tilted her face to the rain. My city girl had a wild streak in her. "But yes, I think she'd go for that."

Holly tilted her head, her black hair sweeping over her shoulder. "You're trying to smoke him out of hiding. Force him to play his hand before he's ready." Her mouth tipped up in a sly smile. "It's not a bad plan."

I grunted as I buckled the pack down. "Lennon's idea. She doesn't like fighting ghosts. She wants him out in the open where she can hit him."

"Dammit," Holly grumbled. "I'm actually starting to like her."

With a firm grip on her elbow, I steered her away from the others. "This shit with you and Lennon? It stops now."

Dark brows winged upward. She didn't respond well to being told what to do. I changed tactics. "I know I can trust you, Holly. I need Lennon to know she can trust you, too."

Her eyes flitted back and forth as she studied me. "You want her to stay."

"Yeah. I want her to stay."

She turned away, but not before I saw the hint of a smile on her lips. "She can trust me."

We finished the packing. Lennon was safe in the kitchen with Amos and Cecily. She'd sneak out while breakfast was being served and if all went to plan, we'd be an hour away by horseback before anyone realized we were gone.

"We don't know what he'll do when he realizes Lennon is out of reach," I said. "Stay vigilant. No one is above suspicion until we know for sure who we're dealing with. I figure he'll either create an emergency to lure us back early, or he'll start planning his move for the moment Lennon is back. It's probably better that everyone believes you have no way of contacting us."

"He might try to follow you. That's a third option," Seb pointed out.

"Maybe," I allowed, "but I think it's unlikely. We'll have a head start. There are too many trails in Forest Service land for him to find us easily. My guess is he'll take the twenty-four hours we're gone to make a plan. That's what I would do." My gaze flicked to Liam. "Any ranch hands go AWOL, I expect to hear about it immediately."

Liam gave a curt nod. "You got it."

"Seb, you keep eyes on the guests," I continued.

"Mateo, I don't care if you have to stare at a screen until your eyes bleed. I want every single one of Lennon's subs verified and checked out before we get back."

Mateo pushed his glasses higher on his nose. For once, he looked completely serious. "I'm on it."

"Good. Holly—"

"I know. If we solve the mystery before you return, I'll handle it." She smiled widely.

"Keep him alive." That could have gone unsaid with anyone else, but it was better not to take chances with Holly. "We want him in prison, not you."

Seb's gaze went over my shoulder and he jerked his chin. "Here comes your girl now. You sure you want to do this?"

"We're doing it." Everything I needed was walking toward me. The circumstances sucked, but twenty-four hours alone with this woman, nothing but stars and trees and mountains for company? That was my idea of heaven.

"Hey, you," Lennon greeted me. "You ready to piss off my psycho stalker?"

Whatever reservations I had—and I had plenty—I pushed aside. "Hell, yeah, honey."

Her lips curved and she bounced on her toes. Déjà vu. That day we'd gone into town for boots, she'd bounced exactly like that. Fight or flight. But I'd read her wrong in that moment. My girl wasn't a bolter. She was a fighter.

Her stalker, for all his *we* and *us* bullshit, he didn't know her as well as he thought he did, and I had the feeling that was going to be his downfall. I almost felt sorry for him.

Almost.

But then the wind rustled the leaves and Lennon whipped around, searching, and my gut clenched. Fuck that guy for putting that mix of fear and fury in her expression. I didn't feel sorry for him at all. He better be praying to the Patron Saint of Jackasses that the police caught him before I did.

Holly laid a hand on my arm. "Keep her safe, okay? Lennon makes a good nemesis. It's been a while since I've had one of those. She got the best of me twice. *Twice*, Jay. No one does that." She shook her head in disbelief. "I never saw her coming."

Me, either. A month ago I had no idea who Lennon Graves was, and now I didn't know how I was supposed to keep breathing without her.

THE GUARDIAN

He took her from me.

Keeping a bland smile on my face while Liam shared the news was hard. I wanted to scream and rage and throw something. But I kept my cool. I imagined Jeremiah floating in the sky like a balloon, a string tying him to Lennon. I imagined cutting the string with a pair of scissors. I imagined Jeremiah getting smaller and smaller as he floated up, up, up and away until *poof!* He was gone. My smile went from forced to genuine.

Camping. Honestly. Did he even know her at all? With a derisive snort, I turned on my heel and stormed to the parking lot. Lennon didn't want to go fucking camping. It was dirty and gross out there. She wanted to sit on a porch and enjoy nature from a safe distance away, with running water and flushing toilets and a soft bed.

There was no way she would really go on a three-week pack trip. No fucking way. She could have this night with him—he better bring her back without so much as a goddamn scratch, or I was going to push him off the cliff like Miguel—but not three weeks. It was good, actually. Twenty-four hours camping with Jeremiah would make her miserable. She'd realize she needed to end things with him before this became her life and she was stuck with these camping trips forever.

Except...Lennon didn't have the best track record, honestly. Men were a real weakness for her. She craved stability, and she thought men were the way to get that. Fucking dumb. Like men could be counted on for anything.

But I understood it. The world was unfair. Men had everything—they had *taken* everything. Power. Money. She thought if she played by their rules, she could win. I had believed that, too, once. Now I knew better.

But Lennon hadn't learned her lesson yet, apparently. Like that time one of her subscribers told her he liked Pokémon Go, and instead of laughing at him like she should have, she cosplayed as a female avatar while baking him a cake for his birthday. Of course, he'd given her a *huge* tip for that, which only reinforced her belief that if she twisted herself into his perfect woman, a man would take care of her.

Now she was doing the same thing with Jeremiah.

He was steady. Loyal. In possession of an apartment with an extra bedroom and a great view.

Oh, goddammit.

She was really going to do it, wasn't she. Lennon was actually going to go on a stupid three-week pack trip with him. She would make herself miserable just to make him happy. He didn't deserve that, but he would take it from her anyway. As long as he got what he wanted from her, he wouldn't even notice she wasn't happy. Men were never as ashamed of themselves as they should be.

I couldn't let him do that to her. I couldn't let her do that to *herself*.

I threw my bag on the passenger seat of my car and peeled out of the parking lot. Tomorrow I would take my camper van to work instead of my car.

Tomorrow I would be ready.

Thank goodness I was here to save Lennon from herself.

33

LENNON

MY MUSCLES SCREAMED IN PROTEST AS I THREW MY RIGHT leg over Indigo's rump and dismounted. I wobbled on the landing and my knees buckled right out from under me, causing me to roll onto my back like a goddamn turtle. I rolled back up on my feet again just as quickly, brushed my ass off, and peered around to make sure Jeremiah hadn't noticed. Indigo gave me an unimpressed look.

"You good?" Jeremiah asked mildly. The brim of his cowboy hat obscured his face as he worked at the knots securing the packs to Ruby's saddle.

Swear to god, that man had eyes in the back of his head. He didn't miss a damn thing. "I'm good," I chirped back brightly. "My legs forgot how to work, that's all."

It was hard to tell if that sound he made was a muffled laugh or a grunt of effort. I decided I didn't care. I was new to all this outdoorsy shit, but I didn't mind looking like a fool while I figured it out. There was a time I didn't know how to pose for a camera or roast a chicken either, and look at me now: a master of both. I liked a challenge.

The moment I loosened Indigo's girth, he let out a big sigh and bobbed his head. "You're welcome," I crooned, giving him a brisk pat on the neck. Then I started in on unpacking him.

"It doesn't seem right that I'm sore but Indigo did all the work," I said to Jeremiah as he unloaded the saddle bags and swapped Ruby's bridle for a halter.

"Indigo has eight hundred pounds on you and two extra legs. Plus he's half Arabian, so he was bred for long distances. He's a good pack horse."

Once we'd gotten Indigo and Ruby untacked, Jeremiah secured hobbles to their front legs so they could move around a bit but wouldn't go far.

"Is that how we keep them from running away while we're sleeping?" I asked.

"Nah." He shook his head. "The hobbles slow them down, but they tend to adjust. If we left them like that overnight, we'd wake up to find them long gone. We use a highline. We'll take care of that first and then get the tent set up."

He showed me how to string the rope at chest height

between two trees. Then we clipped lead ropes to Indigo and Ruby's halters and tied them to the line, close enough that they could hang out together, but far enough apart that they couldn't touch.

"It's so beautiful here." I had thought the ranch was the prettiest thing I'd ever seen, but that was only because I hadn't seen *this*.

I pressed my hands into my lower back and arched backward, stretching out the kinks from sitting in a saddle for the last three hours, and took it all in. A green river shimmered about two hundred feet away. Everywhere I looked, jagged peaks met vivid blue sky. Except that one on the far side of the lake that looked like its pointed peak had been lopped off.

"What's the name of that mountain over there?" I asked.

Jeremiah looked where I was pointing. "Squaretop Mountain."

"Fitting."

He grinned. A laugh bubbled out of me. It was the damnedest thing. I should be scared right now, scared of what was waiting for us back at the ranch, but I wasn't. I felt as light as the air rustling the pine needles.

I loved it here. I loved the mountains and the trees and the horses. I loved making breakfast and lunch for the ranch hands and guests.

And the cowboy who had promised to keep me

safe...well, I wouldn't let myself think the L-word where he was concerned.

But I couldn't stop the feeling from taking root deep in my chest.

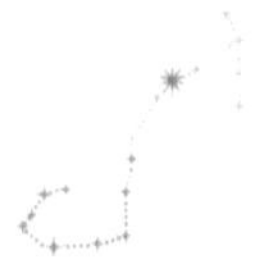

"DID YOU PACK ME A TOOTHBRUSH?" I asked after we had cleaned up from dinner.

"Toothbrush, toothpaste, biodegradable wipes—but don't bury them, we'll pack them out when we leave—and your hairbrush are all in the red toiletries bag."

I rummaged through the bag. Wipes, brush, condoms, toothpaste—aha, there was my toothbrush—

Condoms?

I blinked as my brain caught up with my eyeballs. Condoms. "Jeremiah," I called out, still staring down at the three foil squares. "Why are there condoms in the toiletries bag?"

"Seemed like the obvious place for them," he said in a matter-of-fact way, like we were discussing dental floss instead of the possibility of him losing his virginity, but he rubbed his palms on his jeans and there was a wash of color cresting his cheekbones. "We don't have to use them, though. I figured it would be better to have them than not."

I considered that, tilting my head. "I've always used condoms, but I'm on the pill. Didn't want to risk a faulty condom, but mostly I hate getting my period and sometimes I just want to opt out, you know? Anyway, I was tested for everything at my last gyno appointment. No diseases. And you're a virgin, so...No, we don't have to use them."

"I..." His voice trailed off and he huffed a laugh, spearing his fingers through his hair and tugging. "Hell, Lennon. I meant, we don't have to have sex if you don't want to. With everything going on right now, I'd understand if you wanted to slow things down. I wasn't trying to get out of wearing a condom."

"Oh."

We stood there awkwardly, looking at each other peripherally without allowing a full-on collision. It was all I could do not to burst out of my skin. I could feel my heart beating in my throat, in my fingertips. My palms were starting to sweat.

I was *nervous*. Like I was the virgin here, not him.

Maybe because I had never done it with all these *feelings* swirling inside me. This was uncharted territory for me.

I needed to pull myself together. I wanted to make this good for him. Thirty-eight years he'd waited for this. He didn't need his first time to be with a nervous wreck.

"Jeremiah." My voice came out steadier than my

heartbeat, much to my relief. "I want to, tonight, with you. And if you also want that, then I want your first time to be the full experience. If that's what you want." Christ. How many times could I say *want*?

He rubbed his bottom lip, finally looking at me. "I want that."

"Good." I crossed the four feet of dirt and grass that separated us and kissed him lightly on the lips. "Then that's what you get."

He swallowed hard. "Now?"

I chuckled softly. "Whenever you want."

He glanced around like he was making sure we were alone. The sun had dipped behind the mountains, leaving a velvety purple twilight. Birdsong had been replaced by the hum of crickets.

"I want to watch the stars come out with you." He pressed his forehead to mine. "Can we do that?"

"Yes. We can do that."

We unzipped both sleeping bags, spread one out on the ground next to a fallen log we could use as a backrest, and pulled the other one over top of us. He draped an arm around my shoulder and I snuggled into him, resting my cheek on his chest.

"Do you know any constellations?" I asked.

His body shook with laughter. "You have no idea how glad I am that you asked that."

I craned my neck to look at his face. "Why?"

"Because until a month ago, I could reliably find the

Big Dipper, but that was about it. And then I saw a pretty girl standing outside in the tiniest pajamas, looking at the stars, and wouldn't you know it, I found myself a new hobby."

"You did not!" I pushed off him a little so I could see him better.

He grinned. "I did. I downloaded an app on my phone and practiced every night. Now I don't even need the app. Are you impressed?"

"Impressed? *Jeremiah*. I am delighted." I leaned in so my lips grazed his earlobe. "Tell me all about the constellations, so when I fuck you under the stars I know all their names."

I heard the hitch in his breath, felt the flex of his hand on my thigh. It was the only warning I had before he hauled me into his lap. He kissed me, hot and desperate, like I was the oxygen he needed to breathe. I twisted so we faced each other, my thighs straddling his hips.

I couldn't get enough of him. His slick tongue against mine. The scrape of his callused fingers on my ribs beneath my shirt. And then my shirt was gone, my bra was gone, and Jeremiah leaned back against the fallen log and stared at me with a look of pure awe.

"Fuck, Lennon." He swallowed audibly. "*Fuck*."

His eyes moved over me like he was trying to take in everything at once. I felt his gaze like a physical caress.

The evening air chilled my skin and I craved the warmth of his hands.

"Touch me," I whispered. "Please touch me."

There was a tremor in his fingertips as he grazed my jaw. "I have to tell you something, Lennon."

"Now? Can't it wait until morning?" I didn't want to talk. I wanted to take off his clothes.

"It has to be now. Before..." His breath shuddered as I covered his hands with mine and brought them to my breasts. "No unclean thing can enter the kingdom of heaven. You, Lennon...you're my heaven."

His words set off an earthquake inside me. Broke all my jagged pieces apart and fit them back together in a new shape. I was left rearranged from it. The way this man treated me...it altered everything I thought I knew.

I kissed his temple, his nose, his lips. "There is nothing you can say that will make me want you less."

His eyes met mine. "I killed my uncle in cold blood."

His words shocked the hell out of me. I sat back and looked at him. With anyone else, that might have given me pause. But I had never known anyone who felt the weight of his own soul as keenly as this man. "I'm sure he deserved it."

He laughed hoarsely and lowered his forehead to my chest. "You can't absolve me without hearing my whole confession."

"Then tell me."

"When they banished me, my uncle promised to watch over my sister. Ensure she found a husband who was godly and kind. I believed him. Trusted him. I sneaked into the compound to see her before I went to basic training. By then I'd been out for long enough that I understood it was a cult and had no interest in returning to that life. I wanted Hannah to come back with me—my foster parents said they'd take her in. But she refused. She was still just a kid, and this was all she'd ever known. So I left her a sealed envelope with money and instructions for how to contact me. Two years later she used it."

I held his hands between us, wanting to comfort him. "You went and got her."

He nodded. "She was already married. Fourteen fucking years old, and my uncle made her his fourth wife."

My stomach roiled. I couldn't speak.

"I took her back with me. Got her settled in a new life. I wanted to be named her guardian, but with all the travel I did, it was better for her to stay with my foster parents. I stayed there with her when I was home. And then I heard he was taking a new wife. Thirteen years old." His hands clenched around mine. "Holly covered for me when I went AWOL. Rowed him out to the middle of the lake and pushed him in. Told him he could confess to the FBI, or he could keep swimming." His shoulders rose on a deep breath. "He drowned."

My heart ached for Jeremiah. He had carried the

guilt for so long. "But he didn't have to. Your uncle made a choice."

"I'm not sorry," he rasped.

"Neither am I." I kissed his bowed head.

His gaze snapped to mine, seeking.

I wasn't a religious person, but I'd seen enough bumper stickers proclaiming *JESUS LOVES YOU!* to understand the gist of it. We were born in sin and kept right on sinning until we drew our last breath. No one *earned* a place in heaven. It was given through grace.

I couldn't give him absolution. Forgiveness wasn't mine to give even if I wanted to. I wasn't the judge and jury of his life. But I could give him something else. The words that had terrified me earlier bloomed in my chest.

I held his face in my hands. His heartbreakingly beautiful face. "Look at me."

His eyelids fluttered open. He swallowed as our gazes locked.

"I love you, Jeremiah." And then I said it again. "I love you."

34

JEREMIAH

Lennon was more than heaven. She was my salvation.

The truth had set me free, and when I kissed her again, it was with the knowledge that this time, I wasn't going to stop until I had emptied myself inside her.

My heart beat a frantic pace in my chest. Her mouth was hot and open over mine, and I wanted in. Her mouth, her pussy, her enormous fucking heart that brought me back to life. I wanted in everywhere. It terrified me, this all-consuming need to possess her in every way I can.

Normally I hated feeling exposed. Maybe it was how I was raised to believe that bodies were shameful and to be kept covered and out of sight. At the compound, we wore long sleeves and pants even in the high heat of summer. But now, here, with the mountains and river bearing witness, I craved it. I wanted her touch on every inch of my skin. I reached behind me, grabbed hold of my shirt, and tugged it over my head in one swift motion.

Immediately her hands started exploring with feather light touches. Her fingertips traced my collar bones, then sifted through the sparse hair on my pecs. It was such a fucking relief to finally have her hands on me that I almost wept. I kissed the curve of her neck, then sucked gently at her skin as I breathed in her scent. Fresh air, sweat, Lennon.

Her breasts filled my palms to overflowing. I squeezed, learning the shape of them, then dipped my head to kiss one nipple and then the other. Her head tipped back on a quiet moan. It made me greedy for her. I loved the way she pushed into my touch. Those sweet little sounds she made. I rubbed my lips against the stiff bud of her nipple, then bit gently, just enough to make her squirm on my lap. She liked the nip of pain with her pleasure, judging from the way her hand dove into my hair to hold me against her.

My jeans were too tight for me to comfortably be this hard, so I eased her backward onto the sleeping bag and stood. She watched me shuck my jeans, and then with her gaze locked on mine and a small smile hovering on her lips, she slowly flipped open the fly of her own and wiggled her pants and underwear down her hips and kicked them aside.

Fuck, she was pretty. I could have looked at her all night.

"Get down here before I freeze to death," she ordered.

I couldn't let that happen. I lowered myself to my side next to her and pulled the blanket over us. I couldn't stop touching her. So many fucking curves. Her shoulder, her breasts, the dip of her waist, the flair of her hips. Her skin was so smooth, so soft, that I stroked her again and again like she was a cat.

"Jeremiah," she purred. She nipped at my earlobe, then wiggled closer. With a little smirk, she playfully walked her fingers over my side and then pressed her palm to my spine. "Come here."

"Where?" I nuzzled her neck.

She parted her legs and put pressure on my spine. "*Here*."

With a laugh, I rolled on top of her, settling my hips between her thighs.

And then I stopped breathing. My cock was nestled along the slick channel between her legs, so hard I could feel it throbbing between us. I couldn't help but grind myself harder against her, just to ease the ache.

"Oh, *fuck*." The word gusted from her lips. "If you keep doing that, I'm going to come before you get inside me."

"Maybe that's a good thing. I don't think I'm going to last very long."

She laughed, pushing my hair back from my forehead. "Then we'll do it again. We have all night."

Gritting my teeth, I rested my weight on my elbows and peered down at her. I was shaking with need, my skin damp with sweat despite the cool air. Always shaking with this woman. Back when my job meant facing death regularly, my hands had been steady as a rock. Lennon knocked me off balance and shook me to my core.

I needed to be inside her. But the ground was hard beneath the sleeping bag, and I had to know she was comfortable while I could still form a coherent thought. "Is this okay for you? Do you need—"

"I need *you*." She arched up and kissed me hard on the mouth. "Please, Jeremiah."

I sighed with relief and pushed my hips back until the aching tip of my dick notched against her warm, wet opening. The earth stopped moving. The forest held its breath. My heart threatened to pound right out of my chest.

"Lennon," I whispered, my gaze desperately searching hers.

Her lips curved. "Jeremiah."

Her fingers danced down my spine to the curve of my ass. She pressed the heel of her palm there, urging me to move. I pushed in, her body yielded, and a ravaged groan tore from my throat.

I pushed in deeper until her pussy restricted and her breath stuttered. I pulled back, and fuck, that felt every bit as good, but my body wouldn't let me savor it before it demanded I thrust in again. Harder, deeper, more. The urgency to be inside her was like nothing I had ever experienced before. It was primal and desperate. A gun to my head couldn't have stopped me now.

And then she made a sound that wasn't entirely pleasure and I froze in place, my stomach dropping into a black hole. Fuck, had I hurt her? "Lennon?"

"You're so *big*. Hang on a second."

She huffed as she shifted her hips, widening her legs and changing the angle just a little. Suddenly everything felt even better.

I sank the rest of the way home with a deep groan. "Oh, *fuck*, honey."

"Mmm," she agreed. "Just like that. I love being stuffed full of your cock."

My dick jumped eagerly at her words and I gasped. "Don't say shit like that. I'll spill."

"Oh, yeah?" A devilish smirk tilted her lips. "Your cock—"

I clapped a hand over her mouth, but that was a mistake. She sucked my middle and index finger between her lips and fucked my fingers with her tongue.

I felt it everywhere. My fingers, my dick, the base of my spine.

"You're going to be the death of me."

With her eyes on mine, she slowly slid my fingers from her mouth. "You can't die now. I haven't come yet."

Her slick walls clenched around me and I squeezed my eyes shut and held perfectly still, gritting my teeth. Tight. She was so fucking tight. Heat licked up my skin. *Not yet, not yet. Fuck. Not yet.* When I had myself under control, I opened my eyes.

"Tell me how."

"I need pressure here." She canted her hips as she spoke, rubbing her pussy against me. "Push up when you thrust—*yes.*" She hissed a breath. "Oh, god, yes. Like that."

I did it again, my gaze locked on her face, riveted by the pleasure I saw there. Again, and she whimpered. Again, and again, and again, until her nails dug into my back and her teeth bit down on my shoulder. Her pussy convulsed around me and my balls drew tight. She whispered my name and it reverberated like a thunder-clap inside me.

I pounded into her until I came hard enough to see stars. For one blinding moment, I felt shattered, a million pieces of me scattered to the universe.

But there was her hand trailing my spine. There was her smell. There was her voice, murmuring my name. I wasn't scattered to the universe. I was hers. Always hers.

"I love you, Lennon."

"I love you, Lennon."

35

LENNON

"HOW IS THAT THE MILKY WAY IF EARTH IS ACTUALLY part of the Milky Way?" I nestled in the crook of Jeremiah's shoulder as we took in the heavens.

"All the stars we can see with our eyes are part of the Milky Way, but that's the Galactic Center. It's the brightest part. We probably call it the Milky Way because it sounds better than Galactic Center."

"Oh." My fingers curled against his chest. My eyelids felt heavy. "What's that red star? Is it a planet?"

"Not a planet. That's Antares. It's part of Scorpius."

"And what's that one?"

"Which one?"

I flicked my wrist at the sky. "*That* one."

There was a pause while he shifted beneath me.

Then he laughed softly. "Your eyes aren't even open, honey."

"Hmm," I agreed, snuggling closer.

I fell asleep with a smile on my face.

I woke up the same way, even though my hips were sore from hours of riding followed by hours of sleeping on the hard ground, because the ground wasn't the only thing hard this morning. Jeremiah's mustache tickling my inner thigh was my new favorite way to wake up.

"What are you doing?" I asked, even though it as perfectly obvious what he was doing.

He sent me a wicked grin. "Breakfast is the most important meal of the day."

He was different this morning. Seeing him like this made me realize I had never seen this man truly relaxed before. He was composed. Serious. Always responsible. But now it was like some weight had been lifted from his shoulders and he could breathe a little deeper. He savored my pussy with languid strokes of his tongue like we had all the time in the world.

An orgasm slid through me like a rolling wave. It was as gentle and relentless as the ocean, a slow-rising tide of heat and pleasure that somehow left me both satisfied and needy. My pussy was aching and empty and I needed him to fill it.

He stalked up my body, blue-gray eyes glittering with intent, and kissed me slow and deep. I could taste myself in his mouth. Every glide of his tongue against mine made my pussy clench desperately.

He rubbed his hard length against my clit, teasing me until I couldn't take anymore. I pushed on his shoulders. I didn't have a chance in hell of moving this bear of a man, but he allowed it, rolling onto his back so I could climb on top of him.

I reached between us, palmed his dick and swiped my thumb over the weeping slit. Kept my gaze on his as I lapped the moisture with my tongue. His hips jerked beneath me.

"Dammit, honey. Don't make me spill before I get inside you."

I leaned forward, bracing myself on his shoulder with one hand, and used my other hand to guide his cock to my entrance. "When we're home and have access to a shower, that's exactly what I'm going to make you do. I'm going to make you come all over me."

His groan was deep and desperate. "Fuuuuuuck."

Slowly I lowered myself on his body. Together we watched his thick cock disappear inside my pussy. I paused, then lifted up and slid back down again. Rolled my hips. Did it all again. Slowly.

His brow furrowed with intense concentration and his teeth sank into his bottom lip. With one hand on my hip to hold me steady, he slipped his other hand between us and found my clit with his thumb.

My back arched and my eyes damn near rolled out the back of my head with ecstasy. "Oh, my *god*."

I moved faster, harder. So did his thumb.

And then my second orgasm crested over me. I fell forward, hands clawing at the hard swells of his shoulders, and slammed my hips down on his as hard as I could, rocking against his hand.

His control snapped. He wrapped his arms around me, crushed me to his body, and bucked his hips up into me with a ferocity that sent another orgasm straight on the heels of my last. With a long, low groan, he bucked one more time, and warmth flooded inside me.

"Gunff," I mumbled against his throat.

His arms loosened their hold, letting me breathe. We panted in each other's arms several moments longer. His body was hard and safe beneath mine. The sun warmed my skin. I wanted to purr with contentment.

I never wanted to leave this man.

36

JEREMIAH

RIDING SOUTH TOWARD THE RANCH FELT LIKE RIDING straight into a headwind. Everything in me screamed to turn around, to hunker down in the mountains with Lennon until the danger had passed. Whatever was waiting for us back at the ranch, I'd rather take my chances out here with the mountain lions. Mountain lions might have teeth the size of my thumb, but at least they weren't evil postcard-writing motherfuckers.

I glanced back over my shoulder for the twentieth time since we had started down the trail. There was no reason for me to believe that Lennon was anywhere other than right behind me. I could hear the steady clip-clop of Indigo's hooves on the dirt, for fuck's sake. But still, I couldn't stop myself from checking, just to be sure.

"We're almost there, aren't we?" Lennon called. "I'm pretty sure I recognize that tree. The one that looks like it's going for a run."

I laughed at her description of the large evergreen with an arch hollowed out at the bottom of its trunk. "We should be back at the ranch in another ten minutes."

She was quiet for a moment. "Someone would have called you if my stalker set the ranch on fire, right? No bloody rampages or anything like that in our absence?"

"Liam said everything's been quiet since we left. Exactly what we expected to happen. The ranch isn't his target. You are."

"So are you."

We didn't say anything else the rest of the way home.

Lennon was uncharacteristically quiet as we untacked the horses. We set them free in the pasture and then headed straight for the lodge. Not taking any chances, I did a quick sweep of the apartment, even though I had left the door locked and there was no sign of a forced entry.

"Give me your phone, honey. We're putting Life 360 on it. Should have done that days ago," I muttered as she handed it over.

"You, too," she snapped.

My eyebrows went up. "What's going on, Lennon? Twenty-four hours ago, you were ready to drag this jackass out of hiding by his ball sack."

"I'm scared, Jay. I'm scared he's going to go after you instead of me. Last night changed things. I don't know how to explain it, but the thought of something happening to you makes me…" She swallowed, blinking. "I don't care if you're a SEAL. I need to know you're safe."

I had to bite back a grin as I pulled her into my arms. Of course I didn't like Lennon being scared, but I had to admit it felt good that she cared so much. "All right. Whatever you want." The tension eased from her muscles somewhat, but there was still that worried crease between her eyebrows. I smoothed it with my lips. "Everything is going to be okay."

"You don't know that." She leaned into me. "I'm so sorry I got you into this mess."

"I'm not."

"What?"

"I'm not saying I'm *glad* there's a psycho after you. I'm saying, consider the alternative. No stalker means you'd still be in New York. And I'd still be a virgin." I nuzzled her neck, brushing my mustache right where she was ticklish. She squirmed and giggled, and I grinned.

"Now, that would be a shame," she murmured. "That dick of yours is too good to waste on celibacy."

"I'm glad you think so, honey."

Just as I finished getting our phones set up with the tracking app, my phone buzzed with a text from Holly.

HOLLY:

Ducky is ready to talk when you are.

Ducky—who everyone else knew as Ciaran Doyle—had been one of Holly's university professors long ago, but he also moonlighted as a consultant with the FBI. Profiling was his specialty. Particularly psychopaths. Before Lennon and I had headed out yesterday, Holly had suggested reaching out to him and getting his take on who we might be dealing with.

I typed a quick message back.

Me:

Meet me at the office in five minutes.
Bring Mateo.

Sliding my phone into my back pocket, I glanced up to find Lennon watching me shrewdly.

"What's going on?" she asked.

"Holly and Mateo are waiting for me." I handed her phone back to her. "Stay here. Take a shower. I'll be back as soon as I can."

She glanced at the time on her phone. "I might go down to the kitchen and help Cecily and Amos clean up from lunch after I take a quick shower. I feel bad that I left yesterday without telling either of them I wouldn't be there this morning."

I didn't like the idea of her leaving the apartment

without me, but the kitchen was still in the lodge, and Amos and Cecily would be with her. "You'll keep your location on and text me if anything feels weird. No matter how silly. Got it?"

"Got it." She rolled up on her toes and kissed me. "And the same goes for you, so don't you forget it. Don't go anywhere by yourself."

"Understood." I dropped another kiss on her upturned face. "I love you, Lennon."

MATEO AND HOLLY were already talking to Ciaran on Holly's laptop when I pushed into the office. It looked like he was calling from his house in Seattle. I could see the Puget Sound shimmering out the window.

I scooted a chair between Holly and Mateo so I could see the screen. "Ciaran. Thanks for helping us. I know this isn't the kind of case that usually interests you." Ciaran was highly educated, extremely intelligent, and easily bored.

He pushed his shaggy gray hair off his forehead and smiled. "Anything for Holly, of course. I must say, I'm surprised you haven't had much luck. Given Ms. Graves's choice of profession, and her particular style in that profession, I'd say you're looking for a white male, aged thirty-five to fifty, unmarried." He arched an eyebrow. "I hate to state the obvious, but have you looked into her subscribers? I'm sure a man of Mateo's talents should have no trouble with that."

I glanced at Mateo. He shook his head. "We're looking for someone with ties to the ranch, or at least fifty miles of here. All her male subs check out."

"The postcards don't give us much to go on, either. It's a shame she didn't keep the others." Ciaran adjusted his glasses. "What can Ms. Graves tell us? Does she remember anything unique about them?"

"Nothing unique," I said. "Lennon said the postcards seemed friendly at first. She didn't consider it stalking until they took a turn in tone and kept showing up even when she moved."

"When did the tone shift occur?"

"Anytime she was dating someone. He'd tell her she made bad choices when it came to men."

That got Ciaran's attention. He leaned forward, tilting his head. "Bad choices? That was the phrase he used?"

"According to Lennon."

"He didn't call her a slut? Anything like that?"

"Lennon didn't mention it."

"Then he didn't." Ciaran steepled his fingers. "Interesting."

"How so?" Holly asked.

"Well, it changes everything, doesn't it? You're not

looking for a lonely middle-aged white man. You're looking for someone lonely, yes. Unmarried, I stand by that. Likely doesn't have children or other family, either. But you're not looking for a man."

My eyes narrowed.

"You're looking for a woman."

37

LENNON

THE KITCHEN WAS QUIETER THAN USUAL WHEN I PUSHED through the swinging door. For a moment I had a horrible thought. What if the stalker was taking out the kitchen staff one by one? First Miguel, then Cecily or Amos, then—

The freezer door opened and Cecily stepped out.

"Lennon. You're back." Cecily kicked the freezer shut behind her. "Nice of you to tell us you wouldn't be here this morning."

I winced at her flat tone. It was so unlike the bubbly Cecily who usually greeted me. "I'm sorry. I should have." Any excuse I offered would be a lie, so I didn't give one.

She studied me for a moment, her lips pursed. Then

she let out a sigh. "I mean, you *are* still a guest. But I thought we were friends, too."

"We are friends." I reached impulsively for her hand and gave it a squeeze. "I love working in the kitchen with you."

That brought her familiar smile back. "You're not really going horse packing for three weeks, are you? Because Liam said you were, but that doesn't make any sense. You know it's exactly like camping, right? There are no showers out there, Lennon. And you have to pack out your toilet paper. That's three weeks of used toilet paper you're carrying around with you."

I laughed. I hated lying, but we had to stick to the plan if we were going to flush this fucker out. "I'm really doing it. I feel like I need an adventure, you know? A third-life crises, if you will." I glanced around. "Where's Amos?"

"He stepped outside for a phone call. He'll be back in a minute. At least, he better be. If that man leaves me with mopping the floor after I already did the dishes, I'll put laxative in his orange juice." Cecily scooped the large crate of eggs from the counter. "Get the door for me, will you?"

I twisted the handle and yanked it open, then kept standing there as she set the crate on a metal shelf.

"You don't have to hold it open," she said. "It doesn't lock from the inside, remember? I just need to make a note of what we're running low on. But you can start mopping if you really want something to do."

"On it!" I chirped. The last twenty-four hours had left me sore and tired, but I was too grateful that Cecily was still talking to me to say no to chores.

I grabbed the yellow wheely bucket thing and used the mop to steer it to the sink so I could fill it with hot water. The outside door opened as I squatted to look under the sink for the soap. "Hey, Amos, where do we keep the—"

"Lennon Graves?"

I froze, the hairs on the back of my neck standing at attention. *He sounds like a mobster*, my mom's voice echoed in my head. *Italian*.

Slowly I pushed to my feet. I turned to see a stocky man around my height wearing unassuming jeans, a striped button-down shirt, and a tan blazer. He didn't look like a mobster, although to be fair, I had never actually seen a mobster outside of movies. But I knew...I *knew*. This wasn't my stalker. This was about Benny.

I smiled despite the queasy feeling in my stomach. "Lennon isn't here right now. If you give me your name, I'll let her know you're looking for her."

He chuckled and pulled a photograph out of his pocket. He held it up at eye level, his gaze flicking from me to the photograph and back again. "Lennon Graves."

This time it wasn't a question. I swallowed. Shit.

"There are a lot of people looking for you." He curled his fingers at me. "Let's go, honey."

Annoyance surged. "I'm not your honey," I bit out. Behind him, the freezer door cracked open and Cecily peered out. Her brow furrowed. I tried to send her a telepathic message with my eyes while not tipping him off that Cecily was behind him. *Stay put. Danger!* "And I'm not going anywhere with you," I added loudly, hoping Cecily would realize something was wrong. All I had to do was stall him until Amos got back. Where the hell was that man?

"Hector said you were a spicy one." His mouth twisted in amusement at the shock in my face. "Oh, haven't you heard? Benny's dead, honey. Hector sang like a bird to save his own hide. Told us all about you."

"Benny's...dead." I struggled to get the words out. It couldn't be true. Could it? Fuck. *Fuck.* My chest felt too tight to breathe and my vision blurred. "No. Please."

"Listen, I understand. We all liked Benny, okay? But he knew too much. And you know too much. Now, let's go." He touched my elbow.

I yanked away from him. "No! I'm not going!" Maybe if I shouted loud enough, Jeremiah would hear me.

His palm cracked against my cheek and I gasped at the blinding hot pain. My hand flew to my face. *Motherfucker.*

I blinked until my vision came back into focus. "I'm not going anywhere," I gritted out.

He opened his blazer. My gaze immediately dropped to the black gun holstered on his belt. "Yes, you are."

Fuckity fuck fuck fuck.

"What happens if I don't?"

He tilted his head like the question confused him.

"You're here to kill me, right?" I prodded. The freezer door opened again. I didn't let my eyes look anywhere but his. "So why don't you just shoot me right here?"

"Someone wants to talk to you first. But I will shoot you if I have to, and anyone else who gets in my way. Or you can come quietly, and no one else has to get hurt."

"*Someone's* going to get hurt." Before I could think better of it, I shoved the bucket straight at his knees as hard as I could.

It wasn't much, but it gave Cecily the opportunity she needed and she took it. She swung the frozen ham hock with all of her might, hitting him right in the temple. He crumpled to the floor. His skull hit the clay tiles with a loud crack.

"Oh, my god." I stared in shock as red slowly pooled beneath his head. I pressed my trembling fingertips to my mouth. "Oh, my god."

Cecily dropped the ham and grabbed my elbow. "We have to go! Now!"

I blinked at her. "We need to find Jeremiah."

"We will. But he didn't come here alone. We'll go somewhere safe, and call Jeremiah from there. Okay?"

She tugged me toward the door. "We can't stay here, Lennon. Hurry!"

Dazed, I let her lead me outside. We nearly tripped over Amos's prone body and I let out a sharp shriek. "Is he dead?"

"Lennon!" Cecily snapped. "Do you want to get murdered? Let's fucking *go!*"

"Wait." I dropped to a squat and pressed my fingers to his pulse. "He's alive. Just knocked out."

Cecily looked around nervously. "They must have someone standing lookout close by. My van is right there. We'll get in, lock the door, and call Jeremiah. Deal?"

I nodded.

"Then run!" She gave me a little shove, and we took off across the parking lot, gravel spraying behind us. Cecily beeped the fob and the side door rolled open. "Get in."

I climbed in. This wasn't just a van; it was a functioning living space. I crawled forward. Rope. Duct tape. A sheet. I frowned. That was weird. "What—"

Strong arms grabbed me from behind. Before I could struggle, something zinged through my body, making my muscles convulse.

"What the hell kind of mess did you get yourself into this time?" a familiar female voice whispered in my ear. "I keep telling you, you have lousy taste in men."

Pain bloomed in my temple, and then everything went dark.

38

JEREMIAH

"The good news is, Lennon only has four female subs," Mateo said. "The bad news is that none of their names are familiar. We've got Allison Watts from Maine, Emery Ballston from Illinois, Dana Matthews from Texas, and Lisa DeWalt from Florida. None of them have any connection to Wyoming, as far as I can tell. I can keep digging, but we might have hit a dead end on Lennon's subs."

I scrubbed a hand over my face. "Dammit. What kind of self-respecting stalker turns up his—"

"Her," Holly corrected.

"*Her* nose at having that kind of access? Lennon made herself available to subs three times a week, and you're telling me her stalker had no interest in that?" I shook my head. "It doesn't make sense."

"I'll keep digging." Mateo spun his chair back to his computer. "Maybe I'm missing something."

I pulled up the tracker app on my phone. Lennon was still in the kitchen. My breath came a little easier. "Maybe Ciaran sent us on a wild goose chase. He could be wrong. Maybe the stalker isn't a woman and we're wasting time focusing on the wrong thing."

"He's not wrong," Holly said. "He's never wrong."

Mateo pushed up his glasses and squinted at the screen. "Everyone's wrong sometime. But we haven't ruled out this theory yet."

I leaned over Mateo's shoulder. "See if you can pull up their driver's license. Maybe their faces will be familiar."

"I already crosschecked their names with our guest records and former employee records. No hits. But I should be able to hack into the DMV and find their photo IDs. The Russians do it all the time. How hard can it be?"

Holly snorted. "Wow. I feel so safe."

"No one's information has been safe since 1999. You know that."

Anxiety got the better of me. I pushed to my feet. "Can we fucking focus, please? We have a goddamn stalker to catch. *Before* he catches Lennon," I added pointedly.

"She," Holly corrected automatically.

I ground my molars together. Lennon's stalker was a fucking woman? I couldn't seem to wrap my mind around it. It hadn't even occurred to me. What else hadn't occurred to me? What else had I missed?

I checked my phone again. Lennon was still in the kitchen. At least she was safe.

Seb burst through the door. "Lennon—"

My blood turned to ice. "She's not here. She's in the kitchen." I looked at the app again to verify. Still hadn't moved.

Seb's gaze swiveled around the room like he didn't believe it. "She's not in the kitchen. Fuck! Amos is down. Liam is calling paramedics. There's a man—he's dead. I don't know who the fuck he is, but he's dead."

Lennon. My lips parted but I couldn't force her name past them.

"Lennon is gone. Cecily, too. I don't know if they managed to hide, or if someone took them. But they're gone, Jay."

Panic punched my chest hard and fast. I tried to breathe around it and only managed a shallow gasp. In through the nose, hold, out through pursed lips. I repeated the instructions to myself that I had given to others countless times. Lennon needed me to focus. I wasn't any good to her if I passed out.

I breathed.

And then I was on the move, Holly at my heels.

"Stay," I barked to Mateo. "Keep looking. We need faces."

I burst through the kitchen doors at a run. My head swiveled as I took in the scene. A body on the floor. Blood everywhere. Amos slumped against the wall, holding an ice pack to his head, his knees drawn up to his chest and his feet flat.

Liam stood next to him, his phone pressed to his ear. He covered the mouthpiece with his palm. "Sheriff," he said.

I nodded and kept moving to the back door. There were a few cars parked in the gravel lot behind the lodge. I took a photo of what was there to check against our records. My gaze roamed over the ground. Gravel didn't tend to leave footprints, but I could make out the faintest disturbance leading away from building. I followed it, my gaze sweeping back and forth.

And then I saw it, two feet away, glinting in the sunshine.

Lennon's phone.

Everything in me seized. For a moment I couldn't move. Couldn't think. All I could do was feel. Terror. I was consumed by it.

Focus. My training kicked in. I picked up her phone and scanned the area again. No blood that I could see, other than the little patch by the door. It was from Amos. On autopilot, I headed back inside.

"Amos." I dropped to a squat next to him. "You okay?"

He grimaced. "Got hit from behind. Didn't see him. I'm sorry."

"Not your fault. Was Cecily here?"

He nodded, wincing. His eyes closed. "She was here. If he hurt her, I'll kill him."

I glanced over at the body. "I think that's been taken care of. Looks like someone whacked him with a ham hock."

His eyes squinted open. "*My* ham hock? I had plans for that."

His words were slurred. I straightened and looked at Liam. "Concussion."

He nodded. "His eyes couldn't follow my finger."

"Come get me when the sheriff arrives."

I stalked back to the office. My throat felt like it was closing up. My limbs felt heavy and numb. Where the hell was Lennon?

Mateo looked up as I entered. "I printed out three IDs. Didn't recognize any of them. Working on getting into the Texas DMV now. Here we go—I'm in."

Mateo's fingers moved quickly over the keyboard, and a moment later, Dana Matthews appeared on the screen.

All the air left my lungs.

"Fuck," Mateo whispered.

The license said Dana Matthews.

But the face was Cecily Shepherd.

39

LENNON

EVERYTHING HURTS AND I'M DYING.

The thought fluttered through my aching brain before I was fully conscious. That dull, steady throb was my entire existence. Maybe I could opt out of being alive for a while. Come back to life when it didn't suck so much. Was unconsciousness really that bad? I pushed back from the pain. The darkness was lovely.

But there was no Jeremiah in the darkness.

I grabbed hold of the pain and dragged myself toward it. My eyelids fluttered but didn't open. It was like they were glued shut. I tried again. Focused on the pain. Moved toward it.

My eyelids blinked open, scraping against my eyeballs that felt as gritty as if someone had poured a bucket of sand in them. Something fuzzy and purple was under my face. A blanket? No, it was shag carpet. Where was I? It was too dark to see much of anything.

I jerked upright and immediately regretted it. The movement caused pain to sear through me. I screamed and clutched my head. There was a lump near my temple. My hand came away slightly sticky. Blood.

What the fuck was going on?

I squeezed my eyes shut and tried to remember. The kitchen. A man. Had he taken me? No, wait, there was someone else—

A door opened behind me and mellow light illuminated the darkness. "Oh, good, you're awake." The familiar female voice was full of relief.

I turned slowly, not making the same mistake twice, and squinted at who stood there. "Cecily?" I croaked. "Are you...are you hurt, too? What's going on?"

"It's going to be okay, Lennon. I'm here now. Here, take this." She handed me two brown pills and an unopened bottle of water. "For the headache."

Gingerly, I took the pills and water from her and unscrewed the bottle cap. Everything felt surreal. I couldn't make sense of what was happening.

She peered closer at the crown of my head. "Yikes, that's a nasty bump. Sorry about that, and the stun gun. I really didn't want to hurt you, but I didn't have a choice. Did you know chloroform isn't like what you see in movies? It takes a while to take effect. You can't just plop a chloroform rag on someone's face and expect them to pass out. Plus, it's super dangerous."

I swallowed down the pills with a long gulp of water while she continued her monologue.

"I guess every method of making someone lose consciousness is at least a *little* dangerous, though. I mean, that guy who attacked you? That was crazy. Boom, dead. Good thing he gave me a chance to practice. I could have accidentally killed you."

I blinked. *Cecily* had hit me?

She burst out laughing. "The *look* on your face. Sorry, I know it's not funny. I'm a little hyped. All that adrenaline, you know?" She took the bottle back from me and took a sip. At least that meant it wasn't poisoned? "Who was that guy, anyway?"

"The one who attacked me?" I rubbed my too-dry eyes. "I don't know for sure, but I suspect it has to do with my ex in New York. He had some shady business dealings." *Benny.* Oh, god. Nausea roiled my stomach.

Cecily tsked, shaking her head. "What do I keep telling you, Lennon? You have the worst taste in men. The absolute worst."

What do I keep telling you?

The puzzle pieces clicked into place.

"It was you all along. You sent me the postcards."

She laughed. "Of course it was me. But you knew that, right? Deep down, you knew it was me."

I hoped my thoughts weren't evident on my face. *No,*

bitch, I didn't know it was you. If I had, I would have whacked you with a frying pan.

She looked at me with hopeful eyes, waiting. I knew what she wanted me to say. I was so damn good at that. Reading people. Telling them exactly what they wanted to hear, even when they didn't know what that was themselves. Usually I found a way to shape it into something true. Sometimes—like with Jeremiah—true was all it was.

With Cecily, I was going to lie my ass off.

"I knew it was a friend," I said. "I *hoped* it was you."

She pressed her hands to her cheeks, her eyes glistening with unshed tears. "I knew you would understand." With a sniffle, she wiped under her eyes. "Come on. You must be starving."

I eased carefully out of the van with shaky limbs. We were at a clearing of some sort. Dense forest surrounded us, blocking any kind of view that might have helped me get my bearings. Not that I could tell one jagged peak from another. The only mountain I could recognize was Squaretop.

My chest squeezed.

Jeremiah must be so worried—

Jeremiah. I felt my pockets. No phone. Cecily must have taken it. Feeling her gaze on me, I looked up to find her watching me with narrowed, mistrustful eyes. "My phone! Is it in the van? Jeremiah put a tracker on it. He'll be able to find us. We can't stay here."

Her expression cleared immediately and she smiled. "Don't worry. I tossed it back at the lodge. He can't find us."

Jeremiah can find anything. I had to believe that. I had to trust him. My only job now was to stay alive.

I looked around. "Where are we?"

"Somewhere safe. We can hang out here as long as we want. I have plenty of supplies, and we're not too far from civilization. We need to avoid the main roads while people are looking for you."

That was too vague to be helpful, but I nodded.

"Sit." She pointed to a camp chair by the fire ring. "I'll make us some dinner."

I lowered myself into the nylon chair. Cecily bustled around. Her purple ponytail bounced happily as she boiled water on her pocket stove. It made me irrationally furious. I wanted to grab hold of it and smash her face into a tree. Because right now I should be wrapped up in Jeremiah's arms. But I wasn't. I hadn't even had a chance to tell him I wanted to stay. Not for the summer. Forever.

Everything hurt. But that hurt most of all.

"Here." Cecily passed me a container of homemade chocolate chip cookies. "A snack to tide you over until the pasta is ready."

"They're not poisoned, are they?" Her expression turned furious and I realized my mistake. Friends didn't poison each other. "Just kidding!" Forcing a light laugh, I shoved half a cookie into my mouth and chewed.

"It's because of Miguel, isn't it? That's why you don't entirely trust me. I didn't want to hurt him either, just so you know. I flashed my brights at him thinking he would steer into the ditch, not off the fucking cliff."

I nearly choked on my cookie. Jesus. She might actually be insane.

"He would have died without me, you know. I went back and saved him because the idiots at the sheriff department wouldn't do their fucking job."

I brushed crumbs from my lap, my mind racing. "I guess I just don't understand why you did it at all. I've never even met Miguel."

"So you could keep working in the kitchen with me. Duh. Amos hates a crowded kitchen. With Miguel back, he would have pushed you to find something else to do with your time." Cecily dumped a quarter box of pasta into the boiling water. "I really like Amos, but sheesh. Men get in the way. They're always trying to take you from me."

I mentally sifted through her words, searching for clues. Normally, I knew when someone wanted to fuck me. Hell, I made a living off *making* people want to fuck me. But I wasn't getting that vibe from Cecily. Something else was going on here.

Evening faded to night. The stars popped out. A million pricks of light in an inky black canvas.

Back in the van, sharing a lumpy mattress, Cecily gave me an apologetic smile as she handcuffed us together. "I know it's uncomfortable, but I'm not stupid. Jeremiah has some weird hold on you. Men are like a drug. We keep going back even when they're killing us. This is for your own good."

"I understand." I closed my eyes.

Come find me, Jeremiah.

40

JEREMIAH

"You need to eat something." Holly smacked my abs with a protein bar. "Keep your strength up for that twenty-four-hour fuckathon you're going to have when you find her."

Mateo rubbed his eyes under his glasses. "Jesus, Holly. Now is not the time."

"What? I'm being a good friend! Seb, back me up."

I ignored them and kept staring at the map we had tacked to the wall of my living room. Sheriff Sherwood had put out a BOLO on Cecily's van. Law enforcement all over the state had their eyes peeled. I doubted Cecily would drive far. Too risky. She'd hunker down somewhere.

Amos had provided the missing puzzle piece there.

Cecily lived in a built-out camper van. He didn't know where, but he did know that the day Lennon and I got back from camping, Cecily had driven it to work. My guess was she'd planned on grabbing Lennon the second she could. She hadn't been expecting Lennon to get attacked, but it provided her with an opportunity.

I tore open the protein bar and took off the corner with my teeth, still contemplating the map. I didn't taste a single bite.

Right now, we were focused on secluded areas where Cecily could park her van. Trailheads, campsites, back roads, rental cabins. Green tacks denoted areas we had checked. Red tacks were places we hadn't gotten to yet. Right now there were more red than green, but we were making progress.

Wyoming was a big state and sparsely populated. They could be anywhere.

But this was what we did. Holly, Mateo, Seb, Liam, and me. We found people. The only difference this time was that it was personal. Fear for Lennon's safety clouded my head. I couldn't think straight. Couldn't see the clues that I knew were right in front of me.

I had to find her. Desperation clawed in my chest. We'd been at this two days now, and it already felt like a lifetime since I'd had her safe in my arms under the stars.

I'd promised her she'd be safe, and I'd failed her. The knowledge of that nearly buckled my knees. The only thing that kept me upright was knowing that wherever she was, Lennon was alive. Cecily—Dana Matthews—didn't want her dead.

But Cecily wasn't exactly in her right mind, either, and that worried me. Two years ago, her boyfriend had beaten the crap out of her, causing her to miscarry their baby at twenty-one weeks. Cecily had landed in the hospital. I had no idea how she had stumbled onto Lennon's camming account, but she had, and best as we could figure, she'd developed a fixation. A parasocial relationship, Ciaran called it. He believed it was platonic in nature, but that didn't make it any less dangerous.

"There's an illusion of intimacy," he'd explained. "Cecily feels like they've had this very real, very emotional bond for much longer than Lennon has even been truly aware of her existence. If Lennon denies the bond, it is very possible that Cecily will treat it as a betrayal. There's no telling how she'll react. But we do know that she is capable of violence. She's already proven that."

"I think I've got something," Mateo said. We all crowded around. "Cecily has an unpaid speeding ticket for Millhouse Road." He shoved his chair back from the kitchen table and moved to the map. "Right here." He pushed a yellow thumbtack into the spot.

"There's no campground near there," I noted. "Maybe she was on her way to somewhere else."

"No campground, but there's a fire road that turns off from there. See? I checked it out on some hiking websites. Apparently there is a single campsite there. From there, hikers backpack the rest of the way to a fire lookout tower."

My brow furrowed as I studied the map. "Could she get her van to the campsite? Some fire roads are only passable by four wheelers."

"Hikers say yes. It's not very popular because it's so hard to get to. Remote, not enough room for more than one vehicle."

"Perfect for Cecily," I muttered.

"Exactly."

"Let's go."

41

LENNON

TWO DAYS IN AND I WAS STARTING TO FEEL LIKE MAYBE *I* was the crazy one.

Run! every cell in my body screamed at me over and over. Sitting around waiting to be rescued wasn't in my DNA. No one had ever rescued me—except maybe Cecily, but it turned out she was actually kidnapping me, so that probably didn't count.

I rescued myself. That was how I survived. *I* installed the bolt lock on my bedroom door. *I* filed the paperwork to get emancipated. *I* figured out how to pay my bills. And when that creepy Uber driver pulled into an alley that was definitely not the way home, *I* jumped out of the car while it was still moving and ran three blocks on a twisted ankle.

My brain told me to run. My heart told me to stay put and wait for Jeremiah to find me. And when I listened to my heart, my brain conceded that several excellent points were raised.

First of all, I had no idea where I was. As best as I could tell, we'd gotten here on an old fire road. We could be miles away from a real road, miles away from a town. She'd knocked me out cold, so I didn't even know how long it had taken us to drive here.

The odds of me finding help before I starved or froze to death were not good. My survival skills pertained to city streets and creepy men, not rugged terrain and wild animals. If I ran, I'd be making it even harder for Jeremiah to find me.

Secondly, Cecily might be crazy, but she wasn't stupid. She was fairly certain I was still lusting after Jeremiah and that made me a flight risk. She wasn't wrong, and something told me that if I pretended I was over him this early in the game, she wouldn't believe me. I needed to gain her trust. Right now, she kept me handcuffed to her at night, but she didn't tie me up during the day.

No, she locked up my shoes instead.

If I ran, I'd be running barefoot.

Jeremiah would find me. I knew he would. The truth of that thrummed inside me, the only thing that kept me sane. For the first time in my life, I trusted someone else to take care of me and make me safe.

"Do you want to watch *Golden Girls*?" Cecily asked.

"Sure," I said, because who didn't like *Golden Girls*? Anyway, there wasn't anything else to do while I waited to be rescued. I scooted over to make room for her on the bed.

She hit play on her laptop. The theme song filled the van. Cecily nudged me with her elbow, smiling. "That's going to be us someday." She nodded to the screen. "You're Blanche and I'm Rose."

Well, that settled it. Cecily was batshit crazy. In no world was I a Blanche. I was a Sophia through and through. I only dressed like a Blanche.

"You are definitely a Rose," I said. "That's for sure."

That seemed to please her. "What makes you say that?"

"I don't know. You're kind. That's what made you go back to help Miguel. And you have a way of always looking at the bright side of things. Rose-colored glasses, I guess. Except when it comes to men." I paused, studying her. "Did something happen?" I asked carefully.

She frowned, rubbing her belly. "I don't want to talk about it right now."

"Okay. Whenever you're ready, I'm here."

"Thank you." She reached into the mini fridge and pulled out two Diet Cokes and a bag of Skittles. "Here. We can share."

She looked heartbreakingly young, the way she smiled at me. Like watching TV together while eating candy was everything she'd ever wanted. What was going to happen to her when Jeremiah found me? She had hurt Miguel. Taken me against my will. She couldn't go free, but I couldn't imagine her in jail, either. She needed help. Professional help. The kind that came with intensive therapy and drugs.

Five episodes and a Diet Coke later, I couldn't hold it anymore. "I need to pee," I said.

Cecily nodded. She grabbed a roll of toilet paper and we exited the van. "Don't go far," she said with a little smirk at my bare feet.

I rolled my eyes. "Are you sure you wouldn't rather I pee right in front of you? Since you clearly don't trust me."

"Gross!" She wrinkled her nose. "I'm not a perv."

I carefully picked my way over the campsite to the trees for some privacy, wincing as a twig got my toe. I did my business and wiped, then buried the evidence.

A loud bang pierced the air and I yelped, startled. "What the hell was that?" I hollered to Cecily, zipping up my jeans.

"We gotta go, Lennon! Move!" She ran to me and grabbed my elbow to hurry me along.

"My feet!" I protested. "I can't go very fast. What's going on? What was that noise?"

"A booby trap. Back at the turnoff. I set a few bombs to go off—"

"Bombs?" I squeaked. "How?" My heart raced in my chest. Who had set off the trap? Was Jeremiah down there?

"There is nothing you can't learn on the internet." She threw open the passenger side door and impatiently gestured for me to get in. "I know another way out. We need to go. *Now*."

I didn't budge. "Someone could be hurt."

"Yeah, your boyfriend, probably," she bit out. "Let's hope." The venom in her tone made me take a step back. A rock bit into my heel but I didn't flinch.

"I'm not going with you." Panic surged through my veins, but I reined it in. "The stun gun isn't charged. How are you going to get me in that van, Cecily?"

"I don't need a stun gun." She unlatched the glove compartment and pulled out a handgun. Pointed it right at me. "I've got a *real* gun."

Fuck a duck. I really should have seen that coming. This was Wyoming. Everyone had a gun.

I cocked my head, watching her but also listening. The silence worried me. What set off the trap? A deer? A car? A man?

"If you're wondering if I'll actually do it, I will. But I'm a good shot. I'll try not to kill you."

I hoped she meant it. Jeremiah might be bleeding

out right now. Deep in my bones, I knew it was him down there. He found me. I bounced a little on my bare toes. Getting my muscles ready to move.

Fuck, this was going to hurt.

I ran.

42

———

JEREMIAH

"THIS IS, WITHOUT A DOUBT, THE SHITTIEST HOMEMADE bomb I have ever seen." Liam looked absolutely disgusted as kicked the front bumper of his 4Runner out of the way. "It barely did anything."

"There could be more," Seb pointed out. "They might be better."

"At least we know we're in the right place," Mateo said.

I cut the engine and exited the now bumperless car. "We go on foot from here. Stay off the road and stick to the trees. Seb, get a call in to the sheriff and let him know what's happening."

Someone screamed my name. "Jeremiah!"

Lennon. I held still, not even daring to breathe, every cell in my body listening.

"Jeremiah!"

There. It came from over there. I took off in that direction. Fuck, fuck, fuck. Did she know about the traps? Any bomb that could take off a car bumper could do serious damage to a human body. "Lennon!" I roared. "Don't move! I'm coming to you!"

Trees blurred as I ran flat out. Branches scraped at my arms and face, but I didn't care. I could hear the sounds of someone crashing through the trees ahead of me.

"Jeremiah!" Her voice was frantic, desperate.

I ran harder. "Lennon!"

And then there she was. Her eyes widened as she caught sight of me. I barreled straight at her. She leaped the rest of the distance and I caught her in my arms, lifting her off the ground.

"Gun!" she gasped. "Bombs! Traps!" Her hands went all over me, like she was searching for injuries.

"I've got you, honey. I've got you." I was never letting go of her again. "You're safe now." I rained kisses on her cheeks, her nose, her lips, every inch of skin I could find.

"She's not safe with you."

God*damm*it.

I gently lowered Lennon to the ground. She made a whimpering sound as I pushed her behind me. "I'm not the one who kidnapped her or chased her through the woods with a gun, Cecily. That would be you."

"She's not safe with you," Cecily repeated. "You'll hurt her. That's all men know how to do."

"I know why you're scared. I know what he did to you. But that's not going to happen again. Not to you, and not to Lennon. I promise you that." I had to keep her talking. Holly was on her six, Seb was at three o'clock, Mateo at nine. I had the feeling Liam was behind me, but I wasn't about to take my eyes off Cecily to verify that. "Put the gun down, Cecily. You're surrounded. It's over."

Her lips trembled but then she squared her shoulders. "It's over for me, but it's not over for Lennon. I can still save her." She wiggled the gun at me. "Step over there. Away from her."

Lennon fisted her hands in my shirt. "No."

I squeezed her thigh behind me. "It's okay, honey. Let go. I'll do what she says." Holly almost had her.

"*No.*" Lennon moved in front of me. I grabbed her around the waist and tried to haul her back, but she latched on like a monkey. "No. You cannot kill him, Cecily. It would break my heart. The same way someone broke yours. Is that what you want? Do you want to break me?"

The gun lowered slightly. Her eyebrows drew together in confusion. "I—"

Holly pounced.

There was a sickening crack of bone, one sharp scream, and then it was over in less than thirty seconds. Holly held the gun in one hand and Cecily's broken wrist in her other. "We're good!" she called cheerfully. "You okay, Lennon?"

"I'm—" Lennon's voice died as a tremor wracked her body. Her knees buckled.

I caught her, then hefted her into my arms bride style. "Easy there. You're okay."

"I thought..." She buried her face against my chest. "I thought you had gotten blown up."

"Nah. It wasn't a very good bomb."

She choked out a sound that was half laugh, half sob. "I have never been so scared in my life as I was in that moment. Don't ever do that."

"What? Get blown up by your psycho kidnapper?" I joked because if I didn't, I would sit my ass right down in this forest and fall apart. I'd almost lost her.

Later.

Later I could fall apart. Right now it was Lennon's turn. I needed to be the one to hold her together.

"Don't ever die on me, Jeremiah. I mean it. Promise me."

My shirt felt wet. I looked down and saw tears streaming down her face. My girl who had never met an emotion she didn't want to bury six feet under was *crying.* "I'm not going anywhere, Lennon. I can promise you that."

Liam approached. "Sheriff is on his way. Another twenty minutes—" He broke off, frowning. "Lennon, what the fuck happened to your feet?"

43

LENNON

THREE WEEKS LATER

I KICKED my shoes off with a groan that was half agony, half relief, and flopped on the sofa with a tired but happy sigh. A mobster and stalker couldn't take me down, but my mad dash through the woods had resulted in three stitches, a staph infection, and a strained tendon. Doctors had ordered me off my feet for three weeks, which meant that Jeremiah's fulltime job was carrying me around. Neither of us were complaining.

But now I was finally cleared to use my feet again. Today had been my first day back in the kitchen. It had been weird, being there. Memories of Cecily were everywhere. I kept turning our conversations over in my mind, looking for clues. Amos was shaken to his core. He loved Cecily—still did. He'd visited her twice at the in-patient facility where she would be for at least the next year. She was doing okay, considering. I wished I could see her, talk to her, scream at her, hug her. But her doctors said seeing me could set her treatment back. Maybe someday.

Jeremiah entered the apartment smelling like hay and sunshine. He noted my shoes by the door and me on the couch and shook his head. "I told you to ease into it. Don't do a full shift."

"I'm fine. A little sore, that's all." I tilted my face up for a kiss. "How is your day going?"

"Busy. Do you still have your key to the Orion cabin? Someone booked it for August." He dropped his phone on the coffee table, swiped the bottle of lotion, and sat on the couch, pulling my feet into his lap.

I tensed even though his hands felt like magic on my tight, aching feet. We were at the end of July—the end of my reservation. We hadn't talked about what came next. I'd started putting feelers out, figuring out options. Leaving Mercy River was *not* an option. But other than that...Hell. I didn't have a clue. I'd thought maybe I could extend my reservation. Kick the question down the road for another month. But with all the cabins booked for the rest of summer, that wasn't an option, after all.

"Why are you grimacing like that? Too much pressure?"

"*Way* too much pressure." I flopped my head back on the armrest and contemplated the ceiling. His hands gentled and I craned my neck to look at him. "No, not my feet. I mean..." My voice trailed off.

I didn't know how to tell him all the fears running through my mind. A relationship started in a pressure cooker was bound to explode, right? Jeremiah was so precious to me. We needed to do this right. I had never had a relationship like this before, but I was pretty sure couples who moved too fast didn't last long. I'd watched my mom move boyfriend after boyfriend into our small trailer, and none of them had lasted more than a year.

Jeremiah raised his eyebrows at me, waiting for me to continue. His phone buzzed on the table and he kept watching me while he answered it. Then his whole demeanor tightened as he gave the phone his full attention. A loud, muffled voice pricked my attention. Whoever was on the other end of that call was frustrated...and familiar.

My breath caught. I lunged forward, snatching the phone from Jeremiah's hand.

"Hector?" I asked breathlessly.

"Lennon." He heaved a sigh. "Jesus, honey, you gave

me a scare. I've been calling you every day for three weeks. Benny was about to send the cavalry for you."

"Benny?" I croaked. "He's alive?"

"Of course he's alive. You would know that if you returned any of my calls."

I blinked. The phone Hector had given me was in the nightstand. Dead, probably. I hadn't checked it since I'd been kidnapped. Thinking about Benny hurt too much.

"We got wind that one of Benny's former associates would be paying you a visit. They planned to use you to send Benny a message. Keep him from talking. But it had the opposite effect. He didn't take kindly to them threatening you, so he told the FBI everything he knew. He's in protective custody now, but he left a little something in an account for you. He said you'd know how to access it. And you can stay at his apartment as long as you want."

My brain felt like it was processing everything in quicksand. "The New York apartment? It's safe for me to go back?" Jeremiah's hand shackled my ankle.

"It's safe. You can come home now, Lennon."

I hung up, stunned. *Home.* I lifted my gaze to Jeremiah. "Benny is alive."

"I'm glad, honey." His voice was rough. His hand tightened. "Don't go."

My heart threatened to beat right out of my chest. God, this man. Didn't he know there was nowhere I'd rather be than right here with him? "I wasn't planning on it."

He smiled and it was like the sun breaking through a storm cloud.

"I need a job. And a place to live," I said.

He looked genuinely puzzled. "You have both those things already."

"Until tomorrow, I'm still a guest here. You need to *officially* hire me to work in the kitchen. And you just gave away my cabin, remember?"

"What do you need a cabin for? You moved in with me a month ago."

"I didn't move in with you. I stayed at your apartment for safety reasons while my stalker was on the loose, and then I stayed at your apartment while my feet healed, and by the time *that* was done, it didn't make sense to move back into the cabin when I would be checking out soon anyway, so I stayed a little longer."

He stared at me.

I braided my fingers together. Why was I so *nervous*? "Emma said I could stay with her and Blair while I figure out what to do."

"Or you could just stay here."

I wanted to say yes so badly. The thought of sleeping without him was honestly *sad*. I felt homesick for him and I hadn't even left yet. But...

"Jeremiah," I said softly. "I want to. So, so much. I—" I took a deep, shuddering breath. "But it's only been two months. That's how long we've known each other. We can't move in together after only two months. That's ridiculous."

"Someone once told me that life was a lot more fun when we don't confuse *can't* and *shouldn't*. We can, and dammit, Lennon, we *should*. Maybe two months isn't enough time for other people, but it is for us. If you tell me you need to slow things down, all right. I'll accept that. But for me, it doesn't matter if it's two months or two years. More time won't change a damn thing. I know what I want, and what I want is to spend every moment I can with you."

I searched his eyes. "Are you sure?"

He laughed and pulled me into his lap. "It's not two months for me. It's thirty-eight years. I've been waiting my whole life for you, Lennon. You've been a long time coming, and now that you're finally here, I'm not letting you go. I'm settling in for forever."

I held his face in my hands. Kissed his mouth. "I love you."

"Then stay."

Happiness broke over me like a wave, sweeping away all the doubts. "Okay. I will."

44

LENNON

"We should do this every Sunday," Emma said. With her eyes glued to the shirtless, sweaty cowboys battling through a brutal game of Blood Ball, she leaned over her iced tea, searching for the straw with her mouth. She grimaced when it bumped against her lip.

"No argument here," I said.

With Blair at a friend's house, we had decided to have a lazy afternoon. We had shamelessly set up lawn chairs facing their game. Jeremiah looked like some kind of superhero mashup. Half golden Viking, half dirty cowboy, one hundred percent delicious.

"So, Grace was asking about you the other day." Emma finally managed to get her straw in her mouth and sipped her iced tea. "She wants to know if you're still going to look into getting tested for dyslexia."

"I thought about it. But to be honest, it seems more hassle than it's worth. It's not easy to diagnose an adult, and I'd have to drive pretty far to see a specialist." Jeremiah knocked Seb down, and I grinned. *That's my man.* "A diagnosis won't change anything for me. I'm not in school, and I don't have the kind of job where it matters a lot. Mostly I just wanted proof that I'm not stupid."

"Lennon." Emma squeezed my forearm. "You're not stupid."

"Thanks. But I'm actually feeling pretty good about my intellect lately. I mean, I escaped my stalker and made the most wonderful man in the world fall in love with me. Pretty damn smart of me, *I* think." I smirked. "I do struggle with reading, though, and maybe Grace could help me with that."

"I'm sure she would love to." Emma's attention was back on the game now. "I'm so glad you're staying. Mercy River needed another woman around. I love Tamilee, but she has no interest in gawking at half-naked cowboys."

"I'm here whenever you need me. Happy to be of service."

She giggled. We watched Liam swing his mallet, sending a ball flying with a loud whack, the muscles in his back as defined as a Greek statue. Emma sighed.

I glanced at her curiously. From the pictures I'd seen in her house, Liam looked a lot like his younger brother, Daniel—Emma's deceased husband. "Is it hard for you?" I asked carefully. When she gave me a questioning look, I continued, "Seeing Liam all the time. He looks so much like Daniel, doesn't he? I don't mean to pry," I added hastily. "But if you want to talk about it, I'm here."

She blinked, looking a little surprised by the question. "Huh. I don't..." She paused rolling her lips. "I think about Daniel a lot. But Liam doesn't remind me of him at all, to tell you the truth. They're so different. Liam is...Liam." She shrugged. "So, no. It's not hard for me having Liam around. If anything, he's made everything so much easier. I don't know what I would have done without him after Daniel died. Liam and Grace held me and Blair together. I—"

The sound of tires skidding over gravel cut her off. We both pushed to our feet to see a forest green sedan swerving up the road. The cowboys noticed it to, halting their game and moving toward us.

We gasped as the car swerved again and clipped a boulder with the bumper.

"Are they drunk?" Emma shouted. "What the hell!"

The car careened to stop ten feet from the lodge. Dust flew into the air. We were already jogging closer when the door opened and a woman stumbled out.

"Help!" she called. "Please!"

She reached for me with one hand, her other

pressed to her side where a large red stain seeped through her shirt. "Please—"

Her arms went around my neck just as her eyes rolled back in her head and suddenly I was buckling under her dead weight. I took us both down to the ground as gently as I could. "Help!" I shrieked. "Jeremiah!"

But it was Seb who pushed me aside to check her pulse. "Move!" he barked.

I moved. He dropped to his knees and started CPR.

"Come on, baby," he muttered. "Don't do this."

Baby? I stared wide-eyed at his blanched face. "Who is she?"

"My wife."

EPILOGUE
JEREMIAH

Five Years Later

I did a quick headcount.

Two having a cartwheel contest across the stretch of grass, seeing who could do the most in a row.

Three in the chicken coop with Holly, meeting the newest chicks.

Another two sitting on the tire swing.

One clinging to my wife's leg.

And one fast asleep on my chest.

Kids everywhere. They weren't all mine, but I felt the weight of responsibility for their well-being as if they were. It was starting to feel like I was running a daycare instead of a cattle ranch.

Hannah laughed. She knew exactly what I was doing. "They're fine, Jay. All here and accounted for."

"Just making sure."

"You haven't lost anyone yet."

I shook my head. "Not true. I lost Isaac in the corn maze yesterday, remember?"

My sister pushed her glasses up on her nose and rolled her eyes. "For, like, thirty seconds."

"Longest thirty seconds of my life," I muttered. I should have known better than to take my three-year-old son into a maze without a leash. He was a verified bolter.

"It was so much fun!" Hannah grinned at me. "You should do this every year."

I groaned. Mercy River Ranch hosted an autumn harvest festival to raise money for our non-profit side of the business. The proceeds from yesterday would enable us to build three new cabins and pay for the stay of half a dozen first responders.

It was worth it, but it was a lot of work. Hannah and her husband, Zack, had come up to help us and brought their kids Caleb and Rosie with them. Yesterday had tired out all the grownups and left us in recovery mode today. Unfortunately, after a good night's sleep, the kids had energy to burn.

Hannah and I had claimed the rockers on the front porch of the lodge. It was the first moment we'd had alone together since their arrival three days ago. She had an embroidery project in her lap and a mug of tea next to her feet, keeping me company while six-month-old Jessica napped on my chest.

I pulled the blanket tighter around her plump little body. The September afternoon was full of mellow sunshine, but there was a nip in the air. The first snow wasn't far off.

Lennon let out a peal of laughter, clutching her chest, as Zack waved his arms like he was describing something. They were too far away for me to hear what they were saying, but I could tell they were having a good time. No surprise there. They'd hit it off from the moment they first met.

Hannah looked up from her embroidery. "What do you think they're talking about?"

I snorted. "Us."

"Of course they are. Comparing notes on what it's like being married to someone raised in a cult, probably."

I looked at her. Neither one of us had gotten out of the compound unscathed, but at least I hadn't been married off to my uncle at fourteen. The fact that we both sat here now, happy and free, was nothing short of a miracle. I never took that for granted.

But it wouldn't hurt to check in. PTSD had a way of smacking you down when you least expected it.

"How are you doing, Hannah?" I asked.

She smiled in understanding. "I'm good. Truly. How are you?"

"I'm good." My gaze cut to my wife and son. I rubbed Jessica's back gently. "The best I've ever been."

We watched Lennon and Zack laugh together.

"They're so *normal*." Hannah sounded baffled.

"We're normal," I protested.

She wrinkled her nose. "We're a little odd, Jay." Suddenly Zack and Lennon were looking back at us. Hannah drew in a sharp breath and let out a laugh. "But I think they love us, anyway."

"I know they do."

I could see it shining in her eyes. I could see it in the soft curve of her smile. Joy, hope, laughter, and sex. Lennon had given me so much these past five years. Things I had never dreamed would be mine.

But the greatest of these was love.

Sign up for Elizabeth Bright's newsletter and receive a bonus epilogue! https://dl.bookfunnel.com/zx64di43i1

Stay tuned for Seb's book, *Long Way Home*, coming October 2026!

ACKNOWLEDGMENTS

Some books are easy(ish) to put on the page. Others, you have to open a vein and bleed the story out. That was this book. I couldn't have done it without all the wonderful people in my life.

First and foremost, my daughters. Balancing single motherhood to two teens, a full-time day job, and this author career is so damn hard. I often feel like I'm dropping all the balls. Time and time again, my daughters have given me grace when I had to be a hermit to write, and only complained the teensiest tiniest bit when I made them do chores.

Jonathan—I probably would have starved without you cooking so many meals so I could glue my butt to the chair and my fingers to the keyboard.

Nicole and Lori, the best friends a girl could ask for. Thank you for checking in to make sure I was still breathing, and thank you for understanding when it took a few days to reply.

My beta readers were rock stars, and each one helped me shape this book into the story that needed to be told. Lia, Amber, Christine, and Kelly—huge hugs to all of you.

And Colby—I have so much to thank you for. I wouldn't be where I am today without you.

Lastly, thank YOU. I am so grateful you are reading this book. Thank you for making my girlhood dreams come true.

ABOUT THE AUTHOR

Elizabeth Bright is a USA Today bestselling author of romance with heart, humor, and heat. She loves sassy heroines, protective cowboys, and banter and spice. Elizabeth lives in Washington, D.C. with her two daughters and very needy dog.

Sign up for Elizabeth's newsletter at
www.elizabethbrightauthor.com

Also Available From Elizabeth Bright

Lodestar Ranch

A Cowboy in the Streets
Just Say When
Wild, Wild Cowboy
Call Me Yours
Carry Me Home

Hart's Ridge

Make Me Love You
Don't Call Me Sweetheart
Trust Me
Christmas at Hart's Ridge